A WOMAN ALWAYS KNOWS

ALSO BY LIBBY BELLE...

A Woman Always Knows

stories

Libby Belle

Pure Luck
Press

A Woman Always Knows
Stories by Libby Belle

Copyright © 2021 by Libby Belle Bryer
Cover Art by Jake Bryer

Published by, Pure Luck Press
LibbyBelle.com
Austin, Texas

ISBN02: 978-0-9985165-0-9 (Ebook)
ISBN: 978-0-9985165-1-6 (Print)
Printed in the United States of America

Library of Congress Registration Number:
TXu 1-889-816, TXu 1-805-949 and TXu 2-092-284

*To my brother Marshall
and all hopeless romantics*

CONTENTS

PREFACE

How do I create my stories? Well, it's a lot like making stone soup. You may recall that wonderful old tale in which hungry strangers convince an entire town to contribute ingredients for their pot of soup containing only water and a crummy stone. Hoodwinked into sharing, in the end, they all enjoy a delicious meal together. Very clever!

The ingredients for my stories are given to me freely and are right at my fingertips. By simply listening to everyone and everything around me, the tasty tidbits I collect are gently stirred in with my quirky ideas. While simmering, I sprinkle in a few spicy words with a generous drizzle of love and *voilà* a story is born. The best part of this recipe is the flavorful garnish that *you* add to these stories by allowing your sweet imaginations to soar.

Welcome to my kitchen. I enjoy cooking up fiction for you, and I love being inspired by you. If you have an inkling to tell me which story touched you the most or any other helpful thoughts, or ideas, please email me. It's a thrill hearing from my readers.

A little tip when reading this book: Try not to overthink, let go, be silly, and mostly, be kind to my characters. There's a little bit of all of us in them.

Lose yourself, find yourself, enjoy!

Cheers!
Libby Belle

"Reach out! Take a chance! Get hurt, even,
but play as well as you can."

— Maude from *Harold and Maude.*

A' LA MODE

It begin as an innocent flirtation, and before she knew it, Kate had slid feet first into a full-blown affair.

At the time, she was fresh out of her divorce, fragile and vulnerable, and even though Gavin was secretly seeing her on the side while involved with another woman, Kate seemed indifferent to the situation – practically numb to it. Remove love from the equation and anything is easy. Fashionable even. What a fool believes.

They were three months into it when Kate learned who the other woman was, and you'd think it would have changed everything, but it didn't. When her second cousin, Nina brought Gavin to their family reunion after an impulse wedding in Las Vegas, Kate was completely dumbstruck. Hiding in the shadows, she watched every woman in the room fall instantly in love with the new husband – her lover. Lured by his Scottish accent and envisioning what wonders lie beneath his tartan kilt, they dreamily hung onto every word he spoke. Even the little girls vied for his attention, twirling madly around him in their frilly skirts. And the smile on her grandmother's face while watching Gavin dancing with a two-year-old in his arms convinced Kate even more that he was something special. Only Aunt Mable eyed him warily and kept tabs of his every move the entire evening. Catching her keen eye more than once, Kate feared that her shrewd aunt knew something about him that everyone else didn't. So, she made it a point to stay as far away as possible from the suspicious old broad. That was when the screaming started in her head.

Even so, the affair continued as usual. It was all too easy. As a traveling salesman, Gavin could dictate his own calendar, and Nina could predictably be found at the local elementary school where she taught first grade. Kate worked at home at her own pace, creating websites and keeping books for several builders. She had planned to travel after the divorce, but now, all her plans revolved around her Scottish lover. She knew in her heart the affair could not last – on an honest day, she knew it should not last – but she would not be the one to let go.

Peering over a second cup of coffee while holding her breath each time she spotted a figure walking past the plate-glass window, Kate sat apprehensively inside the coffee shop counting the minutes. Too often Gavin had left her waiting. Glancing repeatedly at the plastic clock hanging crookedly on the wall only added to her frustration. She squirmed in her seat, avoiding a necessary restroom break, fearing that Gavin might show up and think she had left. Unlike her, he was not one to wait; his patience wore much too thin for a man of thirty-five. The uneasy feeling that he was pulling away from her weighed heavily on her heart. Lately he had been showing signs of disinterest, and when she asked him if something was wrong, he simply shrugged and said, "A man is entitled to his own thoughts now and then, isn't he?"

Who was she to argue with a Scotsman?

A slight buzz in her fingers suggested that a third cup of coffee would be a mistake. She nervously folded up a napkin five different ways, anxiously eyeballing the door. Thirty minutes, then forty-five, and when the clock read an hour had passed, anger set in – not as angry with Gavin as she was with herself. *I need to get off this runaway train!* The screaming seemed to get louder with caffeine.

The door opened just when Kate grabbed her purse, ready to leave. A tall man with a white George Strait cowboy hat perfectly situated on his thick, curly hair, wearing cowboy boots and the tightest jeans possible, slowly walked in. His boot-scooting stride lead him right to Kate's table.

"Howdy, ma'am," he said. "Are you by any chance Kate Duncan?"

"Yes, I am," she replied, craning her neck to see his eyes overshadowed by the rim of his impressive hat. "How can I help you?"

"Your cousin, Gavin, told me that you'd be here, and he suggested that I stop over and visit. I understand you do the bookkeeping for several builders in town," he offered, his steady hands resting on the back of a chair. "Do you mind if I sit down?"

"Uh, sure, please." The first thought in her head was not about business or even curiosity about the good-looking stranger. Instead, the easily irritated inner voice screamed, *How dare Gavin think I would still be here!*

"Is Gavin with you?" she tepidly asked, looking over his shoulder toward the door.

"No, he's got his hands full with my sister. He was nice enough to show her around, since she recently graduated from college and doesn't know anyone here. He's quite the salesman, and that man can *sure* tell a story. Can't help but like him. By the way, where's *your* Scottish accent?"

"What? Oh, we're not blood cousins, just cousins by

marriage." *And barely that.* Feeling the heat rise on the back of her neck, she gave him a tense smile and moved the conversation back to the matter at hand. "So, what kind of business are you bringing here?"

"I'm here to build townhomes and a strip center, and the first thing I need is someone to handle my books. I understand that you know the construction business very well." The cool cowboy pulled a shiny business card from his front pocket and handed it across the table. "Tom Tyler's the name. Do you think you'd be interested in taking me on?" he asked, leaning back and crossing his arms and his legs – the red, snake-skinned boots catching Kate's eye.

Kate read the card carefully, suitably impressed by the name boldly printed in gold. "I read about your company in a biz journal. You're on a pretty large project," she said, sitting up taller and considering his offer. "I imagine I will take on a lot more hours working for you."

"Yes, probably at first. My kid sister wants to learn the business, and she could eventually pick up the slack. This job will keep you busy for the next two years."

"Hmm." For a moment Kate was excited about the new opportunity until Gavin popped up in her thoughts. "Since this is obviously an informal interview, which I have not been given the opportunity to prepare for, just what else did Gavin tell you about me?"

Tom smiled and let out a small chuckle. "If you don't mind me saying so, I'm from the south, and we don't mince words. Other than you're the best in your field, he told me that you're not currently involved with anyone, and since I'm a single man myself, he suggested that maybe you could show me your fine city." He sat perfectly still and set his eyes directly on Kate, as if studying a blueprint.

So, now the bastard is volunteering my time? "I'm sorry, I uh, well, I…." Kate felt the heat from earlier rise in her cheeks, followed by a wave of nausea. Practically knocking over her chair when she stood up, she explained, "Um, not to be rude, but I've had two cups of coffee and well, um, please excuse me, I'll be right back."

In the restroom, Kate dabbed cold water on her face, trying to avoid wetting the thick mascara she had applied earlier, along with the rouge and lipstick that she knew pleased Gavin. She felt a disturbing mixture of sadness and anger wrapped in a whirl-wind of confusion. "Not seeing anyone, he said!" she growled at her reflection.

Someone knocked on the restroom door and startled her. "One moment, please," she said so softly the person obviously didn't hear and began to knock harder. "I said, one moment!" she shouted and pulled on a paper towel so forcefully, the container popped opened, and a stack of brown folded papers flew out all over the floor.

"Oh, crap!" Kate protested.

"I really have to go!" a child's tiny voice whimpered, followed by rapid knocking.

Shuffling through the scattered towels, Kate quickly opened the door, recalling when she was a child standing outside the bathroom holding herself and wriggling in discomfort while her brother stood smugly in front of the mirror shaving one by one the sixteen hairs on his pimply face that he had proudly counted for the whole family at the breakfast table.

The little girl brushed past her and pulled down her panties, but not in time to reach the toilet. She stood there frozen as she watched urine gush down her small, white legs; her tiny fists held stiffly by her side. "Mommy!" she yelled. "Mommy!"

"I know just how you feel, kiddo," Kate sympathized, stuffing a wad of paper towels in the child's hands and handing another wad to the mother who had rushed frantically into the room. Stepping back, she watched the mother lovingly rescue her child.

The scene triggered a sad memory – one she thought she had buried.

Blowing on a hot cup of coffee, Tom gave Kate a lazy smile when she returned to the table. "Sounds like a young lady in distress back there," his smooth tone resonating a line from an old western movie.

Kate forced a laugh, but her smile came easily until Tom announced, as if reading a newspaper headline, "Gavin said that you don't have children."

"That's right, I don't," she answered, somewhat defensively. *What about the mole under my left breast, did he tell you about that, too?*

"Well, then, could we get together over dinner tonight and talk about my offer?"

Kate picked up Tom's business card and pretended to read it again, avoiding his alluring, steel blue eyes. His flat eyebrows slowly lifted, anticipating an answer. She felt her lips turn in, and she squeezed them hard to fight back the anger bubbling up inside her. *Gavin is trying to leave me, I just know it!* Bowing her head, she let a deep sigh escape, completely unaware that she had closed her eyes. "It's probably time," she whispered, shaking her head slowly in the face of reality.

"I beg your pardon, miss?"

"Oh, oh," she muttered, snapping to attention, "I mean, it's probably time to take on some new work. One of my builders is about to complete his project and will be moving on to another city. So, yes...tonight...sure."

"Excellent!" Tom exclaimed. "I'm staying at The Worthington. Shall I pick you up, or shall we meet somewhere? I know of only two good restaurants here, and if you don't mind, I would really like to go somewhere new. I'm from Houston, and we have the finest restaurants."

"Well, I think Fort Worth can match those. Here's my card. Why don't I meet you at your hotel bar at six, and I'll drive you to the best restaurant in town."

"Now, that's a plan." Tom gave the thumbs up and a friendly nod.

"Will your sister be joining us?"

"No, Gavin is taking her to some of your finer nightclubs for the evening. He did say he'd try and get his wife to go, if her ankles weren't too swollen." His voice softened as he reminisced. "I remember my first wife swelling like that when she was carrying my boy."

"Oh? Well, my cousin's not pregnant," Kate corrected him.

"Hmm, somebody better tell her husband then, because he sure thinks so."

Kate's jaw clamped down so hard she bit her tongue. The pain was unbearable. She clutched her purse to her chest and told Tom she'd see him later and rushed toward the exit. Tom watched her struggle with her purse strap that got caught on the door handle causing her sunglasses to fall off the top of her head. They flew across the room and landed near the counter. The barista snatched them up and handed them to her. Kate thanked her and backed clumsily out of the shop, slamming the door with such force, she stuck her head back inside and meekly apologized.

Tom turned to the woman at the next table who was also curiously watching the scene and said with a grin, "High octane."

The woman chuckled, leaned in, and whispered, "You should see the mess she made in the restroom."

Tom took her comment as a warning and left his coffee cooling next to Kate's empty lipstick-stained cup.

Back in her car where she let it all out, Kate drove blindly around in circles babbling to herself, trying to deal with these new and bizarre feelings bursting from her pores. Winding up driving past Nina's house, the reality sunk in when she saw Gavin's last name written on her mailbox. The affair was clearly over, and the rat sent a stranger to do his dirty work. Good heavens, Nina is pregnant!

It had been a while since she had the luxury of a long hot bath, and Kate desperately needed to calm down. While the tub was filling, she discarded the silk robe she wore when Gavin visited and put on a comfy cotton one instead. Throughout the divorce and especially during the affair she had conveniently isolated herself. Now, she wished she had someone to talk to.

Unconsciously, she picked up the phone and called her ex-husband. He had always been there for her, until the divorce. In fact, they were best friends before they decided to tie the knot. As soon as she heard his voice, she skipped the ordinary salutations and went straight to the reason for the call.

"I know we haven't talked in a while, but can you take a few minutes to have a heart-to-heart with me?"

"Who *is* this?" Richard asked, convincingly.

"It's Kate. Geez! You forgot the sound of my voice *already*?"

"Just kidding. I knew it was you, silly. Just so happens, I *can* talk. I'm having a bad day and have just sat down with a cold beer to see if I can soon forget it," he spoke with the sweet, wistful tone he used when they were in love. "Nice to hear your voice, Kate. What's up?"

"So, you're alone?"

"Quite."

Kate put her feet up on the edge of the bed and propped a pillow behind her back. Sitting in the old leather chair, a hand-me-down from her parents, brought a sense of honesty that she needed to keep intact in order to share with Richard her latest revelation. "Look, I want to tell you something, something you will probably understand more than anyone, and I need you to be kind."

"OK."

"And honest."

"OK."

Kate stayed silent, wishing she hadn't said it that way. She waited for him to follow up with something derogatory, or funny, or even an intolerant sigh that might stop her from telling him the ugly truth and sparing her the humiliating self-deprecation. It was not to be. He was unusually quiet.

"You told me once that you were really sorry for your affair. Did you really mean it?" she asked, listening to him swallow a big gulp of beer, expecting a satisfying burp to follow.

"Yes, and even more so now," he said tenderly, without belching. "I am more than sorry. It wasn't worth it, and I'll never understand why it happened. And I'll say it again...it wasn't because of you, Kate. It's important to me that you remember that."

Kate reveled in the words that he had said many times before he finally agreed to sign away their marriage. This time she understood them and why. "Well, brace yourself, sweetie. This is not easy to say, but...," she took another deep breath, "I had an affair with a married man, and I don't understand why it happened either. Before you say anything, let me explain. I knew it was wrong and even sick, but still, I was afraid to let it go. What I need to know is...is this how you felt? Stuck? Crazy like that?"

"Oh, Kate. You left me because of my immoral and careless act. How could you do what you hated?"

"Hell if I know! I'm trying to understand myself, Richard. Maybe it was self-loathing? I don't know. I felt worthless when you cheated on me...when I lost the baby...I mean...no excuses...oh, I really don't want to go there." Kate felt her humility slipping away. "Look, just answer my question, please. Is this how you felt, like it was a drug that you couldn't stop using?"

"Yes, something like that. I never told you this, but I was grateful when you found out. I wanted it to stop. I wanted my life back. Talk about feeling worthless. But you...you are so full of good and a much better person than me. This is not like you, Kate. What can I do to help?"

"You just did," Kate said. "I want my life back, too. I didn't realize how much until today. And for the record, I'm not better than you, Richard. I don't want to be better than you." Absorbing her words, Kate sat up straight with a sudden epiphany.

"But you know in some weird way just being able to say all this out loud sort of shatters the illusion, doesn't it? I mean, I fell off my pedestal too, so now we're like, well, on the same side."

"Kindred spirits," Richard said. "We always were."

The reflective pause between the two was long enough for Kate to hear the gurgle of the water reaching the overflow. "I think my tub is about to run over! Let's talk again tomorrow. Would that be OK?"

"Yes, of course. Call me anytime. And Kate..." he yelled into the phone before she could hang up.

"Yes?"

"End it. End it now before too much damage is done. I wish I had," he sighed heavily.

"It's over...I'm pretty sure it's over. Now, I just have to forgive myself." Caught off guard by her own admission, she hung up before too much more was said.

Kate sank deep into the tub, sensing relief and a familiar sweetness toward Richard that she had not allowed herself to feel until this very moment. She had found solace in his kind words and that he didn't say more about the miscarriage, yet the question of forgiveness stayed with her. How could she forgive herself when she could not even forgive Richard? She knew, without a doubt, it was the right thing to do, and soon. With such intense awareness came an overwhelming sadness, realizing that while in her bubble of selfishness, she had not even bothered to ask

Richard about his bad day. Kate choked back another reason to cry.

～

Tom Tyler, like most good businessmen, came to the bar early and drank water while waiting for Kate to arrive. He offered her a beverage, which she kindly refused, then she talked him into leaving immediately, after hearing an embarrassingly loud rumble erupt from her stomach.

The restaurant was full, and Kate felt odd walking through the crowd of people as if they were all watching her. Of course, she thought, what do I expect after slinking around with a married man. She had felt more than enough shame for one day and refused to entertain the sin any further.

"It's pretty crowded for a Thursday night," she announced.

Tom looked at her curiously. "In my neck of the woods, the weekend always starts on Thursday. When was the last time you were on a date?"

"I'd have to get out my diary to remember," she laughed.

"Well, in that case, little lady, you are officially my date." Placing her arm through his, he escorted her to the bar. "How about that drink now before we eat?"

The drinks went down smoothly and so did the conversation. Tom was quite the charming and agreeable Texan, and Kate felt at ease sitting across from him discussing business and getting to know each other over the finest cuisine in the city. For the first time in months, she ate everything on her plate.

Later, while they were waiting for the valet to bring the car, a couple began chatting with them and suggested that they try the jazz club just a few blocks away. Kate and Tom agreed and decided it was an ideal evening for a walk.

The nightclub was classy, with big leather chairs and booths dimmed by soft-lit candelabra lights in finely etched, glass globes.

From every seat around the U-shaped bar, patrons could look across at each other. It felt cozy and sexy, and everyone seemed very relaxed. Kate studied the room and the sophisticated over-thirty crowd. She liked the way the soft light made the women look demure and the men look harmless. On the small stage, a few feet from the band, people were slow dancing. Kate hadn't thought about Gavin hardly at all until she saw him coming toward them, following closely behind a beautiful, tall, young woman with the whitest Colgate commercial teeth.

"Brother, darling. How lovely to see you," the beauty said, reaching out and grabbing Tom's chin. "Gavin has turned out to be quite a perk and has been showing me a fantastic time tonight." Turning to wink at her escort, she asked him, "Haven't you?"

"I have indeed," he said, smiling at Tom, and then seeing Kate peer around Tom's big frame, he dropped his smile.

"Hi, cuz!" Kate said, almost too cheerfully.

"Oh, hi," Gavin said, with a delayed obligatory smile. "It looks like you've met Tom."

"I have indeed," she mimicked Gavin's earlier remark, "and he's turned out to be quite a perk, too." Then she turned to Tom's sister and put out her hand with an introduction. "Kate Duncan...possibly your brother's new assistant."

"Well, that's just perfect. I'm Ceniza Tyler. Glad to meet you."

To avoid sitting next to Kate, Gavin moved hastily past Ceniza to sit on the only stool next to Tom. Ceniza pouted and let out a sigh of disappointment like a teenager that got passed over for cheerleader. Kate coaxed her over to the stool next to her and started up a light conversation, while Ceniza kept looking over Kate's shoulder to try and get Gavin's attention. She was already smitten with the handsome devil, and Kate could see the desire in her eyes. It's too late, she thought, he has her in his clutches, just like he had me. Only, I knew better.

Within seconds, Ceniza slid off her stool and asked Gavin to dance with her again. He was almost giddy with acceptance. When the two were out of earshot, Tom said under his breath, "He's quite the charmer, isn't he?"

Kate whispered in his ear, "You have no idea."

"Well, he *is* married, so I suppose my sister's safe."

Kate held her tongue. Her attitude when seeing Gavin was totally unexpected. Not the typical rejected woman, poor pitiful me feeling, or even the jealousy that comes naturally when seeing your former lover with a younger, more vibrant woman. She was feeling an innate concern for Tom's sister. Ceniza was apparently immature, twenty-three, and fresh out of college, an easy conquer for a man like Gavin. Since her conscience had returned after confessing her hypocrisy to Richard, she felt a responsibility to do something to stop him.

Tom ordered another drink and turned to see Kate frowning in serious thought. "You look like you could use a dance, too. Want to give it a whirl?"

"Another thing I'll have to look up in my diary," she said. "It's been a long time. Can you take it easy with me?"

"Honey," Tom ribbed her, "it's just jazz." He took her by the hand and led her to the dance floor.

Gavin was holding Ceniza much closer than a gentleman should. When he spotted Tom towering above the others coming toward them, he put some space between himself and his partner. The music ended none too soon. Gavin faked a yawn and said to Ceniza, "I think we should leave now. Workday tomorrow, you know. I'll gladly drop you off at the hotel."

Kate caught an impish gleam in Gavin's eyes and a tacit approval in Ceniza's smile. "Gavin's taking me back, Tom. I'm bushed. Don't stay out too late," she teased and dashed through the crowd, her escort trailing behind her.

"Is it time for you to call it a night, too?" Kate asked, hoping he'd say yes for his sister's sake.

"Oh no, I'm having a great time. Another dance?"

"Lovely, but I think maybe soon, though. You have given me a lot to think about with this new job, and I'd like to meet you tomorrow to go over the details."

"One more drink at the hotel little lady, and off you go."

Later in the hotel parking lot, Kate drove up and down the aisles looking for Gavin's car, explaining to Tom that she was seeking out the widest parking space for her new convertible. When she spotted his black Mustang near the back, nearly hidden by a dumpster, she clutched the steering wheel and swallowed the lump in her throat.

"You picked a lovely place to stay," she managed to say, as they passed through the hotel revolving door. "Are you sharing a room with your sister?"

"Oh no, I'm afraid she couldn't put up with my snoring, and I certainly couldn't put up with her playing on her cell phone all night long."

Through a mirthless chuckle, the lump in Kate's throat returned when they entered the bar and saw neither Ceniza or Gavin. Tom ordered drinks, while she anxiously darted off to the ladies' room.

Stopping at the front desk, she was disappointed to find no one there, until a girl popped up from behind the counter.

"Oh!" they both let out a yelp.

"I'm sorry," the girl said, "I got a run in my stockings and was trying to paint clear nail polish on it before it got worse."

Kate sniffed the air. "I can smell it. I've used that trick before, and it does work," she smiled agreeably, an attempt to gain the girl's trust.

Before the girl could launch into a story about how she got the run, Kate asked, "Can you tell me if Ceniza Tyler checked in yet? Her brother and I are in the bar waiting for her."

"Oh yeah, Ceniza. She's nice. She's the one who told me

about the nail polish trick. She and her cousin went up about ten minutes ago. Want me to ring her?"

Her cousin? "No, no, no, that won't be necessary. I'll go on up. Maybe we'll just have a drink up there. Let's see, her room number is…"

"Two-twenty-four," the girl proudly shared.

Kate peeked around the corner to see if Tom was still seated at the bar. He looked content, talking to the man next to him who was laughing out loud. Then she took the staircase up to the second floor and walked quietly down the hall. When she found the room, she pressed her ear against the door and strained to listen. She heard Ceniza giggling. Gavin had started out with her like that – playfully and innocently charming her pants off. She could hear her heart racing, and a crazy urge to pound on the door came over her. Instead, she tapped it lightly with her knuckle.

She heard, "Shhhh," before she knocked again.

Ceniza peered through the peephole and stepped back. "It's Kate," she whispered to Gavin.

Before she lost her nerve, Kate knocked again – this time louder.

Gavin went out on the small balcony beyond the sliding glass door, and Ceniza shut the drapes behind him.

"Coming," she said sweetly and opened the door slowly. "Oh, hi Kate. Is Tom with you?"

Kate looked at Ceniza's mussed hair, smeared lipstick, and lopsided smile, relieved that her clothes were intact and that she had probably gotten there in time. "No, your brother is downstairs at the bar. I need to talk to you Ceniza, it's very important. Can I come in?"

"Well, I…I was just going to bed. Can this wait until tomorrow?"

"No, it can't." Kate looked at her sternly.

"OK, then," she stammered, "I'll just put on my shoes and

come down to the bar with you. I *am* very tired," she said, suppressing a phony yawn. "I guess one more drink won't hurt me."

"Or me either," Kate said, surveying the room, wondering where the coward had hidden.

When Tom saw Ceniza enter the bar with Kate beside her, he patted the chairs on both sides of him, motioning for them to join him. "So," he leaned over toward the bartender, "who's the luckiest man in the room?"

"Tom," Ceniza said, refusing to sit and looking annoyingly at her brother, "I was just going to bed and Kate brought me down here to talk about something important. What's going on?" She turned to Kate.

"I may regret this." Kate took a deep breath, drumming her fingers on the bar, thinking of where to start. "Well, it's really pretty simple, and pretty ugly, but here goes. I've been having an affair with Gavin, who, as you now know, is married to my second cousin and expecting a child." Oh, that sounded awful, she thought, imagining devil horns sprouting from her head.

Tom sat up straight, crossed his arms and set his eyes on Kate's. "Well, that's a true disappointment, Kate. Is there a reason you're telling us this?"

"Well, yes. I believe Gavin used you to let me know that we were through. I was waiting for him at the coffee shop and well, anyway, not only did he use you for that, but he also used you to tell me that his wife is pregnant."

Ceniza kept her eyes peeled on her fidgeting hands, her mouth closed tightly shut. Tom shook his head and grabbed her around the waist. "Hmm, this is an awkward situation."

Kate would not let the shame prevent her from saving Tom's innocent sister. "I'm not proud of this, and I'm only telling you this because you are good people, and I don't want to see you hurt by the likes of messed up people like Gavin...and me."

Kate's eyes began to water. She was compelled to say more.

"I lost my husband to an affair. You would think I would know better than anyone else how much damage this kind of thing does. So, that's why I had to tell you this, Ceniza...Tom."

Tom appeared quite confused. "Look, I appreciate your honesty, I really do, but I don't understand why you feel the need to tell us such personal things. A simple warning about Gavin would have been enough."

Ceniza placed her hand on her brother's shoulder and said meekly, "No, Tom. I know why she's saying these things." Kate looked up and gave Ceniza a tender smile of encouragement. "Because of me. Gavin's waiting in my room right now."

"What the hell?" Tom rose from his chair, knocking over the drink sitting at his elbow. "Is this true?"

"Yes, it is. He's awfully fun to flirt with, and I didn't try that hard to keep him from coming up. But now, but now, I don't want this kind of thing. I don't want this at all!" Ceniza burst into tears and threw herself on her brother.

Tom held his baby sister close and peered over her head at Kate. "Would you mind sitting here with Ceniza until I get back?" he asked.

Kate nodded, knowing where Tom was heading. Ceniza handed him the key to her room without a single word.

The ladies moved to a bistro table and sat quietly taking turns eyeing the door to the bar for Tom's return. Keeping the conversation light, Kate asked Ceniza, "Tell me, did you have a lot of friends at the university?"

"I had a few, and a boyfriend, but he had to go back to Chicago."

"I bet you miss him."

"You wouldn't believe how much. I guess my actions don't show it," she said, fiddling with a button on her blouse to keep from looking at Kate. They sat in silence until Ceniza broke from her thoughts. "By the way, thank you for stopping me from doing something really foolish. I should know better. I'm an idiot."

"No honey, I'm the idiot."

Tom walked into the room. The women sat upright, waiting for him to speak.

"You said you were really tired earlier, sweetheart," he directed the comment to Ceniza. "Why don't you run off to bed and meet me for breakfast in the morning." His stern expression clearly indicated that this was not merely a suggestion.

"OK, goodnight. You'll tell me everything in the morning, right?" she asked, squeezing his hand.

Tom chuckled. "Mostly everything. Goodnight."

On her way out, she turned to Kate and said, "It was nice to meet you."

Kate smiled. "You, too."

The bartender brought over a complimentary drink to Tom and asked Kate if she wanted something. "No thank you, I'll be leaving shortly."

"That was a pretty big sacrifice you made," Tom said. "Thank you."

"No, thank *you*, Tom. I think you might have been sent to help me out of this one. As for Gavin…"

Tom smirked, "I think he'll be a much better husband after tonight…for a while, anyway."

Before the sting from his words began to soak in, Kate abruptly stood and stepped back from the table. Through a tight smile, she said, "Good luck with your new business, and in case you didn't know it, Ceniza has a boyfriend in Chicago who she misses a great deal." And before Tom could say anything more, she fled the room.

When she exited the hotel and felt the night air slap her care-worn face, something deep inside erupted.

～

Kate stood at her apartment door and couldn't remember driving home. The long day had to end. Fully clothed, she threw herself on the bed and wept until she couldn't concentrate on anything else but a pounding headache.

She woke to the school bus stopping across the street; its squeaky breaks reminding her that it was nearly eight o'clock. Yesterday's work was piled on her desk, and the answering machine had been turned on silent. Kate contemplated leaving it on mute, but the blinking message indicator light suggested it was time to get back to business. She turned the sound up and went to the kitchen to make coffee. Looking at the calendar on the wall, she was startled that it was already the end of the month. No longer in a daze, she threw her head back and asked herself, "Where have I been all this time?"

"Kate, Kate," a man's voice boomed from the recording device. Thinking it was Gavin, Kate stood paralyzed against the kitchen sink. But when he spoke again, she realized it was her ex-husband. She let her body go limp and sat down at the table, enjoying the familiar voice.

"Can you come over for dinner tonight?" Richard continued. "I really miss you and after our talk, I think we can help each other." He paused and breathed into the phone. "Well, we said we'd always be friends, remember? Maybe it's time. Please call me back." And before he hung up, he said, "Oh, by the way, I ran into Nina's sister. Looks like another baby's going to be added to the fam. Congrats!"

Kate took a cup of coffee out on the deck. She felt lighter than she had in such a long time. The everyday anxiety she had experienced when waiting for Gavin to call had so far disappeared, and so had the dreadful screaming. For a moment she felt bad about ruining the opportunity to work with Tom, but then she felt better knowing why. The sacrifice had been worth it, in its sick and strange way.

By noon she had most of her desk cleared, the kitchen cleaned, and she even ironed the clothes on the closet floor that had been piling up during the entire affair. She was about to tackle the refrigerator when the phone rang. Kate hesitated, catching it on the fourth ring.

"Are you always this late to appointments?" a male's smooth voice spoke.

"Excuse me? I think you have the wrong number."

Before the phone reached the cradle, the man yelled, "Kate!"

"Yes?" she replied, timidly.

"It's me, Tom Tyler. I thought we were meeting to discuss our business plan?"

"I, well, I thought after last night…"

"Exactly. After last night, I knew for certain that I wanted to work with you. Kate, we all make mistakes. Admitting them and learning from them is what we humans are all about. I'd say you're way ahead of the learning curve."

"I don't know what to say."

"You can start with, I'm sorry for being late, and meet me at my new office in an hour."

Kate didn't take time to analyze the situation and made a beeline for her clothes closet. She picked out her best designer jeans and felt around the floor beneath a line of skirts for her western boots. She hadn't worn them or the soft blue shirt with pearl buttons since the last Fort Worth Stock Show and Rodeo. Thinking that Tom Tyler would surely approve, she smiled in the mirror when she tucked her hair under an Outback straw cowgirl hat.

Before she left, she looked for a nice outfit to wear to Richard's later that evening. She chose a dark, plum colored dress that would easily blend with Chianti and red sauce stains, certain that he was cooking her favorite dish, spaghetti and meatballs.

She would complement the meal with a simple dessert of humble pie.

Just when she locked the door behind her, the phone rang. When the caller reached her answering machine, he said sheepishly, "Tha mi duilich. It means, I am sorry. But, of course, without regrets." A long pause filled the device before Gavin spoke again in a muffled, raspy whisper, "Kate, meet me tomorrow."

SPARKLES

Her name was Maude in that other life, long before she changed it to Sparkles. Back when they were blessed with three fine daughters, a four-bedroom home, a Cadillac in the garage and a Ford Pick-up in the driveway, keys to the community pool, Friday night cookouts, Saturday nights at the dance hall, (Maude so loved to dance), and Sunday morning vigilance – you get the picture. "Living the dream," her husband used to say until the little weasel decided to step out of that dream and seek pleasure elsewhere. And not just once, she would learn from the neighbors, but more than enough to wreck a marriage and keep her searching for guilt in the eyes of every woman she passed in the grocery store aisles. How fooled she had been, and it hurt like hell.

The daughters were well on their way to their own lives when the divorce was finalized, and Maude soon found herself miserably alone in a house too large for just one lonely divorcee. At the time, she was still a vivacious forty-five-year-old, but there was no getting rid of the sour taste in her mouth as long as she stayed in that neighborhood with all that judgment surrounding her. When opportunity knocked, and just in the nick of time, she sold the house and joined up with a group of like-minded people seeking adventure in Alaska. Four men to every woman! Men who were most eager to help her recover from the humiliation of a cheating husband did wonders to restore Maude's confidence. Many would say, including herself, that she went wild. Hog wild!

When her girls started having babies and begged for mama to come home and grandparent, Maude abandoned the geographical cure of "The Last Frontier" and dutifully returned to an ordinary life. In her spare time, she enhanced her culinary skills, and soon her sexual appetite and any foolish thoughts of love were replaced with countless new recipes devoured in front of old movies. Stuck in this routine, she gained an ungodly amount of weight – ninety-five pounds, if you really want to know. "Egads!" her ninety-two-year-old mother exclaimed, after calling her by her dead aunt's name. "Geeze, Louise, that's a buttload of fat!"

Nothing hurts quite like a mother's shaming except for watching her ex-husband, with his ridiculous facelift and bad hair weave, marry three more times – her daughters embracing each new skinny wife right in front of her. Soon Maude was filled to the brim with shame and resentment, blaming it all on the father of her children and the boatload (not buttload, she informed her ill-mannered mother) of extra fat she carried around for the next ten years.

Of course, the grandchildren in their selfish teens went different directions, leaving Maude purposeless and trapped in the daily grunge of her tedious job. Eventually, she moved to the outskirts of the city into a small condo with a long-distance view of the Houston skyline. Even with a change of scenery, designer clothing, pedicures and manicures, hair coloring, teeth whitening and the finest Mary Kay make-up, depression was just inches from her doorstep. Death lurked closely behind. And men? Ha! Nada! Zilch!

Often, while lying in bed, immersed in the soft light of the candy swirl lava lamp, she would imagine her broken heart giving out in the middle of the night and how they would find an overfed, pathetically lonely woman lying dead in between 600-count sheets, above her taped to the ceiling a poster of Burt Reynolds stretched out in the nude smiling wickedly on a bearskin rug. At the foot of the bed on a feather-filled euro sham covered with silk scarves, her little Yorkie, Brando would be playfully licking his master's toes in a vain attempt to revive her. "Farewell, cruel world!" she cried to Burt on those lost, lonely nights.

But each morning like clockwork, Maude would awake at the break of dawn, alive and well and always hungry.

Sixty-five hit like a stifling hot August wind off the Galveston coastline. Most women who face the Medicare age surrender to their body's betrayal, but not Maude. Something had to give! The answer came from her hairdresser who told her a story about a miserable obese man who had elected to have a gastric bypass at the age of sixty. Sixty! So what if he died on the operating table, at least he was courageous enough to do something, anything, no matter the consequences. The story motivated Maude to have the same operation and by the very same doctor. Finally, a way out! She couldn't make the arrangements fast enough.

Several cancellations had just been entered into the system, and the day for surgery was soon upon her. Perfect! No time for second thoughts. With her place all tidied up and a will set out on the kitchen table, she gave Brando to another lonely and needy neighbor and took a final step toward the beginning of a new life, or a quick ending to the old one, however destiny saw fit.

As scheduled, she was lying on the gurney in her birthday suit by midafternoon. "A stretcher on wheels, how clever," she teased the doctor. "Made to roll you right out of surgery and straight to the morgue. One-stop shopping." Maude laughed, and a bit too loud. The nurse chuckled behind his facemask. The doctor stared straight ahead.

So convinced she would die while under the knife, she told Dr. Nankin not to feel bad that his skills may be in question when it was all over, but this time he could rest assured that her death would be in fate's hands and not his. The fretful doctor nervously patted her leg and weakly promised she would awake to a brand-new life, and he would be there to serve her Jello. "Oh? So, you're going to heaven with me, too, Dr. Napkin?" was the last thing she said when the stage curtains fell before her eyes.

But something magical happened while under anesthesia. Maude had a vision. She saw herself being carried in a man's arms. She was laughing. She was happy. And to her surprise, when she opened her eyes, destiny had decided to send her back to earth.

It was said that right after the surgery Dr. Nankin was so overwhelmed with the outcome, he rushed to the nearest bar. A woozy, but vigilant Maude, yelled from the recovery room, "Hey, Dr. Napkin, where's my Jello?"

The transformation that occurred in the following year was simply amazing, and with each pound shed Maude became more of the sexy, exciting woman she was while living in Alaska twenty years earlier. As far as she was concerned, not a day could be wasted, as love was now at her thin fingertips.

Quick weight loss required a necessary tummy tuck and the bags removed from beneath her eyes, followed by contact lenses. The urge to gratify the newly restored sexual impulses flashed in her glazed-over pupils. But if one cared to look closer, they'd see hidden behind that thin veil of lust something entirely different.

A co-worker gladly showed her how to get back in the groove by using an online dating site. She also advised her to use a pseudonym. Because Maude adored jewelry and never left the house without wearing some, she named herself Sparkles. Within a week she had a slew of men lined up. She would tackle each of them one by one, starting with a man guarding a diamond mine in Botswana who wooed her with the sweetest words, although often misspelled. 'How perfectly approppos you name is Sparklee, like my dimonds,' he wrote. He promised they would spend the rest of their young lives making love in sparkling champagne and African diamonds. A mere four thousand dollars was all that he needed from her to fly him across the ocean and into her arms by the end of the month. So be it!

She waited with the excitement of a new bride. When the next month came and another flew by, and the flirty dog mysteriously dropped from sight on the internet, she was convinced that he had faced his biggest fear: (KIA) killed in action.

When she told the outlandish story to the ladies in her book club, not one had the heart to contradict her. Her daughters, however, were not as kind. Their harsh demands that she act her age ricocheted right off Maude's' glossy gullible exterior. She flippantly quoted from an old movie, "Oh my, how the world still dearly loves a cage," and left them with an emphatic, "I will not go back to mine!"

"You're doing it all wrong," her co-worker lambasted her after Maude described in detail the bizarre online affair.

"But it was fun pretending," she explained. "No real harm done. Everyone has the right to make an ass of themselves. You just can't let the world judge you too much."

"Well, fine, but you have to actually date them first before you do anything as crazy as giving them money. Let's get you on a better dating site. You'll have to pay for this one, but honestly, Maude, as much as you love to dress up, it'll be a cinch. Start with dinner first. It may take a half dozen or so to get used to it, and then you can move on to drinks, and dancing, and after that...well."

"OK, but my name is Sparkles now. For real. You can call me Sparkles."

With newfound courage and a new identity, new outfits were bought, and regular dates were set up. It was much easier than Sparkles had thought it would be, but it certainly had its flaws.

The first date appeared to be a regular sort until he got down on his knees, crawled under the table and begged her to show him her feet right when dessert was served. Feigning the need to powder her nose, Sparkles hid in the restaurant's kitchen where she donned an apron and helped scrub the dishes until the date finally gave up and left. The nut with a foot fetish not only ate his dessert, he ate hers, too.

A four-foot-tall man who claimed he was over six feet *before* the accident, nearly had her talked into a second date until he stood on a chair and begged her for a kiss.

Some dates never got past the menu, ending abruptly after the first drink with a standard, "Sorry, we're just not a fit." The men who eventually confessed, right in the middle of dinner, that they were married were the cruelest. Their excuses and stories about their lame wives made Sparkles cringe. Rather than waste the nice meal, she'd wait until the check was paid and the boxed-up leftovers in her hands before going separate ways after firmly announcing, "Just for the record, buster, I used to be one of those lame wives!"

Disenchanted, she put men aside long enough to read more books and watch old movies that spoke to her heart. Fueled with a fresh attitude, more clever one-liners, and ready to face the opposite sex again, she gave dating one last chance.

～

The place was packed. She'd heard from others that The Jacka-lope Restaurant bar was always full of executives on their way home from work. A good sign, Sparkles thought, if this date turns out to be a dud. She had dressed in a tight link-strapped sequin knit dress. A fur collar wrap sat delicately on her shoulders. Her shoes were strapless with a rim of rhinestones around the heel. Layers of delicate silver chains draped from her neck; one with a white swan pendant landing right in the middle of her cleavage. The Aurora Borealis drop earrings complemented the azure sky contact lenses floating on her eyes. Rings on two fingers, one on the middle toe, and bangle bracelets on each arm completed the ensemble. She was more excited than usual about this new date. He was a retired firefighter. And a firefighter who loved to dance.

Dreading the three-block walk in high heels and not willing to trust the valet with her freshly painted 1980 Cadillac Seville, she squeezed her car in an empty space between a backhoe and a pile of lumber on a construction site right across the street from the restaurant. A striking resemblance to Shirley McClain, she noted while examining her face in the visor mirror and singing along with Frankie Valli on the radio. When the song ended, she eased out of the car and discovered that her dress had slipped up to her crotch. Two construction workers nearby were standing next to each other ogling. One yelled out a cat call.

Sparkles stood up tall, stretched, and shimmied the dress back into position. Now, both men were whistling and egging her on. So absorbed in the attention, she hadn't noticed the eighteen-wheeler that had parked just a few feet from her car. Strutting toward it, eyes peeled on the men, she tripped over a piece of metal jutting out from the construction fence and fell face forward. Her feet flew out of her backless shoes, and her purse soared into the air and landed elsewhere.

The workers quickly turned their backs and carried on with their work. Stunned, Sparkles pulled herself up to a sitting position and stretched out her legs. Checking for broken bones, bruises, cuts, and, oh dear Venus, please no rips in my dress, she didn't realize she was sitting within inches of the eighteen-wheeler. Just when she pulled her knees to her chest to try and stand, the rig began to move. Right before her eyes a huge set of tires rolled over her bare foot. Mortified, she fell back on her elbows and watched the monstrous truck move sluggishly past her.

A delayed, "Ouch!" flew from her mouth once she realized what had happened. "Ouch!" she yelled again. "You ran over my foot!" The truck came to a complete stop, and the driver frantically flew out of the cab and ran her direction.

"Oh my God, lady, are you alright?" he asked in a panic, kneeling next to her, scoping out her body for mangled bones and blood.

"My foot, my foot! That giant tire ran over my foot!" She held it up in the air, surprised that there was no sign of damage of any kind, other than a black line of tire tread smeared across her big toe. Dazed and confused, she sat staring at the polished toenails, still sparkling even in the soft dusky sunlight. Then for no apparent reason, she started laughing.

The driver stepped back at a distance and waited until she finished before offering his hand to help her up. Too shaken to pull herself to a stand, he wrapped his arms around her waist and hoisted her to her feet.

"Ohh!" Sparkles squealed. "You're strong."

"Can you walk?" he asked with an anxious smile while awkwardly tugging at her dress that had climbed up her thighs.

"Maybe, but where are my shoes, and oh dear, my purse?" Realizing they were not in plain view, she freaked out. "I can't see out of my right eye! My contact has fallen down into my eyelid!"

"Here they are, here's your shoes, and, oh, look, there's your purse, hanging on the No Parking sign." He nervously gathered them up.

Sparkles placed her hand on his shoulder and steadied

herself, while he slipped her high heels back on her feet. From her good eye, she glared at the construction workers apparently quite entertained at her expense. "Cowards!"

"What?"

"Those men over there," she said, pointing their direction, "they didn't even bother to help me."

The driver looked their way and shot them the bird. The workers dropped their cheesy smiles, turned around and went back to digging. Sparkles muffled a laugh. "Thank you."

"Do you want me to take you to the hospital?" he asked, allowing her to lean on his arm.

"No, I've seen enough of those. But I'm certainly not in any state to be in public now. Geesh, my hair is a mess!" She blew at a lock of loose curls. "Do you live close by?"

"Not too far from here." He gave her a confused look. "Why?"

"If I could just sit quietly for a while, get this contact back in my eye, I'm sure I can determine if my foot is broken or not. And then you can take me to the hospital, if need be. I imagine your company would expect you to do that," she implied with a sudden formal demeanor. "By the way, what's your name?"

"Harry. I, uh, well, what's your name?"

"Sparkles. You can call me Sparkles," she said almost dreamily. Then she lowered her voice to sound more official. "I should get your driver's license number next. I think that's protocol after an accident."

"OK, I'll give it to you when I get you settled in your car."

"I'd prefer now, if you don't mind," she demanded, but not in a harsh way, more like parental chiding.

Harry presented his license, and he knew at that moment he was at this woman's discretion. He must be careful. This was not his first infraction, and he needed to keep the job. Sparkles stuffed the license in her purse and the car keys in his hand.

Relieved that she didn't mention calling the cops, he picked her up and carried her to her car.

"Oh my, I can't remember the last time I was swept off my feet," she giggled. The feeling of déjà vu stayed with her all the way to Harry's home.

The story was a long one, she had warned him. Nevertheless, Harry was determined to hear her out. *After all, it was me who ran over her foot*, he admitted to himself, while hurriedly scrubbing three days of grime from his body before the hot water ran out in the shower.

Refreshed, but still a little skeptical about the stranger sitting on his sofa, he returned to the living room and poured her another glass of Pinot Grigio from the bottle left behind by Bernadette, the girlfriend who never came back.

"You clean up nice," Sparkles said, sipping the cheap wine like a real lady, her pinky waving at the same time her eyebrows lifted in flirtatious approval at seeing him out of the soiled overalls and in a nice clean shirt and cargo pants.

Harry dropped his head to his chest and soaked up the compliment. His eyes roamed the room looking for the beer he had started earlier. He spotted it dripping condensation all over a poem he had been writing. He snatched it up, wiped it off on his pants and hid the poem behind his back. When he swallowed the last of the warm beverage, his stomach growled. Turning to his guest, he asked, "Are you hungry? I could rustle up something while you rest your foot and finish telling me all about yourself."

"That would be wonderful. I was supposed to have escargot if I hadn't ended up here," she said, with a hint of disappointment. "It would have been a first. I love firsts, don't you, Harry?"

"Firsts…oh, sure…but I'm afraid I don't have much in the fridge. I'm rarely here." He opened the pantry, slipped the poem under a four-roll pack of toilet paper and sorted through the goods. "Tuna, chicken spread, a big can of peaches, half a bag of elbow macaroni, and what do we have here…a package of Saltines.”

“Now that I think about it, swallowing slimy snails is rather disgusting. Let's have a smorgasbord and open them all, Harry. I'll hobble over to your cute little bar and help you prepare it.” When Sparkles tried to stand, she fell right back down on the sofa. “Ow, it hurts even more now. I guess there will be no dancing for me in the near future. That's a shame. I so love to dance.”

Harry stood over his guest looking down at her shimmering gold toenails. The big toe was now accentuated by a mound of pink puffy flesh, and the tire tread marks were still there. “You're right, it is swollen,” he observed, guiltily. “Keep it elevated. I'll make you an ice pack.”

While Harry popped out the ice cubes from the plastic tray, Sparkles leaned her head back, closed her eyes, and sang a Cat Stevens tune. So deep in the moment, she did not know he was standing over her with the baggie full of ice watching her bosom rise and fall as she sang. “If you want to sing out, sing out, and if you want to be free, be free…there's a million things to be, you know that there are.” The swan pendant caught in her cleavage looked as if it was struggling to get free.

Nice rack for an old gal, he thought. I wonder how old she is. Got to be older than my mom. Uncomfortable with his impure thoughts, he cleared his throat and woke the woman from her reverie. He placed the ice next to her with a subtle suggestion that she should apply it herself and went back to the kitchen to prepare the appetizers.

In between nibbles, upon Sparkle's insistence, Harry told her a little about himself, his short stint with Bernadette, and the two years of college ten years back when the world was his oyster. “I inherited this rusty old mobile home from my grandfather. Mobile? Ha!” he said jokingly, “this metal box has never gone mo-bile.”

He confessed he'd never been out of Texas, either. Pasadena is where he rests his stiff muscles after weeklong trips delivering heavy equipment from one end of the state to the other. Uncomfortably aware that he sounded pathetic, he went back to the task at hand – spreading canned chicken across a piece of frozen white bread. "You were going to tell me how you got the name, Sparkles," he reminded her.

Transfixed by Harry's meticulous distribution of the pasty spread, making sure each corner was filled perfectly to the edge of the crust, Sparkles felt the alcohol kick in. She sighed wistfully and answered in a mellow voice, "Better brace yourself, Harry, it's a long, long story. It all began the day I stopped backing away from life…."

She rambled through chapters as far back as she could and surprisingly without tears. "There's so much more I can tell you, Harry, but it seems my glass is empty." Sparkles nudged the sleeping prince at the other end of the sofa.

Harry had not realized he had drifted off, his face smashed against the lumpy cushion that smelled like his grandfather's Vicks VapoRub, until he felt Sparkle's fingers tickling his side. "Oh, sure, yes, of course." Glad to be rid of the last reminder of Bernadette, he cheerfully uncorked the wine.

Feeling more at ease with Sparkles, he sat down next to her and popped open another beer. "So, after all that, you're still online dating and still single."

"Yes, and thanks to Dr. Napkin's skilled hands, I'm still shapely," she said, gliding her hand seductively along her hip down to her thigh.

Harry gave her a thumbs up along with a cutely bashful smile.

"How about you, Harry? Are you dating?"

He ran his fingers through his damp hair and thoughtfully rubbed his chin. "Nah, I've been giving it a rest. Pretty busy doing other things these days."

"Like writing poetry?" she ruefully suggested.

"Oh, you read my poem, huh?" Harry folded his hands together and waited glumly for her critique.

"Couldn't resist. It's good, Harry. You must really love her."

"Love who?" He looked at her curiously.

"The girl in the poem."

"No, no, there's no girl. It's just kind of how I see me loving someone someday. A perfect girl like her probably doesn't even exist…anymore."

"Not even Bernadette?"

"Not even," he sighed. "She was, let's say, a trial run."

"Well, you know Harry, it's best not to be too moral, you cheat yourself out of too much life." She removed the melting ice bag from her foot and stretched out her leg.

Harry sat quietly considering Sparkles' vaguely familiar words. He refrained from telling her that the girl of his dreams had died while he was in college, and she was the real reason he quit school and why no one could take her place. Afraid he'd lose his composure if he even said her name, he tried to subdue his feelings. He did not hear himself let out an exasperated moan.

Rescuing Harry from his apparent agony, Sparkles placed her foot gently on his thigh. "Look, the ice is helping with the swelling."

He forced himself to focus on her jiggling toe. "Guess it's not broken," he surmised. When she didn't move her foot, Harry picked it up and placed it next to the other one. "Maybe you should be taking me back soon to get my truck. You can drive, right?"

"I'm not sure I can. Let's just give it a little more time. Pass the peaches, please."

"I just have to say," Harry began, placing his hand over his heart, "that I am really sorry I ran over your foot. I didn't see you there. Just how was it you were so close to my rig?" He had been holding back this question, worried that Sparkles might sue him, but now tipsy with wine and in his entrusted care, he felt more comfortable asking.

"I was leading up to that earlier…until you fell asleep," she teased, lightly shoving his shoulder. "I'll spare you the details again, and there were a lot of them, some you shouldn't have missed."

"I'm sorry. These trips take a lot out of a man. I usually go straight to bed when I get home."

"Ohh?" Sparkles gave him a slow wink over the rim of the plastic wine glass.

"Ahem," he mumbled, trying to hold back his smile. She had such a youthful air about her, he found he was easily charmed. "But I'm all ears now. So, you were standing so close to my truck for *what* reason?"

"I was meeting a date at the Jackalope, right across the street. I could not find one lousy parking spot, and I drove forty miles for this guy. I thought it was a good sign that I found that spot until you ran over me."

Sparkles heartily laughed after reliving their unusual introduction. She threw her head back on the sofa and proclaimed, "I might be the only person alive that can say I was run over by an eighteen-wheeler and lived to tell the story."

Harry laughed with her. She was a good sport after all. Although, he saw in her demeanor a sadness he had not seen before – a refreshing vulnerability hiding behind her laugh. Somehow it made it easier for him to tell her personal things about himself.

"Harry's my nickname. I'm not that crazy about my real name, so I'm guilty of using Harry a lot."

"Well, sure can't be any worse than Maude."

"Maude?" Harry choked on his laugh. "I'm sorry, it's just that I have an Aunt Maude…she's, well, she kind of resembles a full-back with a bad attitude. If you don't mind, I'll just call you Sparkles."

"And I'll just call you, Harry. And that's the end of that."
They clinked their glasses together in a pact.

"I used to be like your Aunt Maude," Sparkles spoke softly,
reflecting on unhappy times. She shook off the impending
sadness with an exaggerated shiver of her shoulders. Later, after
sharing much more, the tears were harder to shake.

In the still of the night, hesitant to wake his guest sleeping so
soundly next to him, Harry was left to contemplate his own dull
existence. Eventually, he had let his weary head land on the soft
furry wrap resting on her shoulders, and soon the low, contented
hum of her snoring lulled him to sleep. It was like cuddling up to
a mama bear.

The next morning, back at the scene of the accident, Sparkles
placed her fur wrap around Harry's neck and thanked him for a
lovely evening.

"My girlfriends are going to be so jealous when they find out
I had a sleepover with a handsome young truck driver," she
teased.

"Ha, you're funny, Sparkles," he said, defusing the comment.
"My mom called it a pajama party in her day."

"Well, that's somewhat true. But back then, we actually wore
pajamas." She pulled her sunglasses down her crinkled-up nose
and gave him another one of her mischievous smiles.

"You're the queen of hoots!" Harry decreed, removing the
furry wrap and placing it back on her bare shoulders. He didn't
have the heart to tell her about the rip in the back of her dress.

Inside the car, Sparkles held her arm out and dropped her
hand, gesturing to Harry that he may kiss the hand of the queen.
So, he did. "Go and love some more, Harry," she said, tossing the
fur wrap his direction. She jerked the gear into reverse and
backed out so quickly she nearly rolled over his foot.

The construction workers leaning on their shovels had been watching them with big dopey grins. "Run over a woman and she takes you home with her," one said to the other. "I'll have to try that on Mary Jo at the office."

"Aye yi yi," the other one crooned.

The doctor said that it was merely a fracture, too small to worry about, although Sparkles had to wear an ugly boot for five days. "You're messing with my style," she told him.

He laughed, until he realized she really meant it. "Well, look at it this way young lady, you can take full advantage of the sympathy."

"Oh, you're absolutely right." Sparkles' frown switched to a wicked grin. She whispered in the doc's ear, "Maybe I'll wear it five extra days. Or better yet, keep it in the car when I need it."

From there, she drove straight to the salon and had her toenails painted blue – the color of the boot mixed with a dash of silver glitter. During the entire session she told the whole story about the eighteen-wheeler and the very handsome driver. She had the technicians and the customers in stitches. When she ended it with the pajama party, less the pajamas, and passed Harry's driver's license around so that there would be no doubt of her story's validity, the laughter changed to barely audible sniggers.

Harry had felt a kind of muddled relief watching her drive away. The whole thing seemed too close for comfort, yet Sparkles had managed to tug at his heartstrings. Never had he met someone who shared so easily and spoke so clearly with little reserve. Her life was an open book. She had a father that used his hand more than his brain. "Poor soul died before he could apologize. Apologies are very healing." The divorce had scarred her heart forever. "Scars remind us that we've truly lived." Dating wasn't nearly as much fun as she thought it would be. "But they bring zing to my stories."

She had said that finding a companion was nearly impossible, and he didn't even have to be particularly angelic or handsome like everyone expects, just witty and kind and one who notices things around him, like the differences in flowers.

So charmed by her, Harry had forgotten the thirty-five-year difference. He even found himself talking about the girl of his dreams who was killed in a skiing accident. In between tears and laughter, they had talked for hours until the last thing Sparkles said while falling asleep in Harry's arms: "I'd like just one honest kiss before I die. I'm lonely, Harry."

Throughout the day an unexpected chuckle would burst out when reviving those scenes. Giving Sparkles a fake phone number, Harry convinced himself, was the right thing to do. Forgetting to get his license back from her was just pure stupidity. Or was it? What were the odds he'd ever run into her again?

He went to bed alone with his thoughts and Sparkles' furry wrap on the pillow beneath his head. Meeting her had been an interesting, no, an extraordinary event, and there was no one he could trust to share it with.

The next day, Harry met a woman squeezing avocados in the produce section of the grocery store. While trying to find the perfect avocado, they chatted about the disparity of the poor fruit, unjustly named a vegetable. He surprised himself when he accepted her brazen invitation to meet for drinks the following Friday. But he was even more surprised when at that precise moment he thought of Sparkles and her challenging words of encouragement, "Reach out, take a chance, get hurt, even. But play as well as you can."

~

After hearing Sparkles' unusual but entertaining excuse, the retired firefighter was very understanding about being stood up and agreed to meet again, same time, same place. Sparkles would not risk being run over by anything with more than four wheels and parked in one of the five empty handicap spaces at the Jackalope restaurant. She left the big blue boot on the dashboard as proof of her disability.

The place was packed with drinks all around. The patrons were smiling and seemed relaxed, eager to begin the weekend. Suits and loosened ties were everywhere – about two men to every woman. Sparkles nearly swooned.

She pressed her way through the crowd to the bar. Noticing how the women looked dainty drinking from fancy glasses, she dropped the idea of a hearty whisky and ordered a lemon-drop martini. Delicately pinching the stem between her fingers, she scoped out the men, hoping to recognize the firefighter. From his online picture, she looked for broad shoulders, a thick neck and rippling muscles, a head held high with pride. She wondered if his pores still carried the scent of burnt forest.

Across the way, she spotted Harry sitting alone in a booth for two. An enormous smile seized her face, and she found herself advancing toward him.

"Oh my, if it isn't the man who almost killed me," she embellished, clinking her glass against Harry's beer mug.

"Sparkles!" He acknowledged her with a boyish grin.

"Yes, tis' I," she said, accepting his cheery smile as an invitation to sit down across from him. "So good to see you, Harry. *Really* good."

"Good to see you, too. What a nice surprise," he said mean-ingfully.

"What brings you here?"

"ME," a woman announced flatly, seeming to appear out of nowhere.

"Oh, yes, Sparkles, this is Reba. Reba, this is Sparkles." He stood up to give Reba his seat. She huffed while claiming it. Harry stood awkwardly without a place to sit.

"Here, Harry, sit by me. I can squeeze you in." Sparkles patted the cushioned seat with such enthusiasm, Harry obeyed. He looked over at his date who was not smiling, apparently uncomfortable with the change of events. Sparkles noticed her discontent and said, "Oh don't worry honey, he's an old friend. Matter of fact let me tell you the story of how we met. Harry ran me over with his eighteen-wheeler…."

Teetering on the edge of the seat, Harry nervously laughed in between gulps of beer, while Reba maintained a look of irrita-tion. When Sparkles got to the part about falling asleep in his arms, his laughter came to a halt. Reba looked at Harry in disgust. Her face crumpled as if a festering boil had suddenly appeared on his nose. She turned to Sparkles. "Aren't you kind of old for him. I mean come on lady, you have to be at least twice his age. And you, Harry, have you always slept with older…elderly women?"

"I didn't sleep with her," he protested. "I was just being kind. I mean, after all, I did roll over her foot."

"Just being kind?" Sparkles reached for Harry's arm and gazed into his eyes. "You *are* kind, but I thought we liked each other, Harry. I mean, we did share a lot that night."

"I think this date is over!" Reba slammed her drink on the table and stood up. "Next time you see me at the grocery store, pretend you don't know me, Harry. And you," she leaned in and said directly to Sparkles, "why don't you find somebody your own age? You look like his mother!" She rolled her eyes in a slow condescending manner. "Sparkles! How ridiculous!"

Harry moved quickly to stand up and slipped off the cushion onto the floor. Humiliated, he picked himself up and rushed after Reba, not looking back once at Sparkles' doleful eyes.

The cruel and worthless words Reba had said dissolved in the air like soap bubbles. But Harry's reaction wounded her heart. Profoundly disappointed, she considered leaving, until she spotted her date at the bar. At least she thought it was him. He was the only man in the room with a handle-bar mustache. She mustered up the courage to greet him.

"Are you by chance a firefighter?" she asked, tapping the man on the shoulder who swung around on the stool to address the question.

"Depends on who's asking," he said, looking Sparkles up and down, expressionless.

"Well, I was supposed to meet an online date here, and I have only a distant picture of him, but you sure do have the muscles for a firefighter. Are you Phil?"

"I am, and I was supposed to meet a woman here, too, but she is, well…no offense, but how old are you anyway?"

"Not old enough to be your mother," Sparkles retaliated. "How old are you? You look to be in your sixties." She sized him up with one raised eyebrow.

"I suppose I am, but I only date women of a certain age. I think there's been a mistake. You can't be the woman I met online. Are you...are you Sparkles?"

The look on his face almost made Sparkles deny her identity. But she would not cower, not now, not ever. "I am. But right now with the way you're looking at me, I wish I weren't."

"Well, I should probably at least buy you a drink for the trouble. You're a nice-looking lady, but I just don't have an attraction for…"

"Women your own age?" Sparkles challenged him.

"Yes, I guess you're right. But hey, tell my lady friends here about being run over by an eighteen-wheeler. That was a seriously funny story!"

Sparkles' lower lip went slack. Telling the story to Reba had taken the fun out of it. Even though it was so worth repeating, she hesitated, noticing the younger women huddling at the bar listening to the conversation and rudely whispering behind cupped hands. They snubbed Sparkles and sat up taller upon seeing the good-looking man who suddenly appeared behind her. The man placed his hand on Sparkle's shoulder. Startled, Sparkles turned to see who was getting all the attention, as well as taking the liberty to touch her.

Harry kissed her on the cheek. "I'm so glad you waited for me," he said. "Can I buy you a drink?"

"Oh!" Sparkles eyes widened and every rotten feeling up to then dissipated. Bolstered by Harry's timely rescue, she gave them all a bashful smile. "Phil has first dibs on buying me a drink. Don't you Phil?" Before Phil could respond, she turned to Harry, "But you can buy the next one."

Through a round of drinks, Harry, himself, told the story of how he and Sparkles had met. He ended it with them falling asleep on the sofa and leaving that tidbit for his captive audience to digest, he whisked Sparkles away. Before they reached the exit, she pulled away from him, went straight up to the firefighter, leaned in, and like a dog, she sniffed his neck. "Yeah, I thought so!" she said with a smirk. Holding her head high, she linked arms with Harry, and they casually strolled out of the establishment.

In the parking lot, Harry remarked, "You sure do have a way with people."

"Well, they're my species! Like it or not."

Looking at her sideways, Harry was visibly puzzled. "What was that sniffing all about?"

"I wanted to see if he smelled like burning forest. He did not.

He smelled like cheap cologne. Firefighter, my foot!" She opened her purse and added more lipstick to her lemon infused lips. "Hey, what you did back there...that was very sweet of you, Harry. What made you do it? What about Reba?"

"Besides telling me she doesn't date truck drivers, Reba was wrong to treat you like that. I pretty much told her so." He paused and added sheepishly, "Although, I kind of wish you hadn't told the part about falling asleep together."

"Well...you told it back there to Phil and his harem."

"Yes, I know. I did that for you. You do know nothing happened between us, don't you?"

Sparkles looked down at the ground and pinched her dress. "Yes, I know that. It just felt so good pretending that someone liked me, especially someone kind and vibrant like you. I'm sorry I made you so uncomfortable."

"And I am sorry I'm so uncomfortable with the idea of being with an older woman. I really don't know why that is, but it is."

"A much older woman," Sparkles conceded. "If I were to be really honest with myself, Harry, I probably *should* be uncomfortable with the idea of being with a much younger man. Weird, huh?" She fished through her purse again and held up his driver's license. "I tried to get this to you earlier, HAROLD, but I guess you wrote down the wrong phone number."

Harry looked away in shame.

"It's probably best you don't go in the Golden Nail Salon on Third. Everyone working there knows who you are now." She covered her mouth and giggled. "Good night, Harry...and thanks again." With a little wave of surrender, and a misty-eyed farewell, she turned to walk away.

"Wait, wait!" Harry frantically stepped toward her. "How's, how's your foot?"

She turned around slowly, surprised to see the anxious look on his face. "Thank you for asking. Working just fine...see?" she said, breaking into a Texas two-step in her fancy high heels. "Too bad the firefighter won't be taking me dancing any time soon."

"It must be great to feel younger than you are. I hope I feel like you do when I'm your age, Sparkles. Well, heck, I'd like to feel like you do right now, at *my* age. And you're so refreshingly bold…and honest. In my opinion, that firefighter is missing out. You're much more fun to be with than any girl I've ever met."

"I am?" Maude sucked in a sniffle.

"Yes, you are." Harry shuffled his feet. "Do you think we could be friends?"

Maude stood silently basking in the request. A playful chuckle leapt from her throat. "Only if you promise not to run over my foot again."

"I'm afraid I can't make that promise. I have two left feet, but I'll try really hard not to step on your foot on the dance floor." Harry cocked his head and offered his most sincere smile.

"And I would really like to ride in your monster rig…wait! Dancing? Did you say dancing?" Sparkle's moist eyes twinkled.

"Yeah, let's go dancing, Maude."

"Oh, what a fine idea, Harold!"

Then it hit them both at the same time. "Harold and Maude!"

"Oh my gosh!" Maude squealed with delight. "That's my all-time favorite movie."

"Mine, too!" Harold bellowed and gave her a high five. "Wait a second, that's who you've been quoting all along!"

"The earth is my body. My head is in the stars!" Maude recited, swirling around in a circle, her arms reaching for the sky. "I've been trying to live the rest of my life like that wonderful character."

"Who sends dead flowers to a funeral? It's absurd." Harold mimicked, looping Maude's arm around his as they walked into the darkness.

"Everyone should be able to make some music. That's the cosmic dance," Maude recounted tenderly.

Harold stopped and looked up at the heavenly stars above.

"Maude?"

"Oh my, I never liked my name until just now hearing you say it like that. Say it again, please, Harold."

"Maude…do you pray?"

"Pray? No. I communicate," she said easily, looking up and joining him in his gaze.

"With God?"

"With life."

And in that perfect illogical moment, Harold gave Maude an honest kiss. And he was not just being kind.

RANDOM REFLECTIONS

Do you remember when you were a kid and you played outside for hours until just before dark your mom would call you in? You would run and hide behind a tree, thinking that if she didn't see you, she'd go back inside. Fat chance! Moms do not give up. And when you did finally reveal yourself, it was only to beg for more time. "A little longer, please!" If you whined loud and convincingly, she would give you your wish. "OK, ten more minutes!" And those ten magical minutes, that usually rolled into twenty, but felt like five, became the most exciting part of your day.

A LITTLE LONGER

Reason woke up invigorated as usual. Exhaling a full-bodied yawn, followed by a long gratifying catlike stretch, she stood on the porch and watched her aunt robotically toss corn to the chickens as she did every day that summer. She squinted toward the sunrise and observed the dew rising from the moist earth, gradually heading toward the sky. It appeared to her as rain falling in reverse, leaving the blades of grass standing erect, begging. Lighthearted birds flew from one tree to the next, each trying to be the first to spread the news that morning had broken. Reason enjoyed their erratic chirping, sounding like a chamber orchestra warming up.

Surrendering to the new day, she stepped out into the early sunlight. Nearby a rooster stood balancing on a fence post, growling like an old man at her presence. Ignoring him, she watched her "Good morning" whisper float gently on a feather across the yard toward Aunt Delores where it landed softly on her ear.

"And good morning to you, sleepyhead," Aunt Delores shouted, startling the chickens, her words fluttering back to

Reason like a rabble of butterflies. "Breakfast will be ready soon. Uncle Sonny is preparing it now. Why don't you give him a hand?"

Reason nodded and turned to go inside. She paused before opening the door, recalling the exact moment she had first arrived on the lovely Southern Minnesota farm. Nearly three months had passed since her spirit had inherited this young healthy eighteen-year-old body in this time, and in this space. "Trust your instincts," the superiors had told her repeatedly, and one last time for good measure as she materialized at the door of Delores and Sonny Rainwater – an old suitcase in hand, a cloth purse slung over her freckled shoulder, on her head a floppy straw hat – a Norman Rockwell image if ever there was one.

Although she had not been given a middle name like all the other girls in the county, her last name made up for its absence. Rainwater. Reason Rainwater. The name pleased her and fit perfectly because she had a never ending desire to learn her purpose – a reason for living. The thick, wavy auburn hair, and the lily-pad green eyes had been chosen by her superiors. The long, muscular legs were her choice, and like a wild horse, she would run them often. Freckles? Perhaps they were there to remind her that she was human.

The assignment had been selected specifically for her, and it was quite clear and simple: observe and learn as a member of the human race. There were a few guidelines, but mainly she was instructed to log everything she would experience in the leather-bound journal they had provided. When she would return was unknown, and she was instructed to keep it out of her mind, lest it interrupt her studies.

At first, the daily challenges seemed overwhelming, heightened by Reason's eagerness to learn. But as the lazy summer days slowly went by, she began to ease into her new skin and the comfort and love provided by her aunt and uncle.

Standing there in the doorway, her thoughts were interrupted by a sudden shiver. She had yet to get used to the morning chill or the goosebumps that seemed to appear out of nowhere, and she knew that the best place to warm up was in the kitchen.

Uncle Sonny was whistling while standing over the stove pressing bacon into the pan. "Coffee's ready," he said, without looking over his shoulder. The smell of the heavily salted pork wafted throughout the room and clung to the ceiling. Reason stuck her tongue out, licked the air, closed her eyes and swallowed. She poured herself a cup of the thick Italian roast coffee, adding just enough cream to make it look less threatening. Early on she had decided that this was her favorite time of day, and she wanted it every day for as long as possible.

"Brandon is coming over to help me chop wood this morning," her uncle spoke with head still bent, focusing on ironing out the bacon strips. "Would you like me to invite him to lunch? After all, I think he's really coming here to see you."

"Oh, you think so?" Reason stood behind him, peering over his shoulder, inhaling the thick grease as it rose above the stove. "What makes you suppose that I want to see him, too?"

"Well, I am assuming nothing of the kind, my dear. Simply telling you what I think is fairly obvious." He turned to see if she was smiling or frowning, uncertain of how his presumption had been received.

Reason put her hands on her hips and managed both a smile and a frown. "Uncle Sonny, I like Brandon very much, but...," she looked down at the floor searching for the words that would be closest to the truth, "he is a bit, well, a bit simple."

"Oh, like your old uncle, eh?" A slow grin inched across his weathered face.

Sensing that she may have chosen the wrong words and somehow hurt her uncle's feelings, Reason reached around his denim overalls and embraced him in a tight squeeze. "You're not simple. You're like a big bear that scratches his back on a tree and thinks only about honey and sleeping and all the good things in life." Just then, she realized that was exactly what she also liked about Brandon. It had been hard resisting him from the moment they met. He came boldly riding up on his horse, wearing a most confident smile, and within minutes Reason found herself on the same saddle racing through the fields, hugging Brandon's strong body from behind, just like she had just hugged her uncle. No matter how much she tried, she could not get the young man out of her mind, and her uncle was not making it any easier.

"Does that mean Brandon can come to lunch?" Uncle Sonny rephrased the question.

"Of course," she said, squeezing him tighter, "if you think he can find me out in the cornfield. I have a lot of writing to do. I might just be out there most of the day."

"I imagine that boy will find you. He's got the nose of a bloodhound," Uncle Sonny assured her. "Now, call your aunt in for breakfast before I eat all the bacon."

Breakfast with her new family was the best. They sat outside on the covered porch where the breeze gently curled up the ends of the napkins, flowing just softly enough to keep the conversation light. Afterwards, her aunt and uncle took a second cup of coffee and strolled around the farm arm in arm, taking inventory of what needed to be done or bought at the store the next time they drove into town. With her tablet in hand and a pen behind her ear, Reason stood a few minutes longer watching the purplish aura dance around them, radiating from the timeless love the happy couple shared with each other. Her keen ears heard her uncle say tenderly to his wife, "I don't ever remember a time without you, Dee Dee." The sweet words bounced from his lips into the air and rocketed straight toward the sun. Delighted, Reason watched the elderly lovebirds until they disappeared inside the barn, and then she turned and ran excitedly toward the cornfield to write down, in the comfort of her private sanctuary, the scene she had just experienced.

Squeezing between the cornstalks, she located the spot that

she had carved out when she had first arrived, the perfect place for writing and meditating. The imprint of her body was molded into the hay that she used for a pallet. After writing down what she had learned, along with her own personal thoughts and feelings, she stretched out on her back and watched the clouds roll by as the ears of corn held steadfast framing the scene. The corn was due to be harvested by the end of the month and her aunt had encouraged her to enjoy the beauty of the field while it lasted, as it would not look or smell the same afterwards. Lying there in nature's bliss, Reason could not begin to imagine the impending change of her surroundings. She closed her eyes and let her body sink into the earth. After a few shallow breaths, she felt weightless as a moth – her head clear of all thought.

In a deep trance, she didn't hear the cornstalks being carefully separated as Brandon moved slowly through them, intent on surprising the girl he had grown fond of that he was told could be found somewhere in the middle of the cornfield. When he spotted her bare feet, all ten toes pointing upward toward the golden sun, he stopped in his tracks, not yet wanting to reveal himself. Peering through the tall stalks, he strained to see the rest of her body. His eyes slowly trailed the familiar tan leg from the ankle to the bottom of her blue denim shorts, and recognizing the brown birthmark shaped like a star on the side of her thigh, he let out a pleasurable sigh.

"Reese," he whispered. When she didn't respond, he cleared his throat to warn her before going forward. She didn't move a muscle, both arms resting beside her, palms up, her head perfectly still. She could have passed for dead until he noticed her mouth twitch. Looking closer he saw tiny flecks of gold floating out from the corner of her slightly fluttering eyelids. "What the...?" he blurted, stumbling backwards, barely stopping himself from falling.

Reason shot up from her sleep and turned to see Brandon bracing his fall with his body wrapped around a tall stalk. The gold flecks disappeared the second she opened her eyes. "Well, it's not harvest time yet and if it were, I doubt that's the way to pick the corn," she teased, sitting up on her knees and looking sideways at the clumsy boy.

"Oh, hi Reese. I was looking for you and…well, I guess I found you," he said, unraveling himself to an upright position. Steadier on two feet, he leaned in to look closer at her eyes.

"What are you looking at?" Reason demanded. "Do I have a bug on my face?" Imagining the ugly creature climbing into her mouth, she swatted the air and shook her head to make sure before he answered, and it was too late.

"No, no bug, I just thought I saw…oh, never mind, it was nothing." He stepped closer and asked, "Can I join you?"

"Well, it looks as though you already have." She reached for the journal and tucked it under the straw next to her.

Brandon plunked to the ground and struggled to sit cross-legged in his dirt-caked boots. "Your uncle invited me to lunch. We just finished chopping a pile of wood. Makes a man hungry," he attested, patting his hard, youthful stomach.

As Reason watched him maneuver his legs in the limited space, his knees grazing hers, she felt a tickle in her tummy and a tiny twitter seemed to fly out of her navel. *Oh my, that happens every time I'm around him.* She smiled crookedly at Brandon, realizing right then that she was more than happy to see him. "I'm getting kind of hungry myself. Sometimes I stay out here longer than I should. I might have again if you hadn't stopped by."

"What are you doing out here, besides sleeping?" He glanced over at the tablet.

"I'm writing. I think better out here in the quiet, and the smell of this sweet corn does wonders for my imagination."

"What are you writing about?" Brandon reached over to pick up the tablet. Reason grabbed it and hid it behind her back.

"Lots of things, actually. It's a daily log of my life here. I'm learning a lot this summer."

"I can't imagine there's much to learn on a farm." He removed his cap and brushed it off. "Besides corn, chickens, field mice, crows and the country barn dance this weekend." Lifting his eyebrows, he winked at Reason and smiled. "Speaking of which, are you planning on going?"

"I hadn't thought about it. I suppose if my aunt and uncle do." Feeling that funny tickle in her tummy again she looked closer at Brandon's face. *Such nice features and what long eyelashes. Those lips, why they look like they are as soft as rose petals. I wish I could touch them.*

Lowering his voice, he spoke with a calm, more serious demeanor, "I'd really like it if you'd go with me."

"You would?" she asked dreamily. Without any further thought, Reason leaned in at the same time Brandon leaned forward and their lips met. *So, this is a kiss.* The words rushed to the tip of her tongue and were swallowed up by his warm breath. Her eyes remained opened and seeing both of his closed eyelids melding into one, she quickly closed hers shut. *Umm, much better.*

When Brandon gently pulled away, Reason stayed perfectly still, eyes closed, lips relaxed and waiting. She was not aware that the kiss was over.

"Another?" he whispered. "No problem." This time he kissed her longer, taking more of her mouth inside his. The words were not readily available to describe this glorious new feeling she was experiencing. When he finally released her lips, she opened her eyes and saw the purple haze surrounding Brandon's head that she had seen earlier on her aunt and uncle. A lighter, playful, perhaps less intense purple, but even so.

Smitten with the girl behind the kiss, Brandon slumped back with glazed over eyes. "Does that mean, yes?"

"Makes sense to me," she laughed, and this time her stomach grumbled the way she heard her uncle's grumble while he stood over his wife's shoulder at the kitchen counter, nibbling on her neck and hoping to snatch a bite before it hit the plate. "All of a sudden, I'm starving. Race you to the kitchen!" Reason sprung to her feet, and in all the excitement, she forgot to take her journal. She ran toward the house with Brandon following, too far behind to catch up.

"She runs like the wind!" he blurted out in between breaths while holding onto the back door at the threshold of the Rainwater's kitchen. "What are you feeding that girl?" Brandon directed his question toward Aunt Delores who had just given her husband a slice of freshly baked bread.

"Well, take a look at my husband here. He's as fit as a fiddle, too. I bet it's my cooking."

"Darn right it is!" Uncle Sonny slapped the top of the table and gulped down the bread before the butter melted onto his hand. "Have a seat, boy. You're in for a treat."

Reason slowly entered the room, having stood unnoticed in the hallway, quietly eavesdropping. She had pulled her hair loose and brushed it, her face still flush from the quick run. She knew, like her uncle, that they were all in for a treat. Aunt Delores took tremendous pride in her cooking and served their meals on her favorite China, explaining, "Why would anyone want to keep this sitting in a cupboard when it is so beautiful. It's meant to be used, especially by special people like you." No one argued with her reasoning, silently agreeing that the mouth-watering dishes looked even more delectable on the lovely porcelain pieces that had survived shipment from Paris, and at one time graced her great-grandmother's finest table setting.

After all the fussing over each bite, and the promise of hot apple pie served outside afterwards, everyone went to the porch to digest. They sat in silence listening to the wind until Brandon stood up and removed his cap. "Mr. Rainwater, Mrs. Rainwater," he addressed the couple, "I would like the honor of escorting your niece to the dance this weekend."

"Oh?" Aunt Delores smiled modestly and looked over at her

husband who was obviously biting away his smile. "Well, Mr. Rainwater, what do you think?" she asked politely.

Uncle Sonny looked over at Reason questionably, not sure if that was what she wanted after she had made the remark earlier about the young man's simple being. He waited for her to give him a sign. Like him, Reason was holding back a smile, pressing her lips together while her eyes twinkled with delight. She gave a little nod and shifted her gaze toward Brandon.

"Well, young man, I think that's a splendid idea. Mrs. Rainwater and I are going, too. We wouldn't miss a chance to get up on that dance floor and cut a rug. Tell you what, we'll bring Reason with us to save you a trip, and you can bring her home. I doubt we'll be able to stay through the entire thing, anyway."

Delores spoke up, "You may not be able to, but I'm certain I could last!" Catching her husband's scolding eyes, she quickly changed her tone, "Oh, but you're right, we'll probably leave early anyway. I, well…isn't it about time for that pie?"

"I'd love some, but after that big meal, I think a stroll with Reese might help make more room for pie." Looking over at the elated girl, Brandon reached for her hand.

Reason locked her fingers with his, and they walked away in silence. Their smiles said it all.

"My, my," Aunt Delores sang, "how did you know, Sonny?"

"Same way I knew about you, sweetheart." He reached over and pulled at Dee's skirt, patting his knee with his other hand. Knowing right where to sit, she slid gently onto his lap, and they cuddled for a while until the old lover's legs fell asleep.

Meanwhile, the young couple strolled across the fields and every time they came upon a haybale they would stop to lean against it and kiss. The purple hue around Brandon had intensified and the warmth that it generated caressed Reason's body and filled her with love. Knowing better she tried hard not to listen to the silent plea, *please let me stay longer, much longer.*

The sun was nearly setting when Brandon left the farm.

Reason stood on the porch and watched him drive away. She whispered, "If this is love, I think I love you," and she blew a kiss his direction just before his truck disappeared. She listened intently, hoping he would return the sentiment, picturing the words flying toward her on the light summer breeze. All she could hear was the quiet of the farm. Just when she moved toward the front door, she heard a high-pitched sound. Straining to see, she spotted a swarm of bats heading her direction. They turned just feet before they reached her and swooped over the house, leaving a distinct message floating in the air meant specially for her. "I love you, Reese."

That night, Reason had a second slice of pie with a cup of hot cocoa. She felt unusually hungry and yet light on her feet. At the kitchen table, watching her aunt roll out dough for the morning breakfast, she cupped the hot mug between her palms and noticing the smile on her face, she asked, "You enjoy cooking, don't you?"

"I do, and most of all, I enjoy seeing my loved-ones happy."

"You and Uncle Sonny are very happy. Why do you think?"

The sincere question made her aunt stop what she was doing. She brushed the flour off her hands and looked seriously at her niece. "Love is an action word, my dear. When you learn what pleases a man, you spend the rest of your days doing those things for him. In return, when he does it back, it forms a special bond that grows bigger than life and brings the best kind of happiness. Keep in mind, it can never be one-sided because we are human. Mature love is kind of like a seesaw...it takes two to balance it."

Reason took the words into her heart. "I think I understand. It's the same with family, isn't it? I mean, both you and Uncle Sonny please me, and I am learning to please you. That's why we are happy to see each other in the kitchen every morning. We all love each other."

"Yes, we do, and before you know it, you will be rolling dough on your own kitchen table like I am right now, just so you can see that wonderful look on that special person's face when he takes his first bite. The look of love." Aunt Delores observed Reason's starry-eyed innocence and chuckled with delight. "Yes, the look of love."

Later, the house was still, inside and out. Tucked under the sheet, her head propped up on two pillows, Reason reached over to get her journal out of the drawer. She had much to write about and was excited to relive it again on paper. Realizing that she had left it in the cornfield she blurted out, "Oh no!" Clenching her teeth, she sat motionless and listened for any sounds of movement within the house. When she was certain that she heard her uncle's snoring, she slipped out of bed and tiptoed from the room.

Easing her body down the narrow hall, she stopped at their bedroom door and listened again. She pictured her aunt's arm draped over her husband's bare chest, her chin resting on his shoulder, their heartbeats in perfect rhythm, just as their love had been for nearly half a century. *I want to love like that.*

Hidden by the clouds, there was not enough moon to light the path through the cornfield but Reason knew it so well, she could have walked it blindfolded. The loose fabric of her pajamas made a different sound when it grazed the twisted leaves on the cornstalks. She took a mental note to write that in her journal when back in bed. This was the first time she had experienced the field in the dark, and she took extra notice of her surroundings.

When she reached the familiar spot, she bent down to feel around the hay for the tablet. Just when she touched it, the moon peeked out from behind a cloud and beamed brightly into the space where she was kneeling. Reason looked up and felt warm air caress her face, and suddenly she couldn't resist sleep. Dropping the tablet, she closed her eyes and fell slowly to the ground. She felt the darkness swallow her up, and the silvery threads of a moonbeam lift her above the cornfield. The roof of her aunt and uncle's home grew smaller and smaller, and then seconds later she found herself running down a wet asphalt road; the stark smell of creosote rising heavily from its cracks after a hard rain. The air was thick and wet with fog, and she heard voices saying softly but urgently, "Run to the tunnel. Run!"

"But I want to stay. Please, just a little longer," she cried. The cold realization of leaving Aunt Dee and Uncle Sonny, Brandon, and the farm shook her to the core of her being. The sadness was overwhelming. She saw the tunnel ahead through blinding tears. It looked as if it were dissolving. When she tried to run faster, she slipped and fell on the wet road, landing on her hands to break her fall. The rough asphalt pressed into her palms. Black grainy crumbles were stuck in her skin and tiny puddles of blood began forming around them. Human blood, she thought, staring down at her hands, momentarily stunned by the sensation. Shaking them loose, she looked up and saw that the tunnel had disappeared. Everything around her faded to black.

Reason woke to the friendly gurgle of the coffee pot percolating. She looked up at the ceiling and then from side to side, taking notice of the dresser where her clothes were neatly folded, a lamp with a twisted candlestick base wearing a lacy fabric shade trimmed in gold fringe, and to her right, the nightstand that held her tablet each night as she slept safely in the soft padded bed her aunt claimed was made for a princess. She was afraid to move. Carefully recounting what had happened, she wondered if she had dreamed it all. Why am I here? Her heart began to beat rapidly with the question. She forced herself to sit up, and when she placed her palms down on the bed, she let out a soft, "Ow!" Turning her hands over she saw small indentions in her skin, tinges of dried blood and scrapes near her wrists. The pajamas she had worn every night since she arrived were damp and stuck to her knees. It wasn't a dream.

Then instantly she remembered the journal. In her haste, she pulled hard on the drawer of the nightstand, and it flew out of its casing and landed on the floor. The noise alerted her aunt, and she came running to her door. "Everything alright in there, honey?" she said sweetly, a natural hint of concern in her voice.

"Oh yes, everything's fine. Just dropped something. Nothing's broken."

"Well, good. Breakfast will be ready in ten minutes. Got your favorite biscuits in the oven now, and Uncle Sonny is making gravy."

As she walked away, Reason could hear Aunt Delores singing a little tune about a muffin man, then stopping to scold her uncle for licking the gravy ladle.

She leapt out of bed and picked up the drawer to find that the journal wasn't there. Throwing on a robe, she ran past her aunt and uncle and said before closing the door, "Be right back!" Trying to hide the panic in her voice, she added, "I left my journal in the cornfield."

Reason ran so fast, she was unaware that she had passed the entry to her hideaway – no longer a secret since Brandon had found it. She stopped and looked around her, not recognizing the surroundings. Disoriented, she backtracked to regain her sense of direction. A sigh of relief poured from her mouth when she found her way to the carved-out niche where she nearly stepped on the journal lying face up and open on the hay. A monarch caterpillar was resting in the fold, its vivid stripes of yellow and black were bold against the white pages. Reason carefully picked up the book and dropped the insect safely onto a leaf. Thumbing through the journal to see if there were more creatures snuggling within its pages, she noticed that all her writing had disappeared. Every page was blank.

She plopped down on the pallet and began turning one empty sheet after another, gasping in between, until she got to the end. In the middle of the last page, boldly written in black ink, was a single *A+*. Reason grinned from ear to ear. Looking up to the bright blue sky, she whispered, "Does this mean I can stay?"

Waiting for an answer, a sign, anything, she closed her eyes tightly and held her breath. The answer came from her uncle's own kind voice traveling melodically through the cornfield on yellow kite tails directly to her heart. "Reason, the biscuits are ready!"

A WOMAN ALWAYS KNOWS

The assignment landed with a loud kerplunk on Ester's desk just as she was taking that first glorious sip of morning coffee. Through the steam rising from her cup, she curiously eyed her boss' rear-end as she strolled back to her office. She had learned over the years how to read the editor's mood by the way she walked. Oh, this must be a good one, she thought, watching the fifty-something-year-old, bad-ass, executive editor of the *Woman to Woman* magazine sashay across the room. And to make sure that Ester understood the importance of the assignment, her boss turned around and winked at her – a sure-fire signal that expectations were high.

All eyes were on Ester as she slowly opened the folder, taking more time than usual just to tease her colleagues. Every writer there knew the procedure – skip the front page stating the professional code of ethics, and go straight to the red tab, the assignment at hand. Taunting her fellow journalists, she deliberately went to the front page and began reading, mouthing silently each word until finally the exasperated spectators resorted to throwing paper clips at her.

"Alright, alright!" Ester playfully protested, throwing her hands up in resignation. But when she read the title of the assignment, her mouth dropped open and the teasing stopped. Snapping the folder shut, she fished a paper clip out of her coffee cup and walked past the disappointed faces out into the sunny, fifty-two-degree Philadelphia morning.

The small park across the street had only one bench under a tall maple tree that would soon produce clusters of beautiful redbuds. On that bench is where Ester did a lot of thinking. She was glad to see that it wasn't occupied and moved speedily toward it before someone else claimed it.

It took two deep cleansing breaths before she could open the folder again. The heading, "Dana H. Moretti Weds Franklin T. Russo" jumped right off the page. Was this a cruel joke? Franklin, known to Ester as Frankie, was once her fiancé just two years earlier. She had not seen or talked to him since they parted on a night she would never forget, and one she would play over and over in her head on rainy days and lonely nights or whenever she watched one of those gooey chick flicks. Even now it pained her to revive the disturbing memory.

Under constant pressure with their demanding careers, Frankie designing film sets and Ester's many travels for the magazine, it was a wonder the couple had any time at all together. Both from strong Catholic stock, they would wait until they were married to share the same bed.

It was during an out-of-town assignment when Ester was ordered to take the next flight home for a second interview with Loretta Youngblood, the up-and-coming actress starring in a movie being produced right in her own hometown. She knew that Frankie was working closely with Loretta on the set, so when the plane landed she hurried to his studio to surprise him with the good news.

Nearly dark by the time she arrived, the old building was closed, but Frankie's car was still in the parking lot. All the lights were off except for one office on the third floor. A tenacious journalist like herself didn't think twice about climbing the emergency stairs. When she reached the third floor, she leaned over the rusty railing to try and see through the window. She caught a glimpse of a woman in a strapless, red cocktail dress, a man's hand resting on her hip. Stretching further for a better view, Ester easily identified her. Loretta! Loretta Youngblood, in all her sensual flesh! She froze when the man's hand moved to the back of the woman and began unzipping her dress. When the man whispered something in her ear and eased around her, Ester cried out "Frankie? Frankie!" When he looked up, the guilty expression plastered on his face jolted her. What happened next, Ester still cannot explain. She was told in the hospital that she had fallen from three flights up and was lucky to be alive. Four broken bones, a serious concussion, and a mean gash in her forehead would all heal in good time. But not so for a wounded heart. Naturally, she ended the engagement.

Ester grumbled from behind clenched teeth. Could she face Frankie after all this time? Everyone in her office would die to get their hands on an assignment like this one. Dana Moretti was the heir to a fabulous, multi-million-dollar estate, and her father had been the mayor of Philadelphia in the early nineties and was so popular that the town named a hoagie after him. Thirty-nine and single again after three failed marriages to men of considerable wealth, Dana was featured often in high-powered magazines and was known as the modern Liz Taylor. Loving the comparison, she used the star's name regularly when describing herself, giving her license to wed as many men as she chose and for any reason. Why the jetsetter decided to make Frankie her fourth husband puzzled Ester. Sure, he was handsome with a schoolboy charm and a good steady job, but certainly not a wealthy man. With no significant position in society, he was mostly important to his own big, Italian family, and at one time, he was of great importance to her.

But alas, such is the life of the rich and famous and those who must cater to them. Ester would take the high road and make her boss proud, as usual.

The crisp morning had cooled off her coffee, so she dumped it out on the grass and walked toward the nearest coffee shop to get a fresh, hot refill. The warm sun felt good, and she lifted her face toward it to soak up its rays, not seeing the little old lady slowly crossing in front of her until they collided – the force knocking the lady off her feet and sending Ester's ceramic cup into the air landing on the sidewalk where it smashed into pieces.

"Oh, oh, oh dear," Ester cried, dropping the folder and her shoulder bag onto the ground. Reaching for the elderly woman's legs with both hands, she pulled them away from an oncoming truck. Its wheel barely missed her foot but managed to run over the cane that she had been using to support her aged body. It snapped in two pieces like a dead tree limb, and Ester was suddenly struck with the ghastly thought that the old lady's leg would've sounded the same way had it been under the tire.

Falling on both knees, she asked the woman lying lifelessly on her back with eyes shut, "Lady, are you alright? Please answer me…are you alright?"

"How would I know?" the woman blurted, and then smiled up at Ester with one eye closed, squinting from the sun. "You don't look very strong. Think you can help me up by yourself?"

Although the woman was not very tall, she was rather stout, and by the look of her double chin, Ester imagined that underneath her light coat was substantially more body than she could lift. She looked around to see if anyone was nearby to assist. Crossing the street directly in front of her was a well-dressed man in a hat. As he approached, he noticed the two women on the ground and hurried toward them.

"May I help you?" he asked, kneeling over the injured woman.

"No thank you, I think I'll just lie here until the buzzards start to swarm overhead," the elderly woman said, followed by a hearty laugh.

Ester covered her mouth and giggled, glancing up at the man to see if he had responded the same. The smile behind his beard was familiar. She sprang to her feet and stepped back in astonishment when she recognized who he was. Lowering her sunglasses, she asked with a squeaky voice, "Frankie, is that you?"

Momentarily rendered speechless, the man stood and made an awkward move to brush off the knees of his pants. "Well, I just can't believe it…Ester Malloy."

"And I'm Queen Elizabeth!" the old lady barked, "and my ship is sailing before dark. Do you think you could help me get up before it leaves my old arse behind?"

"Of course!" the flustered adults answered in unison, jumping to attention.

Together they lifted her up. Frankie kept his arm around the woman's back as she stood, waiting to see if she could stand on her own.

"Oh dear, I'm a bit wobbly," she said. "Perhaps you could walk me to that lovely bench over there at the park." Spotting her cane lying in the road in two pieces, she reached out to grab it.

"I'll get it," Ester volunteered, and looking both ways, she retrieved what was left of the cane and snatched up her purse and the folder. "We'll be your cane for now. Hold on."

When they reached the bench, they carefully seated the portly lady and stood back watching her pull up her support stockings and adjust the green plaid socks she wore over them. Ester tried not to notice Frankie staring at the scar on her forehead and proceeded to care for the woman she had just minutes ago almost killed. "What's your name, please?" she asked. "Do you hurt anywhere?"

"Dear girl, I told you, my name is Queen Elizabeth. But you can call me Queenie. And you asked me if I hurt? Well, of course I hurt, everywhere, all the time. I'm over nine-hundred years old, and if I didn't hurt, I'd be dead."

Frankie chuckled and asked, "Where do you live? We can help you get home." The look of concern on his face appeared to be genuine, and Ester remembered it well.

"That's not important right now," Queenie said with a direct tone that kept both adults from questioning her again. "What *is* important is that you tell me all about yourselves. I'm sure after a while I'll feel good enough to walk." She pointed to the ground. "How lovely, the first new grass of the year, and you get to enjoy it. Sit down, please."

Frankie looked questionably at Ester. "It's fine with me, I guess. I was just on my way over to your office to talk to your editor. You still work there, don't you?"

"Yes, of course," Ester said, eyeing him curiously. Queenie, now pointing with two fingers, motioned for them to take a seat. Frankie took off his light jacket and spread it out on the ground, inviting Ester to sit on it.

"Oh, no," she spoke up, "I have on jeans. You're the one that needs to protect those fine slacks you're wearing." She plopped down on the soft grass before he could object and crossed her legs in a yoga position, hiding the folder underneath her bag.

While Frankie was adjusting himself, Ester observed his very fine attire and Italian leather shoes; a far cry from the usual khaki pants and pullovers with rolled up sleeves that he wore when they were a couple. And what's with the beard? She caught herself staring too long and turned her attention back to Queenie.

"So, you two know each other…ah ha!" Queenie tossed Ester a sidelong glance.

"Yes, coincidentally, we do," Ester said.

"There is no such thing as coincidence, dear girl." Queenie turned to address Frankie, "Now, tell us please, why were you going to see her editor?"

Frankie looked at Queenie and then timidly at Ester. "I, well,

I was going to discuss a certain project that had been submitted recently."

He doesn't know the project's been assigned to me, Ester thought, and she wondered if she should tell him. She decided to sweat him out instead, asking with innocent eyes, "What's it about?"

"Nothing really important." He squirmed. "But what a surprise running into you after so long. How have you been?"

"Just great!" Ester said, a little too cheerily. "Well, you know, I'm always busy working the magazine, traveling and all. How about you? Still on the set?"

"Not actually. Well, I'm changing my career," he said, turning his eyes away and pulling at the grass around his shoe.

"So, let me guess," Queenie slyly interjected, "you were together as a couple at one time, and something broke you apart. Hmmm, let me think…one of you had bad breath. No. You like dogs and she loves cats. No...that's not it. Oh," she paused, looking suspiciously with raised eyebrows, "one of you had another love interest. Am I right?"

Ester's expression froze, while Frankie's eyes were stuck wide open in disbelief at the old gal's candid remark. Ester stood up and said, "Queenie, if you don't mind, I'd like to get you home now."

"Young lady, I do mind," Queenie spoke sternly. "Sit down! I'm not ready to walk, and you can at least appease me until I am. After all, dearie, you almost sent me to my grave just a moment ago."

While Ester sat back down, Frankie was halfway up when Queenie also stopped him. "And you're not going anywhere either, young man. Your friend here will need your help when it comes time to walk me home. I'm certain that you are the gentleman you appear to be." And like a chastised little boy, Frankie surrendered to the demands of the stubborn but persuasive lady and lowered himself back down.

"OK, now, where were we? Which one of you strayed?" The shrewd old fossil continued the interrogation. "Come on, confession is good for the soul." Ester shifted her eyes toward Frankie and then quickly looked away. Queenie raised her eyebrows his direction.

"Well," Frankie began, removing his hat and rubbing the back of his neck, "supposedly, I did, but it was a mishap. I mean, it didn't really happen, but it looked like it did, and well, everything went wrong."

"It sure did," Ester sighed.

"Good heavens, don't leave me to my imagination. Tell me the story, Frankie," Queenie urged.

"I'm not sure where to start, or if Ester even wants to hear it."

Ester squirmed and stretched her legs out, trying not to show any sign of anxiety that was building up inside her. After the accident, she had never allowed Frankie to explain. She saw what she saw and that was quite enough for her. Appealing to Queenie, she begged with her eyes to show mercy. But the enchanting stranger only smiled, and as if she could read Ester's mind, she said, "Perhaps it's the young man's turn to tell his side of the story."

Bewitched by the woman's dazzling green eyes, Ester felt her body shrink and her mind went blank. "It's fine with me. Go ahead."

Frankie began, slowly at first. "I suppose I should start with what happened the day before. I worked all day on a set for Loretta Youngblood...the actress." He stalled, expecting Queenie to respond with excitement. When she offered nothing, he lightly shrugged and resumed his story. "When I told her I was going to my family's Italian restaurant for dinner, she insisted that she come along. Well, I can't say I tried to dissuade her...after all, bringing a beautiful actress to the restaurant would thrill my parents and of course, add to its reputation. Tony Bennett's picture is on the wall twice."

Now that juicy morsel of information initiated a reaction from Queenie. "Oh, I *do* so love Tony." Holding her hand to her heart, she looked up dreamily at a fond memory.

"Yes, well," Frankie continued, "before I knew it, we had stayed until my uncle closed the restaurant, and Ms. Youngblood was not only very content, but very drunk. I drove her to her hotel and made sure that she got safely to her room."

At this point, Frankie moved the story another direction. "I do remember calling you, Ester, when I was at the restaurant. You were in Baltimore on assignment, and we talked only briefly. But anyway, those particulars probably aren't that important."

Ester silently kept her emotions intact. Queenie abandoned her daydream and spurred him on.

"Well, the next day, Ms. Youngblood came in late. She said she had to sleep off the lasagna." Frankie muffled a nervous laugh. "But that slowed us down, and it took until after closing to get everything exactly the way she wanted it. Everyone left, including the janitor who shut off all the lights and locked up. I was about to leave when she asked me to go over a scene with her. She claimed that she needed to get a grip on it before the leading man arrived the next day. Ms. Youngblood came out of the dressing room wearing a knockout party dress and pearls, in bare feet. I admit it, she was gorgeous. She stuffed a script in my hand and went straight into the scene. At first the lines were typical – a man and a woman talking – and then she explained to me that one part of the scene was really disturbing her and asked me to follow directions and walk her through it. I was pretty nervous when she ordered me to reach behind her and unzip her dress. So nervous in fact, I jammed the zipper. And that's when I walked around the back of her to fix it and saw Ester watching me outside the window. I thought I had seen a ghost! She wasn't due back from her trip until the next day, so you can imagine…well, it was awful." Frankie stopped long enough to consider his final words. "When I saw her fall, it was the worst moment of my life. I felt completely helpless."

Ester had not realized that she had kept her eyes closed during the last part of the story. When she opened them, she was surprised to see tears forming in Frankie's eyes, while hers stayed dry. She felt a tinge of shame, realizing that she had never once considered how he must have felt, seeing her fall like that, not knowing what he would find when he ran three flights down to her crumpled body.

Queenie clapped her hands lightly and leaned toward Ester. "I'm very glad to see that you are well and so mobile, dear girl." To Frankie, she said, "I know that must have been difficult to share. Thank you."

Then she reached out for both of their hands. Ester rose to her knees and extended hers first and seeing how easily she submitted, Frankie did the same. The old gal's hands were warm and soothing and when they looked up at her angelic face, the sun beamed directly behind her forming a nimbus around her head. They sat there silent, mesmerized, absorbing her energy, and as they did, the former couple smiled at each other, and in that mystical moment, it seemed all was forgiven.

"Well, that's that!" Queenie exclaimed. "It's time for me to go." She sprung up from the bench and picked up the cane that was now in one piece. Ester took it from her hands.

"Wait a minute, this was broken in two!" She held it out for Frankie to inspect.

"Well, it *was*," he said, twirling the cane around, looking for some sign of breakage. They both turned to Queenie whose smile had widened, stretching across her entire face.

"I'll be going now, kiddos. I feel a whole lot better!" Standing taller, as if she were much younger, she took the cane from Frankie's hands. With lightness in her step, she crossed the street and turned around to wave just as a bus drove by and hid her from view. After it passed, she was gone.

The two stood gazing at each other in silent wonderment until Ester woke to the reality of the moment, threw her hands in the air, and moved quickly to snatch up the folder lying openly in the grass. "I don't know what kind of spell she put on us, but it sure was a doozie!"

Frankie picked up his jacket and dusted it off before putting it back on. "I'll say." Then he reached for his hat and spoke softly, "I suppose I'd better get over to see your editor. There's an article I need to discuss with her."

Ester handed over the folder. "You mean this one?"

Opening it to the red tab section, as he had seen Ester do many times when they were a couple, he read the subject line and nodded his head in agreement.

"I guess this is where I'm supposed to say congratulations," Ester said halfheartedly.

"I suppose…except, well, Dana's a very stubborn woman. The truth is, I need more time to think this over," he explained without looking at her.

Ester took the folder from his hand. "Looks like you better get started. According to this file, you are due to get married next month."

A brittle stick crunched under Frankie's foot. He reached down to pick it up and tossed it to the side. He was clearly at a loss for words and deliberately avoiding Ester's eyes.

Ester placed her hand under his chin and lifted his face to meet hers. "Thank you for sharing." Then she ruffled his curly hair like she used to do, turned, and walked back to her office.

Frankie sat on the bench and watched her gather up pieces of the broken coffee cup shattered on the sidewalk, placing them carefully in her jacket pocket. And as she often did when she was troubled, she took two deep cleansing breaths before entering the building, not once looking back at the park.

Breaking into a sweat, Frankie jumped up from the bench

where Queenie had been sitting. The wood was hot to his touch. Startled, he practically ran the opposite direction of Ester's building, failing to keep his appointment with the editor.

Two weeks went by without a word from Frankie. Ester felt strange wishing he would call. After that crazy episode with Queenie, tender feelings from the past were trying to resurface. But when Dana and Frankie's wedding assignment ended up back on her desk, this time including an invitation to the wedding and a list of prominent guests that she was to interview, no one in the office teased her or threw paper clips, as they could see that Ester was visibly concerned. What a foolish notion that he might want her again. That she might even want him! She tucked the folder under her arm and left the office with her bruised ego.

As she strolled through the park, Griff popped into her head. Griff! She had to share this with Griff – her best friend since middle school. They met often at their favorite pub where they talked for hours over cold beer and sandwiches. Neither were married, had children, or anything breathing to go home to. It was the best kind of friendship, requiring nothing but honesty and the promise to watch the Super Bowl together every year, no matter who they were with at the time.

The Packers were playing on the big screen and a touchdown had been scored, sending the Cheeseheads at the bar into a cheering frenzy. Griff listened carefully to Ester's story without making any odd faces or gestures, allowing her to talk until she ran out of air. She knew he mulled over every word she spoke, and in the end, she posed the unsettling question, "Is it possible I judged Frankie too harshly?" Not easily convinced, and having to check his own motives, for Ester meant more to him than she knew, Griff reserved his answer for a later date.

"What do you mean you can't go with me to the wedding?" Ester whined, slamming the mug down on the bar causing it to splash beer into the air and land on Griff's hand.

Griff watched her frantically wipe up the spill and waited for her to calm down before explaining. "I rather think that my grandmother's funeral tops going to my best friend's ex-boyfriend's wedding," he calmly stated. "You have a photographer going, don't you? What about him?"

"In case you hadn't noticed, Griff, he has a boyfriend."

"OK, I guess that won't work." He twisted uncomfortably on the stool. "Why do you need a date, anyway?"

"You're kidding! I'll be the old maid in the room…I'm thirty-one years old! Plus, I don't want Frankie to think I can't get a date."

Griff knew why Ester couldn't get a date. After the fall from the fire escape and the long recovery period, she lost all desire to start another relationship and spent most of her free time with him. Appearing helpless, he scratched his head in confusion. "You women kill me. Look, if you need someone that badly, I'll ask my cousin, Darren."

"Oh yeah, right," Ester scoffed. "I don't think there's enough fabric around to cover up all those tattoos. And besides, he'd probably upstage the bride."

It was an odd moment for Ester to get teary-eyed, but she did, and she turned her head away from Griff. Her emotions had been running high almost every day since Frankie had told her the convincing story of his innocence and how traumatic the whole horrible scene had been for him. She thought back on how determinedly she had refused his requests to visit her at the hospital. Her parents had strongly agreed with her, and there was certainly no getting past them. None of that matters now, she'd tell herself every time she weakened and let him into her mind. It had taken two years to chisel him out of her heart and only one day to let him back in. Ester blotted her eyes with a napkin and gave a loud, fake cheer for the wrong team.

"Are you nuts?" Griff turned from the screen and grabbed her clapping hands. "I thought we were for the Eagles!"

"Oops, my mistake."

"Are you crying?" he reached out and put his hand on Ester's shoulder.

"No, I mean, yes. Never mind, it'll pass. It always does." Ester stood and excused herself to the ladies' room.

Griff leaned back, let out a deep contemplative sigh and watched her closely as she turned the corner. Ignoring the game, he kept his eyes peeled on the spot of her re-entry. Anyone observing him would have thought he was in love.

With a VIP pass, Ester was able to squeeze past the crowd of folks standing outside the Cathedral of Saints Peter and Paul who were waiting anxiously to get inside for the wedding of the year. When she entered the sanctuary, she was taken back by its majesty, with the copper vaulted dome and the ornate altars on each of the side aisles. She had done her homework and learned that the church was reminiscent of Roman churches, with red antique marble and stained glass in magnificent proportions creating an Italian Renaissance flavor. It seemed apropos that the Italian bride and groom would want to marry in a Catholic church and especially one this spectacular for the likes of Dana Moretti. Ester imagined that Frankie's humble family would feel quite overwhelmed in such a spectacular setting, since they attended a much smaller and certainly less adorned house of worship near their home. Remembering them brought a smile to her face, and since she had made amends with Frankie, she was looking forward to hugging his loveable parents again.

Ester pulled out her tiny voice-activated recorder and turned it on to pick up the happy sounds of the folks meandering around the cathedral. The device came in handy, along with a small pad and pen to make sure she didn't miss anything she might want for the article. She spotted her cameraman setting up in the corner, his cheerful boyfriend acting as his assistant. Her thoughts turned to Griff. If only he were here.

From the fourth row at the end, so that she could get up and move about more freely before and after the service, she looked around to see who she might know. She spotted Loretta Youngblood walking toward her – the woman that Frankie had been caught with and the woman that she never got to interview because of the accident. Loretta had her hand out before she even reached her, forcing Ester to stand up to shake it.

"My dear, Ester, I am so glad to see you," she said. The long silky glove she wore felt strange in Ester's bare hand. "Surely you remember me…Loretta Youngblood," she announced loudly for all to hear. "I couldn't believe it when I heard *you* were the one covering the wedding."

"Yes, I am. It was a shame that I was unable to have that second interview with you. Unfortunately, I was laid up," Ester said, almost apologetically, trying not to remind herself that this was the woman that allegedly stole her fiancé.

"I understand. It was a terrible thing that happened to you. You know, I have wanted to talk to you ever since, but my life has been completely chaotic since I started that bloodsucking movie. Now that it's over, I'm beginning to feel like myself again. May I sit next to you?"

"Well, I, yes, of course," Ester said, reluctantly moving her writing material and the recorder from the seat to her lap.

Loretta sat down, leaned over and immediately started with an unexpected topic. "I had no idea that Frankie was engaged when I met him. He gave me no indication whatsoever that he was dedicated to anything but his job, which he was very good at, by the way."

"Yes, he was," Ester replied, beginning to feel even more uneasy when Loretta moved in closer, pressing against her shoulder.

"Now that you are no longer together, and so much time has passed since then, I want to tell you that you did the right thing by not marrying him." Loretta patted the top of Ester's free hand and left it there.

The woman's remark caught Ester off guard. "Why would you say that?"

"Don't you know?" she said, sounding strangely devious.

Ester sat quietly listening to her own heart pounding in her ears. She looked straight into the cunning actress's dark eyes and asked the question Loretta was apparently quite eager to answer. "Know what?"

"That we were having an affair," she said, almost boastfully. "It started about two weeks before your accident. But again, I had no idea about you."

Ester held her breath and closed her eyes. She was reliving the same awful sensation she had felt when she saw them together that night. This time she would not let it overpower her. This time she would not lose her grip. She opened her eyes and blew out a slow breath. When she felt her diaphragm finally collapse, she slipped her hand out from underneath Loretta's. "Yes, I knew. I've always known."

"But, of course darling, a woman always knows," Loretta said in a slippery tone while reaching for Ester's hand again. "What I really wanted to tell you is after I found out, I broke it off. I do have scruples, you know, even though in my line of work, I don't have to," she explained with a flutter of her fake eyelashes. "Although, he is a cutie, but honestly, do you really think he's marrying that pathetically thin wealthy socialite for love?"

Ester did not want to hear another word, but the journalist in her couldn't stop asking the inevitable question. "I'm guessing you found out about our engagement that day…the day I fell?"

"Oh no, I had to remain in the building, you know, the media, my reputation, etcetera. We carried on for quite a while after that. I didn't know about you and Frankie until later, and it sure didn't come from him." And as if she had just confessed to a priest and received a simple penance of three Hail Marys, Loretta excused herself and hurriedly squeezed past two rows of guests, anxious to claim the empty seat next to the recently widowed mayor.

Shaking her head in disbelief, Ester was completely stunned by the conversation. Then she looked down at the voice recorder still recording in her lap and let out a discreet gasp.

The wedding seemed to last forever, and the thought of Frankie lying so skillfully and easily to her and Queenie left Ester disconsolate. The moment she could, she dashed outside to get some fresh air and regain her composure.

The reception was held just a block away at the elegant Four Seasons Hotel, with the city's most luxurious outdoor venue. As Ester walked toward it, she felt the sun on her face and looked up to take in the warm rays. She was struck with a moment of déjà vu and just before she looked down, she ran directly into a woman, practically knocking her off her feet.

"Oh dear, I'm so sorry," she said, balancing the woman with her free hand.

In the middle of a cough, the old woman started laughing. "If I didn't know better honey, I'd think you were trying to do me in." Then, she grabbed Ester around the waist and hugged her.

"Queenie, what a pleasant surprise!" Ester returned the hug, inhaling the strong scent of lavender in her silvery white hair. "I was just on my way to the hotel where Frankie's wedding reception is being held. What brings you this direction?"

"Fate, I think. Good ole marvelous fate."

"Oh, Queenie. I'm so glad to see you. Can we talk for a minute?" Ester urged, pointing to a nearby bench.

"Naturally, my dear," she said with interest and then smiled upon seeing the bench. "I just love it when places to sit pop up at just the right time. Somebody wonderful must have designed this city." Sighing appreciatively, Queenie sat down and lovingly patted the empty space next to her. "Now tell me what's on your mind, besides the fact that you're not the bride."

"And I'm glad I'm not!" The words flew out fast and loud, followed by a concise rundown of the conversation with Loretta. "The woman is incorrigible! I even have it all on tape," she added, holding up the small recording device.

"A woman always knows, hmm," Queenie repeated the phrase. "And hell, hath no fury like a woman scorned," she laughed through the quote. "We are an interesting species."

Apparently amusing herself, Queenie drifted off with her own thoughts. Ester delicately led her back to the moment. "Queenie, I'm OK, and certainly not scorned. I made my decision back then and right or wrong, I lived with it. I just wish I hadn't let him get to me. Frankie is a jerk for lying to us."

"Yes, all men are jerks until proven otherwise," she quoted. "So, what are you going to do with that recording?"

"What is there to do?" Ester shrugged. "I certainly don't need to listen to it again."

Queenie tapped her finger on her nose while she sang the wedding march under her breath. "Here comes the bride, big, fat and wide." While Ester waited, the warmth radiating from their shoulders touching seemed to relax her. She entertained the idea that the highly spirited and admittedly quirky woman sitting next to her might be her guardian angel.

"May I have it?" Queenie blurted.

"Well, I suppose…why do you want it?"

"I'll explain later," she said and held out her hand with the face of a child waiting for a friend to share her jellybeans.

Once again, Ester was under her spell. With the tiny cassette tucked away in Queenie's pocket, she breathed a sigh of relief. "I probably should get to the reception now. I still have a job to do."

"And so, do I," the flowery scented woman announced.

"I would really like it if you came with me." Ester gently squeezed her confidante's arm. "I feel better with you around."

"Sounds lovely, and I bet everything is gourmet and looks too beautiful to eat...oh, yum." Queenie licked her lips with bright-eyed delight. "And look, I am even dressed for the occasion." She opened her shawl, revealing a purple chiffon layered dress with butterfly buttons. "I'll be there shortly, but first I have a quick errand to run." She tapped her cane on the sidewalk and scooted off, leaving Ester feeling grateful to have a friend to help her through the next few, grueling hours. And not just any ordinary friend either, she was beginning to understand.

The outdoor reception area was more beautiful than the pictures had portrayed. Under the pavilion, the bride and groom sat on velvet thrones and to the far left was a table full of Frankie's relatives. They were quietly reserved − some of them whispering to one another while others craned their necks observing the hundreds of guests mingling in their finest apparel. One of them spotted Ester and practically the entire table turned around and motioned for her to come over.

The warm welcome was genuinely appreciated and after ten minutes of catching up, Ester learned that the family wasn't all that thrilled about the wedding and the mother openly admitted, "We had wished for Frankie to marry you, instead of this high society woman that we are certain is no good for our son." On that note, Ester reminded them that she had been invited only to work on the article at hand and excused herself to mingle with the guests.

Waving enthusiastically, Frankie's father bellowed, "Don't forget to write about us, and the restaurant!"

Everyone was eager to share their names and comments with

the journalist, and Ester was glad that she had an extra cassette tape for the occasion. When the music started, the newlyweds danced first, then the bride and her father, followed by the groom and his mother. Touched by the scene, she let Frankie briefly into her heart long enough to catch his eye after he walked his mother back to her seat. Upset with herself, she darted off to get a much-needed drink.

"I'll have a stiff martini," said a cocky voice to the right of Ester, as she stood at the bar waiting for her wine.

"Queenie!" she greeted her exuberantly. "A stiff martini? Sure you can handle it?"

"I have for hundreds of years," she claimed. "The stiffer the better!"

With drinks in hand, Queenie signaled Ester to follow her. Wading through the crowd, they ended up just feet from the bride and groom. When Ester tried to walk away, Queenie slipped her arm around the reluctant journalist and pulled her directly in front of them.

"Congratulations, Frankie! And to your lovely bride." Queenie lifted her glass and curtsied before the royalty seated on their velvet thrones. She elbowed Ester to do the same.

"Yes, congratulations to both of you, Mr. and Mrs. Russo," Ester said, leaving out the curtsy and refusing to look at Frankie.

"No, no," the bride smirked, "I will be keeping my name. I'm Dana Moretti." Then she turned to Frankie and asked, "Who are your friends, darling?"

"Well," he hedged, stumbling through the introduction, "this is Queen Eliz...Queenie." And looking over at Ester, Frankie said cautiously, "This lady is the journalist from the magazine you hired to cover the wedding."

"Oh, yes." Dana perked up. Apparently not the least bit interested in Ester's name, or Queenie, she brought forth her demands. "I will, of course, want to approve it before it goes to press, and I'd prefer that you focus on this side of the room only."

She pointed the opposite direction from the Russo family table toward a large group of guests consisting mostly of politicians, actors, and a few boney models that looked like they had just exited the runway.

"I understand," Ester responded laconically – wishing at that moment she had a cream pie to throw in the heartless woman's face – while Frankie looked the other way, acting as if he hadn't heard a single word.

Having endured enough, Queenie broke the awkward silence that followed and declared, "And I'm Queen Elizabeth, ta da! And I, too, am keeping my name." She slipped her hand inside her pocket and brought out a small gift box, a tiny bow fastened on top. "A gift for the two of you," she said, handing it to Frankie. "May it be a reminder of your never-ending love for your new bride."

With the sudden realization of what Queenie was up to, Ester quickly covered her mouth to smother a burst of laugher. Queenie gave her a look that would make a pit bull stand down, and then without formally excusing themselves, they retreated to the other side of the room where they could openly relish the humor of the moment. Queenie walked backwards, and with each step she humbly bowed to the queen and king. From the side of her mouth she said, "Don't worry, I made a copy."

Ester exploded with laughter. Doubling over like a drunken sailor, she bumped right into a man standing in her path, spilling the remainder of her wine on his shoe. "Oh, no!" she exclaimed, looking up apologetically.

"Don't mind her," Queenie said, "she's always running over people. Believe me, I know."

The man catching Ester by the elbow laughed out loud.

"Griff!" Ester cried. "You came!" Before he could say anything, she hugged him tightly as if he were a long-lost dog. "Oh, I'm so glad to see you." Turning to Queenie, she excitedly introduced him.

"Oh yes," Griff said, extending his hand as he bowed, "I've heard some interesting things about you, Queen Elizabeth."

Holding tightly to his hand, Queenie eyed Griff curiously. "Yet, I've heard nothing about you," she responded, casting a quizzical glance at Ester. "But I'm certain you'll tell me all about yourself over a stiff martini...or two." Looping her arm in his and motioning to Ester to take her other arm, she gaily led them to the open bar. "Everything...I want to know everything and leave nothing out."

Apparently baffled, Frankie slumped into his chair after watching the scene unfold. He turned to Dana and innocently shrugged.

"What a strange old lady," his wife said. "Let's see what kind of gift could fit in such a small box. Open it, darling."

Frankie lifted the lid and dumped the contents into his palm. He removed the toilet paper wrapped around it and held it at arm's length in disgust. Discarding it, he stared curiously at the item, turning it over and over between his fingers.

"A measly tape cassette?" Dana jeered. Evidently disappointed, she snatched it from his hand. "Well, we'll listen to it later. No telling what that crazy old coot put on it. We may find it amusing." She stuffed it in her fancy handbag and waved excitedly across the room at one of the guests, beckoning her to come over. Delighted to see her approaching, Dana said to her husband, "Franklin, darling, I want you to meet my new friend, the wonderful actress, Ms. Loretta Youngblood."

Frankie went pale.

SLIPPING

"You're dreaming, Helen," he groaned, waking her from her restless sleep that now had him awake in the middle of the night.

"I am?"

"You're talking in your sleep." George yawned and stretched out his left arm, buzzing from having slept on it at the edge of the bed because Helen had claimed most of the mattress. He wouldn't openly admit it, but he missed having the bed all to himself.

"Too bad…" she said groggily, falling easily back to sleep.

George rolled over and squinted in the dark at her youthful face. Her arms were relaxed, palms up, and her legs were comfortably spread apart. Wide awake and somewhat irritated, he asked, "Are you trying to go back to sleep now, or do you want to tell me about the dream?"

"What? Oh, I doubt if I can remember it now."

"You said something about the moon and then you called out a man's name. Sounded like you said, Brad."

"I did?" Helen's eyes popped open when he said the name.

"Are you certain that's what I said?" She flipped over and turned her back to her boyfriend.

"Pretty sure. Want to talk about this *Brad* guy?"

George blew on Helen's bare neck, giving her a sudden rise of goosebumps. "Oh!" she shivered. "Does it seem cold in here?"

"Want me to warm you up?" he asked, nibbling the bottom of her earlobe. "Then you can tell me all about your friend, Brad."

Helen sighed and pulled the blanket up around her neck, forcing George to move back. "It was just a dream. I can't remember all of it."

"Well, try," he said, suddenly deciding to sit up, pulling the blanket off Helen as he did.

"Hey!"

George flipped on the lamp and seeing the ugly tattoo on his girlfriend's shoulder, he recoiled and turned his head. He hated how it stuck out so boldly against her pink skin and how the eyes of the lizard seemed to follow him whenever he moved. He quickly covered it up and sat there quietly seething.

"Let me refresh your memory. You said Brad, I'm slipping, I'm slipping!" George tried to imitate Helen's feminine voice, but it sounded more like Pee Wee Herman's.

"Gosh, I hope I didn't sound *that* bad. No wonder you woke up," she said, with a less than genuine chuckle.

"Well, the point is you were calling for help. What was happening?"

"I can only remember a little. But if you must know…a giant hand lifted me high in the air, and I looked down and saw your house and that silly red rooster weathervane you have on the roof. It got smaller and smaller the higher I went."

George sat very still watching Helen speak slowly and carefully. Her eyes remained shut and nothing else moved but her lips. "Go on. Tell me about the slipping part," he urged.

"Well, I was dropped onto a sliver of the moon. It was like I was sitting on the inside of a cracked-opened pecan shell, my back resting in the curve. Then the weirdest thing happened, the moon tipped, and I started slipping. My bottom felt really hot, like when I was a kid going down the slide at the park, not smoothly like on a water slide, but clumsily, like I was sliding down on hot metal, and I wiggled to stop from burning my thighs. Then I yelled I'm slipping."

"I'm slipping, *Brad*," George reminded her, his patience growing thin. "Then, what happened?"

"*You* woke me up."

"Weird dream, but who's Brad?"

"The man in the moon?" Helen smiled with one eye opened, making her best guess sound reasonable.

"Well, I hope not. You'd think something that amazing would have a regal name, like Sampson or Geronimo. Brad hardly says stellar."

Helen let out a long weary yawn. "Yeah, well." She rolled over and looked at the clock. "It's four thirty-two, I'm going back to sleep."

George molded the pillow under his head six different ways trying to get comfortable. His mind wouldn't shut off, pondering who Brad might be. He thought of the countless people they had met at the parties Helen had dragged him to, now that school was out and the summer fun had begun. All those young people he tried so hard to talk to left him weary. There wasn't a Brad amongst them. The only Brad he could think of was the nerdy guy that owned Clayton's Music just two blocks east. He was in his thirties, George guessed, and had a big, brown mole on the tip of his nose. He had nothing that would interest Helen, he decided, beginning to feel relieved. Then it occurred to him; she had forced him to stay up late the night before and watch a Brad Pitt movie. Seems he had not gone to bed a decent hour once since she moved in. "So, was it Brad Pitt?"

"What?" Helen grumbled, after being startled out of her sleep again. "What about spit?"

"Ah, go back to sleep, Helen. Brad's waiting for you."

Feeling weird with his petty thoughts, George rolled over angry at himself, a thirty-four-year-old man acting like a jealous teenager. It took him another hour to finally fall asleep.

They slept past nine and George woke up stiff and grouchy, clinging to the edge of the bed. "Man!" He rolled his head to get the kink out. "I slept hard."

Helen, appearing completely refreshed, threw back the sheet and rushed to the bathroom. She called out from behind the door, "Hey, I have to leave in twenty minutes. Put the coffee on!"

Slipping into one of her nicer summer dresses, she applied orange lipstick to match the flowers on the belt around her waist. She rubbed vitamin E oil on the tail of the lizard running down the length of her arm and checked her teeth for unwanted intruders. She rushed past George who held in his hands a cup of coffee and a bagel neatly spread with cream cheese and raspberry jelly.

"Um," he cleared his throat. "You asked for coffee."

Turning from the door, she hurriedly snatched the cup from his hand and made a face at the bagel. "Ew, you know I don't like cream cheese."

"Hey, what's the hurry?" he yelled, watching her fumble to get out, spilling coffee on the doorknob.

"I have a second interview for a job. Close the door for me. I'm late!"

"How many interviews does that make, Helen?" he bellowed after her. Two months of job searching and nothing to show for it. "Bye," he muttered with a limp wave, watching Helen drive off without once looking back at him. "Stupid, stupid!" he said under his breath, not knowing why, but that's exactly how he felt.

George gobbled down two bagels and decided to take a walk. He slipped on his jogging clothes and running shoes and after he greeted the hot, late morning sunshine, he decided to stroll two blocks east. Walking past Clayton's Music, curiosity had him turn around. He stopped in front of the dirty glass window displaying faded posters of rap and funk bands barely secured by layers of old brittle masking tape. Like the owner, Brad Clayton, he could see the shop was still unkempt. The last time George visited the place, he left sneezing his head off from the dust particles floating in the air every time he flipped through the stacks of albums. He remembered arguing with Helen and Brad over the word vintage, insisting that it did not include dust or mold. They had never gone back since. Why he was visiting the store again, he really didn't know.

He hesitantly walked in and scanned the small room. The hundreds of record albums were now replaced with rows of outdated video games and CDs. Rap music was piped in by Pandora instead of the old cassette player that had previously blasted out sixties heavy metal tunes. Toward the back was a large sign: Only 21 and Over - Enter at your own risk. Beneath it XXX was boldly printed in a fluorescent orange. "Wow, this place *has* changed," he said, "except for the dust." He sniffed the moldy air and kept that complaint to himself.

"Sure has," said a man from behind the counter. George could only see the top of his sparsely bald head until he slowly rose and revealed himself. "Can I help you?"

"Well, I'm not sure. I haven't been here in quite a while." He looked over at the X-rated section and pointed with a jerky thumb. "That's different."

"You should check it out." The man motioned for him to follow.

George shrugged. "Why not?" He went through the red velvet curtain, glancing over his shoulder to see if anyone was watching. "By the way, whatever happened to Brad Clayton? Does he still own the store?"

"Better than that," the employee said, "he's the star of the place."

"What'd you mean?"

"Heck, he's the biggest porn star on this side of the railroad tracks." The clerk laughed and walked over to a tall shelf. "Take a look for yourself." He handed George a DVD with a man on the front sitting on the back of a woman positioned on her hands and knees like a horse. Holding a whip in one hand and a set of reins attached to the woman's neck in the other, he wore only a Zorro mask and a black cape.

Pointing his finger at the masked man, George asked, "That's Brad?" To avoid looking at the woman underneath him again, he put his thumb over her humongous dangling breasts. "Oh, man, it is him. I recognize the big mole."

"Yeah, that's his trademark. Read the title on this one," he urged, handing him another DVD.

George read aloud, "Where no mole has gone before." Starting to feel disgusted seeing Brad now on all fours, he handed the case back to the employee.

"Aren't you interested in this stuff, man?"

"No, not really. It's not my kind of thing, I guess." When Helen had insisted that they watch one, he had properly refused. He remembered her calling him a prude. "Prude, Prude, Prude!" George winced and looked around the room to see if anything else might interest him, perhaps without Brad and his big mole on the cover.

"Oh wait, there's a new one that's coming out this week," the employee said with some urgency. "If I were you, I'd get on the sign-up sheet for this one. He's only doing a limited number of copies."

"If the women look anything like the woman on the front of these, no thanks." George turned away from the images disturbingly and deliberately facing the patrons at eye level.

"No, no. He's upgraded his models. Here, let me put your name on the list, and I'll call you when it's ready."

The salesman shoved a pen in George's face and pleaded with his eyes. "Oh, alright. But no need to call. I'll drop back in next week."

"Hey, thanks." The man looked down at the list. "Thanks, Dan. You won't be sorry."

Feeling a sneeze coming on, George left the store in a hurry. He spent the rest of the day walking in and out of shops, feeling odd as he did every year when summer arrived, and his days were empty without his students. He was in his ninth year as a high school History teacher, and it usually took him a week or two to settle in with a new routine of sleeping in, late afternoon walks, catching up on his reading, and the occasional drive to the country to visit his parents. He fell into the summer days with ease. But this year he had Helen. She was looking for a job when he met her, after ditching college and sleeping on friend's sofas, and within no time at all Helen had graduated from his sofa to his bed, and her personal things had camouflaged his home to the point that he no longer recognized it.

At first, he had ignored the changes, too busy trying to keep up with her, trying to impress her with his virility. Then after a while he became easily irritated when removing her worn socks from the kitchen table, shoving all her Jello cups to the side to find his craft beer, and he wished she could make up her mind which bathroom sink or razor she wanted to use. And couldn't she just try to clean up after herself, just once? He tried to chalk it off to her age. There was a fourteen-year difference, and he had never been with anyone that much younger.

Passing a tattoo parlor, he caught himself again wondering if he had done the right thing with Helen. The jealous spasm he'd had earlier over her dream was just one of many irritations he experienced since he brought her under his roof. Their conversations had shortened after a while, too, having nothing in common outside the bedroom, and even that was dwindling. Beginning to realize the pretense of it all, his motives remained in question for the rest of the week.

As usual, Helen spent her time running in and out to interviews and visiting her friends, while George re-arranged his books, cleaned out the closets and worked on his bicycle that had stayed broken for much too long. When he thought he had it up and running again, he took it out for a spin.

It was cloudy overhead, and the day was cooling off. The hot summers of Texas made a resident appreciate clouds of any kind, and soon the sidewalks were filled with folks enjoying a sun-free day. George lived a block away from one of the busiest streets in South Austin. Cyclists were respected in this neck of the woods, and everyone politely stayed out of his path. When he came upon Clayton's Music, he braked and looked through the window. The balding employee saw him and waved him in.

"Can I bring my bike in?" George yelled through the door.

"Sure!"

He leaned his sleek Diamondback against the wall and proceeded to the counter.

"It's in, and you're the first to get a copy, Dan," the man grinned – a sleazy look that would normally make George cringe, but lately with his principles being challenged, he allowed himself to be seduced.

"Dan? Oh yeah, uh, right. Sure. I guess I am a little curious. But honestly, I don't watch these things, so I probably won't buy it."

"They all say that," he stated with rolled eyes and disappeared through the thick, velvet curtains.

When the man handed the DVD to George, he read the title first. His brow wrinkled, and he looked down at the floor, trying to remember where he'd heard those words before. A strange uneasiness poured over him. Looking back at the cover, this time it was Brad kneeling on his knees, wearing only long black swashbuckler boots and a tight vest. He held his hands open as if he were catching something. At the top of a big white prop, that badly resembled a crescent moon, was a naked woman with her legs spread wide open, including her large orange mouth, excitedly sliding down it toward his waiting arms. The woman was wearing a mask over her eyes, and when George looked closer, he recognized Helen, her big, toothy grin and short, cropped hair which was now spiked and sticking up like a pitchfork. The tattoo was unmistakably hers.

"She's a looker, isn't she?" the grimy man behind the counter said when he saw George's surprised expression.

"She sure is," he said, inhaling a deep breath. "How much?"

George rode around the city fast and fierce trying to work off the frustration that had finally exploded from the moment he stumbled out of the porn shop. When the clerk reported that Helen had been working for Clayton for over a month, he got angry, then disgusted, ending with a weird kind of self-pity. So sick of the mixed emotions, he made a critical decision right then and there while slurping down a Gatorade in front of the high school where he taught.

Entering his home, the full reality of his messy life sunk in. He methodically picked up Helen's things that were in all the wrong places and placed them in a cardboard box. After scrubbing the bathroom sinks and tubs and emptying the pantry of Helen's opened boxes of cereal that were now filled with mealworms, his anxiety began to subside. It was while standing in the middle of his sparkling clean kitchen when it hit him that he had been used. How could he have traded in a practical and perfectly simple life for an untidy, but sexy twenty-one-year-old liar who quit college to become a pornographic film actress with a mole-faced moronic owner of a creepy, dusty porn shop? The bizarre day called for a couple of ibuprofen tablets and a long nap.

When Helen arrived that evening, George was chopping onions, listening to Paul Simon's, "Slipsliding Away." The song had resurfaced sad memories, including the day his wife had left him, and at that moment he was glad he had onions to blame for the tears.

"Oh, wow, you're cooking. I'm starved!" she said, not noticing George's blotched face while tossing her purse on top of his beautiful Steinway piano. She knew that aggravated him to no end. He would let it go for the last time.

"Yeah, I thought we'd have a nice evening at home," he said disingenuously, carefully rubbing the flat blade of the sharp knife over his fingers under the running faucet. "Did you finally get a job?"

"I sure did. At a vintage store and the owner *really* likes me. He said I'm perfect for the position."

The owner likes me? I bet! George wiped his draining eyes on his sleeve. Then he held the knife up to the light and examined it. "What's the name of the store?"

Helen squeezed past him to get to the corner cabinet, completely ignoring his question. She bent down and reached for a glass. Her short blouse rose up her back, revealing her spine under soft peachy skin, and on each side of it, plump hips squeezed out of tight shorts. He allowed himself one last look.

"Hey, my new boss gave me a bottle of Jim Beam," she announced, proudly holding the bottle up in the air. "Want some?"

When she turned around to face him, George looked into her eyes as if he had just seen her for the first time. *She's just a silly girl. I drank that crappy whiskey in college. Be cool, George, be cool, you fool. Let's get this over with.*

"No thanks," he said without making a face. He reached for a dishtowel and began carefully polishing the knife. "Dinner will be ready soon, and I've picked out a great new movie for us."

"Oh yeah, what is it?" Helen asked, filling her glass a couple of extra fingers higher than sociably acceptable.

"A surprise."

George read a magazine during the entire meal, while Helen played with her cell phone. She seemed to be content with the silence. When they finished, he closed all the blinds and turned out the lights, except for a small lamp in the corner.

"Get comfortable," he suggested. "Do you want popcorn?"

"No, this drink is doing the trick," she cooed, sprawling out on the sofa.

George flinched with a sudden flash of her spreading her legs on the cover of the DVD. Having not taken the time to watch the movie, he braced himself for what was to come. "It's show time!" he announced, sinking back in the armchair.

The title of the movie jumped out into the viewer's face. *Slipping Off the Moon* in bright yellow bulbs blinked off and on, like hazard lights on a car. Helen sat up startled and choked on a swallow of whiskey.

"Great title, eh?" he said facetiously. "Sounds like the dream you had the other night."

Helen stood up and nearly fell over the coffee table. "You rat, how'd you get that?"

"Sit down, Helen. There's nothing to say to each other. Let's just enjoy the show."

Without a trace of shame, she uttered a curse word under her breath and sat back down to watch her performance. "I thought you didn't like porn," she mocked.

Five minutes into the movie, George ejected the DVD. He had made his point, and he surely didn't want to have indecent images of Helen etched in his brain. Seeing that she was indifferent to the matter, he let the speech he had planned earlier fly right out the window.

"Let's go to bed, I'm beat," she said nonchalantly, after gulping down the drink. "And now you know why."

George glanced at his watch. Not a man who likes confrontations, he would be as cavalier about her deception as she was. "I'd prefer we take a walk. I think we need to talk." If he was disturbed at all by the raunchy film and bad acting, the look on his calm face didn't show it. Helen stepped into her flipflops and went outside to wait on the porch. She pulled out a cigarette from her shirt pocket and lit up.

Taking her gently by the arm, George started to say, I thought you quit smoking. It occurred to him that it didn't really matter. Instead, he said, "Let's go this way," and he led her down the sidewalk.

They walked in silence. Helen smoked the cigarette down to the filter, then flicked it into the street. George strolled over and picked it up. He dropped it into a nearby trash can. When they arrived at the front of Clayton's Music, George took her hand and pulled her down the alleyway to the back of the building.

"What are you doing?" she squealed, jerking her hand from his.

Firmly grabbing her arm, he yanked her in front of a door to a small apartment. He knocked on it. "Let's don't make this any harder than we have to, Helen." When the door slowly opened, and Brad stood before them, his mole beaming bigger than ever, he rose up tall and smiled wide at Helen. But when he saw George standing behind her, he dropped his smile and his scrawny shoulders.

"I think this belongs to you," George said with controlled impassivity, and he pushed Helen through the door. "I'll have her things delivered tomorrow."

"But, but...," Brad protested, watching George disappear into the night.

Helen plopped down on the sofa and asked coolly, "So, what have you got to drink?"

Back at his home, George held the DVD in his hand. "Prude, am I really a prude?" He glanced over at the DVD player and slowly walked toward it. He stood in front of it, fixated on the digital clock reminding him that he was due for his nightly shower. Holding the DVD up, his eyes darted back and forth from the clock to the title, *Slipping Off the Moon*. A burst of sweat flushed through his pores, as he contemplated watching it. He snorted through his nose and looked up at the ceiling long and hard. "If anybody's slipping, it's me," he announced to any living thing that might be listening.

Looking around the room, he spotted the empty glass with Helen's lipstick stain on the rim. He picked it up, sniffed the remains of the cheap whisky and felt a slight twinge of sadness. He shook away all doubt from his mind and declared with a gratifying smile, "So be it, I'm officially a prude, and if anyone's listening right now...I like it!"

Looking forward to re-establishing his usual routine, he dropped the porn movie into the box holding Helen's belongings, took a long leisurely shower, brushed his teeth in the clean sink that he preferred, slid into the cotton pajama pants that Helen claimed were gross, and turned out the lights.

"What was I thinking?" he scolded himself for the last time, lying between cool clean sheets. "Well," he chuckled, "she did have a nice body."

Stretching out in the middle of the bed, within seconds he slipped into a simple, dreamless, untroubled slumber.

RANDOM REFLECTIONS

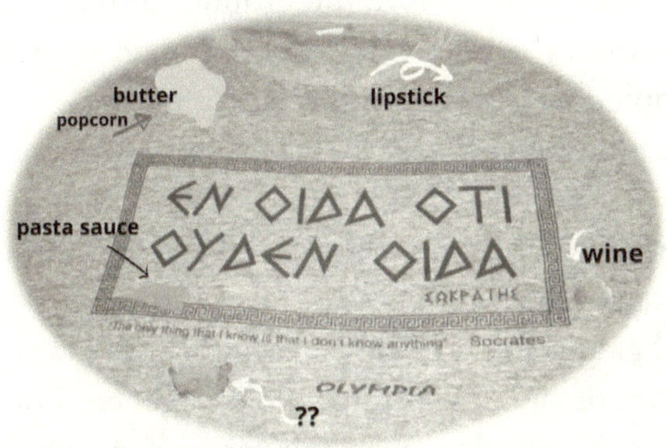

This is my favorite t-shirt, worn, torn, and oh so soft with lots of stains on it. Life is messy, and behind every one of those stains is a story just waiting to be told.
The cool quote from Socrates is a nice reminder:
"The only thing that I know is that I don't know anything."
I remember fondly the Greek god who gave it to me — Johnny Johnson

AN UNCOMMON BOND

Thirty-five thousand feet above the ground, in the middle of the night alone with her secrets, Lucy felt as though she was suffocating. The disquieting scene from the past played over and over in her head, and the pitch-black sky beyond the window offered no relief.

They were on the second leg of a red-eye flight from Chicago to Maui. Wedged in a window seat, her head pressed against her cloth hobo bag, and her size eight cowgirl boots crammed under the seat in front of her, it was impossible to get comfortable while her four-year-old son slept peacefully sprawled out next to her. She shoved her body deeper into the corner to allow him more room. No rest for the wicked, she thought. What exactly does that mean?

Through the subdued light, she saw the passenger two rows ahead straighten her seat, leaving a gap wide enough to see the profile of the man sleeping next to her: a Greek nose sloping toward thin nostrils underlined by a pencil moustache resting atop a luscious full lip shaped like a perfectly drawn heart. Lucy closed her eyes and remembered watching a similar face, but without the mustache, as he slept next to her – his long brown eyelashes curved slightly at the tips, fluttering with his dreams. She let out a sigh and allowed the memory to unfold before her. Yes, no rest for the wicked.

It was five years earlier, and the air was attempting to cool down as autumn tried eagerly to beat the summer heat into submission – a hard thing to do in Texas where heat waves run rampant like teenagers dropped off at the mall. But this year fall came fully armed with unexpected rain that fell in buckets, pounding the dry earth and keeping the stinging rays of the sun at bay long enough to restore hope. Every church service in New Braunfels offered prayers of gratitude for the end of the three-year drought.

Troubled by recent events, Lucy sat barefoot on her porch sipping a full glass of Cabernet Sauvignon, not once letting it rest from her fingers, pouring herself more each time the glass became slightly empty. She sat directly in the middle of the porch swing, controlling the rhythm of movement to her desire. The thunder was getting closer, and she felt the wind become agitated with the anticipation of more rain.

By the time she reached the middle of the bottle, much of the melancholy had subsided along with the sinking sun beyond the hills that surrounded her country home. She had just finished counting the seconds it took for it to disappear below the horizon – something she did often as a child – when it started to rain, and she spotted car lights coming down her long winding drive. It was after eight and unusual to have visitors on a lazy, uneventful Monday. The car eased closer and came to a stop at the end of the walkway. Planting both feet on the floor, she sat perfectly still, peering over the top of the glass waiting to see what the driver would do next.

A full minute passed. Only the windshield wipers could be heard in the rain. The engine stopped. Headlights turned off. A car door slammed, and a man hurriedly approached the porch steps. Upon seeing her sitting there, he stopped abruptly – one foot from the shelter of her covered porch.

Realizing that he was getting soaked, Lucy motioned to him to take the next step. "Come out of the rain," she insisted.

"I'm so sorry to bother you," he explained without delay, "I think I'm lost. I've been driving for the longest time looking for my friend's home. I'm not from around here, so when I saw your lights on, I decided I could use some help with directions."

He seems friendly enough, Lucy thought – the instant assumption enhanced by the alcohol and superseding any ounce of caution. And good looking, too. "Sure, I'm glad to help. I'm just sitting out here enjoying this much needed rain."

The stranger reached out to shake her hand and announced, "I'm Brian Digby."

"Lucy Ellison," the lady of the house said, startled when she felt his clammy wet hand in hers. "Oh, my goodness, would you like a towel?"

"No thanks, it's been so hot, it actually feels good." He smiled with fresh-faced satisfaction as he ran his fingers slowly through his thick dripping hair.

"So," she proceeded, taking note how sexy that looked, "who is the friend you're visiting? I probably know most of the people in this small town."

"David Guthrie," Brian said. "He's an artist and has a gallery in Boerne. We're old college roommates. Do you know him?"

Lucy's eyes widened when he said the name. "Yes, I do." She paused and studied Brian's innocent expression. *He doesn't know about David.* "Um, yes, he and I have been friends since middle school. We reunited a little over a year ago when I moved back here from Rhode Island."

"How about that!" he bellowed and slapped his knee, sending spurts of water flying. "Small world isn't it?"

Searching her memory, Lucy said, "I think I remember David mentioning you. You went to SMU together, right?" When he nodded with an amused smile, she asked, "What brings you here?"

"David invited me to his art gallery grand opening." Brian dropped his smile and scratched behind his ear. "We haven't seen each other in at least two years…actually, since Amber's funeral."

Hoping to avoid the topic of David's deceased wife, Lucy changed the subject and averted her eyes to the nearby wicker chair. "Have a seat, please. How long have you been on the road?"

"Let's see, I left Albuquerque early this morning. I'd say about nine hours. Been trying to reach David on the phone since yesterday. But you know artists…they tend to fly off their orbits at any given time," he chuckled. "I imagine he's…"

"Yes, he does that," she interrupted, "but I don't think you'll find David at home right now, and by the way," she pointed over her shoulder, "his home is at the base of that hill over there. If you look hard you can see it through the trees. Well, maybe you can't. I don't see any lights on."

"Hmm, I was so close. It *has* been a while. Well, if he doesn't show up soon, he told me where to find a hidden key."

Lucy reached for the bottle of wine and held it up to the light. "Would you like a glass of wine while you wait?"

"That is the best idea I've heard all day. Please, I'd love one," he said, dropping his head back and inhaling the earthy scent of fresh rain. "Petrichor," he said dreamily with closed eyes.

Lucy watched Brian in his moment of peace. A sense of pity fell over her, knowing that once she shared the latest news with him, he would no longer be lighthearted as he was now. Determined to make the moment last, she went to the kitchen to collect a wine glass and slice some cheese and apples. From the reflection on the glass cabinet door, she saw that her face was tense, and her eyes drooped right along with her mouth. Even the smattering of friendly freckles were dulled by her mood. She practiced smiling while opening another bottle of wine.

Letting the screen door slam behind her, Lucy put down the refreshments and handed a glass of wine to Brian, along with a towel. He wrapped the towel around his neck and stood up to make a toast. "Here's to David and all his success."

"And here's to the rain," she added nervously, avoiding his eyes when she clinked his raised glass and took an unusually long swig for reinforcement.

As they talked further into the night, they discovered that they were both single, neither had children, and neither had any plans for the future except to carry on with their thriving careers – his as a successful family attorney and hers as senior editor for the local newspaper. They shared how they had first met their mutual friend and several humorous stories, both agreeing that David had been a special person in their lives, and that's when Lucy could no longer avoid the inevitable. In a steady voice, she said, "I have something to tell you Brian, and I think you might want to have another drink before I do." She took the liberty to fill his glass.

Brian took a big gulp, swished it around his mouth and swallowed hard. Then he leaned forward and looked directly into Lucy's eyes, where tears were beginning to form. He sat perfectly still, waiting for God knows what would come from the cute hill country woman's mouth.

She reached out for his hand, and he took hers gingerly in his. Slowly and carefully, her words guarded, she said, "I'm very sorry to tell you this, so very sorry…but…David is in the hospital, in a coma. I'm afraid recovery doesn't look good."

"Oh, my God!" Brian choked, letting go of her hand and rearing back. "What happened?"

"It's an awful story," she warned him.

"Go on."

"Well, what I know is he was in his studio hanging a painting from the top of a ladder, when a man came in and held him at gunpoint." Lucy took a deep breath and steadied herself. "He accused David of being his wife's lover, and he threatened to kill him. David's employee was on the floor hidden behind the counter and heard everything. He said that David tried to plead with the man and convince him that he had the wrong person. But then the employee coughed, and the gunman shot wildly his direction. One of the bullets hit him in the knee. And that's when David jumped from the ladder onto the guy with the gun, and when they fell, his head hit the concrete floor. David was knocked out cold…only, he didn't wake up."

Brian sat quietly wringing his hands, trying to digest what she had said. "This happened yesterday?"

"Yes."

"Are you saying…he's not going to make it?"

"They can't stop the brain hemorrhage. It's severe. We're told it's just a matter of time." Brian buried his face in the towel. Lucy moved next to him, put her arm around his shoulders and wept with her new friend.

After a while they moved to the living room where they talked some more and lamented over David's impending death, until they finally surrendered to the alcohol and dozed off at opposite ends of the sofa.

They slept through the night until Ricky, the neighbor's rooster, jolted them awake. Neither felt the least bit awkward when seeing each other still fully clothed with only their shoes removed. Their common bond seemed to bring some comfort to their aching hearts, and over a fresh pot of coffee they agreed to go to the hospital together.

David's sister was due to arrive from Maui that day, and since she and her husband were to occupy his home during their visit, Lucy insisted that Brian stay with her. She was more than happy to have his company and gave him a key to come and go as he pleased.

Brian unloaded his luggage in Lucy's guest bedroom and took a long shower; his crying muffled by the sound of the water streaming hard on his face. He thought of David before Amber was tragically killed in that horrible car accident. A time when his whimsical friend's extreme happiness reflected in his twinkling eyes and in his lively art. He allowed himself to remember Amber. A beautiful, graceful woman whose death had brought both men to their knees. David would never know how much Brian had loved and coveted his wife. How he had mourned for Amber even while she lived. Why he had abandoned his best friend and stayed away with his pain and guilt.

Brian had accepted the invitation to the gallery opening, intending to tell David everything. Now, it was too late.

The ride to the hospital was reasonably quiet, as both friends privately worried about how they would handle seeing David lifeless on tubes.

When they entered the hospital room, they stood one on each side of David's bed. Brian told him the cute story of how he and Lucy ironically met on a rainy night on her porch, knowing that it would have made David smile since he had relished serendipitous moments. But there was no smile.

After a while of awkward silence, Lucy told Brian in a hushed voice that during a recent lunch with David he had mentioned a woman who he said was bringing him back to life. He did not share her name, but there was a lingering smile when he talked about painting the woman's eyes and her incredible hands.

"I felt hope for his future," she said, squeezing back the tears. "I thought he'd never stop grieving over Amber." Now, looking down at his barren expression, that hope was fading with each shallow breath. "I'll give you some time alone with your friend," she said to Brian, backing out of the room and quietly closing the door behind her.

Brian sighed heavily and bent down to kiss David's cheek. In his ear he whispered, "If you can hear me buddy, I'm so sorry I was not here for you. It's because I…" the words stuck in his throat. "Please forgive me."

Not long after Brian and Lucy left the hospital, David left, too.

The following day they were both invited to David's gallery to pick out a painting that they could keep in memory of their cherished friend. As they somberly perused the rows of art on the walls — expressing in whispers their feelings about each piece — Brian wandered off alone and came across the studio where the artist had created his work. The art in this room was dark and foreboding, a side of David he had not known. Gloomy ominous clouds, battered flying cars with wings, fading faceless figures, balloons struck by lightning, the colors intentionally drained of their vibrancy. In a word, surreal.

Sensing the magnitude of David's grief, Brian strolled around the room feeling closer than ever to his friend. More paintings were propped against the walls, some stacked, some askew, and others that were simply sketches of shattered dreams scattered across a large table. In the corner, by a wall of glass windows where the trees sifted perfect light from the sun, stood an easel, next to it a pedestal holding a palette of oils and several brushes. Brian hesitated before approaching the last piece of art on canvas the artist had created.

She looks nothing like his wife, he thought, cocking his head to discern who the beautiful, nude female with amazingly sad eyes might be. He studied her face, and the heavily textured brush strokes that defined her long wavy hair. Shimmering like a waterfall from the top of her head, down her breasts, and past her waist, the thick strands landed just short of her interlaced fingers. Sitting cross-legged, the tips of her toes seem to fade into thin air.

So engrossed in the painting, Brian hadn't noticed Lucy standing beside him until she spoke. "She's lovely. I wonder who she is."

He responded in a whisper, "Maybe she's the woman he told you about. The one he liked to paint. I've never seen her before."

They stood still, uneasy with their discovery, yet equally entranced by the mystique and beauty of the unknown model who appeared to be floating on a cloud.

"If it's alright with his sister, I'd like to have this painting," Brian spoke up. It was not only a hauntingly exquisite work of art, but just maybe a part of the puzzle he hoped would be solved before he left town.

Lucy fell silent watching Brian stand stoically transfixed on the subject. She left him and the dismal room in search of a more lighthearted piece.

"Take them with my blessings," David's sister insisted, while the paintings were being wrapped. "And please, I expect you both to visit me in Maui. I have plenty of room, and I would like to hear more stories about my brother."

With the carefully packed treasures in the back of her Tahoe, hunger pangs hit them both at the same time. Dinner was next on the list.

Italian food was Lucy's favorite, and the owner always gave her the best table in the cozy compact restaurant. He was pleased to see her not dining alone, for a change, and gave her a little wink when Brian pulled out her chair.

Tired and emotionally drained, Lucy and Brian welcomed some light conversation, and after the second bottle of wine was uncorked and breathing, they began to share intimate details of their lives. Brian had just recovered from a rocky relationship that ended bitterly. Lucy confessed, rather embarrassed, that she had been without a man for at least four years — and after counting the years on her fingers she admitted that it was nearly five. They toasted to the single life and simple things in between bites of homemade pasta. The sauce was mouth-watering and so rich, they passed up dessert.

Back on her porch, sipping Drambuie, Brian asked if he could sit beside her on the swing, explaining that he could see the moon much better from where she sat. The swing was only four feet wide, meant to hold only two, and Lucy was glad she had bought the smallest instead of the wide six-footer. She liked their shoulders rubbing together and the scent of the liqueur mixed with Italian seasonings on his breath when he turned his head her direction. "I bet David would have liked seeing us together like this," she said.

Before she could diffuse the bold statement, Brian said, "I believe he'd like this, too." Holding her chin in his hand, he delicately pressed his lips on hers. She gave a muffled reply into his warm mouth, "Uh huh," and purred it again in his ear while he kissed her cheek and then gently led her mouth back to his.

Turning her body toward Brian, Lucy sat up on her knees and kissed him again, much heartier than she had planned. He was delicious, and she could not deny his response to her touch. Unable to restrain the sexual tension any longer, she found herself straddling him, trying clumsily to keep her balance while the swing shook erratically from her sudden move. Brian pulled her closer and stood up, holding her tightly, his tongue playfully stroking hers. He broke free and looked into her eyes. The answer to the question she hoped he would ask tumbled out of her mouth before he could speak. "Yes, please…more than anything."

Ricky the rooster dutifully and rudely woke the deeply sleeping lovers around five the next morning.

"Someday, I'm going to kill that rooster," Lucy said though a muffled laugh.

"Not today." Brian rolled over, meeting Lucy halfway.

It was nearly eleven when they woke again, this time to the phone ringing. It was the publisher of the newspaper asking Lucy when she was coming back. She said she'd be in within the hour after a quick breakfast with her guest, who she chose not to name.

While Lucy was busy at work, Brian unwrapped the painting of the mysterious woman and sat it on top of the dresser across from the bed where he was supposed to be sleeping while a guest in Lucy's home. He pondered why David had kept her a secret. He understood why he had become a recluse after Amber died, but not confiding in his own sister or best friend was out of character. Brian was deeply perplexed and wondered if this woman was even aware that David had died. He spent the day contemplating that question and hoped that the stranger would be at the funeral the following Saturday. He wasn't quite sure why he was compelled to know her.

Pouring himself some tea, he picked up the local paper from the day before and read the headlines. In the center was an article about David and the details of that awful day. Gerald Damery was the name of the man who threatened his friend. He was now in jail and had not been bonded out. The case was clear cut with the witness alive and well in the hospital recovering from the gunshot wound. The wife of the gunman was not identified at the time of the writing. The article was short and simple, an unfortunate mistake of identity.

Puzzled even more, Brian went back to the guest room and lay on the bed looking up at the enigmatic female, studying her hypnotic eyes for an answer. Sleepily, his eyelids fell shut, only to open them again with a sudden realization. He jumped up, grabbed the painting, and brought it closer to the light pouring in from the west window. He blinked several times to make sure he was seeing clearly and began counting the fingers on each of the model's hands. He counted again, "One, two, three…eleven! Eleven? Unmistakably, there were eleven fingers; an extra ring finger on her left hand.

Lucy arrived early to find Brian on the porch reading. He greeted her at the top of the steps with a welcoming kiss. Coaxing her inside, he led her to the guest bedroom to show her his discovery. Lucy was clearly amazed and equally confused. Had he painted that extra finger in, or did the woman actually have eleven fingers? When Lucy repeated what David had told her about painting a woman's incredible hands, they concluded that she had to have been the new woman in his life. For the time being, it was the only thing that made sense.

Leaving Brian soundly asleep in her bed, Lucy tiptoed out the door heading to her office. She found herself thinking about David and the eleven-fingered woman off and on throughout the day. The more she thought about it, the more her journalistic curiosity got the better of her. Instructing her assistant to call her when needed, she took off for the police station.

The records department was used to seeing Lucy come and go, reading police reports often to match with a crime or accident she would write about in the paper. She read thoroughly through the Damery file, looking for key words that might shed some light on their recent discovery.

She already knew that the assailant claimed David was having an affair with his wife, who had been missing for nearly a month. He had found a letter in her handwriting, referring to the artist who knew her body better than no other, and she called him David. Nowhere in the report was the woman's name.

Sitting there thinking, a friend in the department stopped at the doorway and stuck her head in. "Hey, girl, what brings you here today?"

"Hi, Julie. Glad you stopped by. Do you have any other information you can share with me on the Damery case? I noticed there's no mention of the wife's name."

"Well," she whispered, entering the room cautiously and closing the door behind her, "I don't know anything about her, but I do know that guy Damery told the officer that she had eleven fingers. Imagine that, eleven fingers! He's probably nuts."

Lucy rushed back to her office and spent the afternoon mulling over her latest breakthrough. She was uncertain of what to do. It gnawed at her for the rest of the day.

For the first time since his arrival, Brian decided to visit David's home while David's sister and family were with the Funeral Director finalizing the service arrangements. When he lifted the painted stone by the front door, the one with two fingers forming a peace sign, he found the key he had been told would be there.

Inside, everything looked the same as it had at his last visit, except there were added paintings on the walls. He decided to study them later when he had more time and went directly to his friend's bedroom. He knew David had kept a journal since childhood. He hoped he'd find it now. Combing through the drawers and the closet he began feeling like an intruder. On his way out, he dropped to one knee, searched under the bed and found what he was looking for. "Yes!" He snatched the journal up and hurriedly left the house. When he lifted the stone to put the key back, he took a closer look at the peace sign and saw that both fingers were ring fingers. Startled, he put the stone in its place and promptly drove back to Lucy's house.

The front porch swing was becoming Brian's favorite place to be during this stressful time away from his own home. Waiting for Lucy to return seemed to comfort him. But this time he hoped she'd be a little late, so he could read David's journal.

It began a week after his wife had died. The handwriting was aligned and neatly written, as one generally does when writing for the first time on fresh, white paper. Turning the pages, the elegant writing changed to scribbling, showing that his thoughts were pouring out much faster than his hand could write. He wrote of his sadness, how he missed his wife, and the disturbance in his soul. He described her death in detail, using stark words filled with agony. Scattered across the pages, ink was smeared where tears had fallen. Brian's own tears fell onto the pages, mingling with his friend's and bonding them closer than ever before.

He labored through each page until the words ceased and the next few pages were blank. Thumbing through the journal, he thought there was no more to be read until he found toward the end a series of sketches. They started with the face of the mystery woman, first her eyes, then on the next page her mouth, followed by various parts of her body until the final page put them all together and formed a stunning illustration of a female standing naked from head to toe. She held her hands up, as if reaching for the heavens, and Brian again counted eleven fingers. A loopy letter "I" was written several times in bold ink along the edges. In tiny letters David had written: Dear God, help me, I must have her.

On the next page, he wrote one word: Brian.

Upon seeing his name, he concluded that David had insisted he come for more reasons than to attend a simple grand opening. Did he want to tell him about the new woman? Was she the wife of the crazed gunman? Was he seeking counsel from him? Did he need my friendship? With these unanswered questions bombarding him, he decided to keep his discovery and the journal to himself. Hiding it in his briefcase, Brian took a long drive through the country. Perhaps there was another reason he wanted to keep David's secret lover to himself. He needed to sort things out.

Privy to the information no one else knew, Lucy decided that no good would come from disturbing David's family and friends with the connection between him and the mysterious woman. Affairs are seen as ugly, no matter the circumstances. She would preserve David's beautiful legacy and not even tell Brian.

When she arrived home, she was relieved to find that Brian was not there. She went straight to the guestroom where he had left his things and stood before the painting. When she counted eleven fingers again, her heart sank. But it did not stop her from taking a picture of it.

The next two days were spent busying themselves and ending each evening in Lucy's bed. When he had moments alone, Brian pondered David's lover and found himself staring at the painting often. He read the journal two more times. When he reached up to slip it into the suitcase on the upper closet shelf, a small piece of paper fell from between the pages. On it was written a name. Izabelle. Brian kept that to himself, as well.

～

They woke to the day of the funeral and barely spoke a word to one another. Brian had left Lucy's bed in the middle of the night and slept in the guest room. His actions and the silence during breakfast could easily be construed as a respectful reverie on a very sad day. She would honor his feelings and allow him his peace.

Lucy wore a solid black dress, scooped enough at the neck to show a faint shadow of cleavage. She clipped on a simple pair of pearl earrings and slipped into her black satin heels, while Brian donned a dark blue suit with a crimson red tie, knowing that David would like the contrast.

There were at least a hundred people at the funeral; mostly artsy folks who loved the deceased artist's work and people from the trade merely paying their respect. A dozen or so were family, from both his side and his wife's. Their grieving was etched in their faces as they cried into wadded up tissue, barely acknowledging the funeral proceedings until Brian stepped up to the pulpit. He spoke eloquently and shared some funny stories that brought timid laughter to the sadness of the memorial. Watching him from the second row, Lucy was intrigued, and she knew at that very moment she was falling in love with this man whom she had known barely a week and with whom she shared a common bond. She wept for the loss of David and for the love she felt for Brian. Perhaps someday, when the time was right, she would tell him.

While everyone was mingling and giving their condolences, Brian slipped away to get some fresh air. He looked around for the nearest bench and spotted one in the garden shaded by a beautiful old weeping willow tree. He sat down and rested both arms on the back of the bench, inching down so that his neck would rest on the slat of wood while he gazed up at elongated leaves swaying hypnotically with the wind. This had always been his favorite tree, and he felt at home under it. He closed his eyes and let the warm breeze dance across his face.

"Brian," the voice whispered so low he thought he was dreaming. "Brian" she spoke a tad louder.

Brian sat up and looked to the left and then to the right. A shadow appeared from over his shoulder. He turned to see who it was, and there stood a strange image of a woman dressed entirely in black wearing a thin veil. She came around and sat next to him on the bench. Even through the black tule, he recognized the piercing dark eyes of those in the painting. She held his gaze and said, with a thick Portuguese accent, "Hello Brian, I'm David's lover, and I believe you know me by the painting you took from his studio."

David gulped and spoke carefully, "You have me at a disadvantage. You know my name, but I don't know yours."

"Oh, but I believe you do. I'm Izabelle." He saw her smile with her eyes. "David told me wonderful things about you. I'm glad to meet you, even now."

Brian shifted his body toward her and without thinking, he reached for her six-fingered hand. As he did, she quickly pulled back. "I know about your hand," he said.

She looked straight through him.

"Your painting. I studied it thoroughly." He wanted in the strangest way to see it, but her reluctance told him not to ask. "May I please see your face? I feel like I already know you," he gently coaxed.

Izabelle slowly lifted the veil and gave him an alluring smile. Brian was taken aback by the likeness in the painting. David had captured her liquid-brown eyes perfectly – yet now they appeared even more sorrowful. The questions he wanted to ask melted away at the sight of her. And of course, this was neither the time or place for such intimacy. He asked, "Could we meet soon…to talk?"

"It would only be right. David loved you very much. He would want me to share with you."

"I'm scheduled to leave in two days. Can we meet before then?" he spoke a little breathlessly.

She lowered the veil and got up to leave. Brian stood and faced her. He continued with some urgency. "David's family is leaving later today, and I'm staying at his home. Please meet me there after dark. Is that possible?"

"Yes," she said and hugged him so tightly, when she let go, he thought he might fall backwards. He watched her walk away. Instead of entering the sanctuary as he thought she would, she passed through the heavy iron gates and disappeared.

After the burial, everyone gathered at the gallery for refreshments. David's sister announced to the guests that all the art would be auctioned the following Monday and that the gallery would be sold. The hushed room was suddenly filled with excited murmurs as the guests began writing down the pieces they wanted to purchase.

Lucy was sorely disappointed when Brian told her he'd be sleeping at David's home the remaining nights of his stay. He explained that he had to catch up on a case and had been asked to help with the auction. He promised to see her before he left town. She felt like a silly schoolgirl with a crush when he left after kissing her goodbye standing next to his car. She was glad that she reserved telling him how strongly she felt about him and closed herself up in her bedroom for a much-needed sleep.

Brian settled into the old corduroy sofa that David refused to give up since college and waited for Izabelle. He opened a bottle of wine from his private collection, a 1993 Reserve, and sipped it slowly while listening to Mozart from an old turntable, another treasure from the past. He heard the rain lightly hitting the metal roof overhead. After a while, the back door flew open and before he could reach it, Izabelle entered, brushed past him, and walked straight to the sofa as if she had been there before. She was wet from the rain.

"Let me get you a towel," he said. Returning with a bath towel and David's thin bathrobe, Brian handed it to her, snatched up the wine bottle and went to the kitchen to give her some privacy. He took another wine glass from the cabinet, filled it, and waited a few minutes before entering the room.

He saw her wet clothes hanging over the back of a chair, her shoes tossed on the floor. His eyes landed on her body huddled in the corner of the sofa, tightly cocooned in the robe. She accepted the glass of wine from his outstretched hand. Brian turned off the music and sat down close to her. In silence they savored the wine, while listening to the thunder growing louder and moving in their direction.

Outside, the rain began pounding the roof. Soon lightning struck angrily overhead, and then the lights went out. Izabelle felt her way through the dark to the kitchen and returned with two lit candles. She didn't go back to the corner where she had been sitting, but instead sat down right next to Brian. She pulled at a ribbon that loosened her hair, falling softly over her shoulders. Then she gently placed her hand on his thigh. Without a word, she turned and kissed him; a long adoring kiss, as if he had been her lover all along.

By candlelight she led him to David's bed, where they spent the night making love in silence. When Brian tried to question her, she put her finger to his lips and said, "Shhh, you are my David now. I am your Amber."

Izabelle woke Brian the next morning while caressing his face with six fingers. He lay quietly with eyes closed reveling in the experience. When he finally opened them to acknowledge her, she eased out of bed and led him to the back patio where the morning sun shone the most. She wove her fingers through his to let him see and feel what had given him such pleasure. He felt a mixture of awe and a sense of unease – strangely beautiful and bizarre, and when he lifted the thick strands of hair away from her breasts, he knew he must have her. Aroused to near explosion, he leaned her against the railing and took her again.

Lucy tried knocking on the front door several times before she gave up and went around the back of the house to see if Brian was leisurely sipping coffee, watching the sun rise. She had in her hand a paper bag of breakfast tacos and a cinnamon roll covered in butter that she looked forward to sharing with her new friend. When she rounded the corner, she stopped in her tracks at what she saw. She stood paralyzed witnessing the two in a heated embrace – Brian breathlessly collapsing with his final thrust. He lifted his head from Izabelle's chest and reaching for her hand, he sensually placed her fingers inside his mouth. Afraid to move, Lucy watched the scene unfold in slow motion as Izabelle lured him back inside. Looking over her shoulder, she tossed back her hair and smiled at Lucy while slowly closing the door.

Gazing out the window of the airplane, Lucy could not believe that so many years later the vivid imagery from that experience could still haunt her. Of course, the memories would reappear. She expected them. They began nagging at her the moment she decided to make the trip to Maui to see David's sister, whom she had never told about the mysterious eleven-fingered woman responsible for David's death. Nor had she told her or anyone else about her brief affair with Brian, who had left without saying goodbye, never to be heard from again.

Fortunately, the disturbing image shattered when the pilot announced that they were descending in an early arrival.

Relieved, Lucy looked over at her son – his long, brown eyelashes remarkably like his father's – and gently nudged him from his deep sleep. The Maui sunrise burst through the window and got the passenger's attention. She was glad to have an excuse to wear her sunglasses, not just to ward off the rays, but to hide the tears.

After a rocky landing, Lucy let go of her son's hand and stood up to stretch. She noticed the woman seated ahead of her reaching out to wake her sleeping companion. Lucy counted six fingers, and when the man with the heart-shaped upper lip opened his eyes, he was no longer a figment of Lucy's imagination. It was him, Brian, the father of her child.

As the lethargic passengers sluggishly moved toward the aisle, Lucy's chest tightened, and she felt her hands trembling. She bent down and pretended to tie her son's shoes in hopes that Brian or Izabelle would not see her. When they were far enough ahead, she exited the plane.

At the baggage claim, she anxiously rushed past them. She pulled her son closer and forced the travelers to make room for them in the crammed elevator. Looking over her shoulder, she met Izabelle's surprised gaze – the look on her face was nothing short of astonishment. Lucy smiled at her, as the elevator doors slowly closed between them.

CARLA'S CONUNDRUM

"She has logorrhea," he said calmly, while sorting through the newspaper to find the sports section, discarding the slick ad sheets and the comics, lining up the metro section next with the front page saved for last.

"What's that?" she asked, the sharp knife resting in her hand, tomato drippings slipping down her thumb. Carla loved it when her husband gave her a new word, which he did often and at the most appropriate time – always when she found herself in need of a good word to describe the feeling or subject at hand.

"Pathologically excessive and often incoherent talkativeness or wordiness," he said without pausing to think. "But for your sake, you can say it means diarrhea of the mouth. A compulsive talker."

"Oh, that's perfect, that describes her perfectly. So, is there a drug for that?"

"I may be good at words, sweetie, but I'm certainly not a doctor."

"Well, at least we have a proper word for it now. I feel bad calling her a blabbermouth, or obnoxious, which is exactly what she is. But, if it is a true disorder, maybe she'd want to know about it."

Carla walked over to her husband who now had his head buried inside the newspaper. She gently pulled it away from his hands. "Edgar, please. This is very serious. Just yesterday, Betty told me not to bring her to our wine tasting tonight because she disrupts everything. Remember last week when John invited us to his birthday party, and when I told him I'd bring Jean he nearly bit my head off? He yelled at me as if I had invited an ax murderer, not my own sister."

"I did my part. I gave you the word. Sorry babe, you're on your own with this one."

"But you can't stand it either when she goes from one subject to another, never asks about you, interrupts our talking, refuses to answer a question, always trying to sell us something…."

"I know, I know, but because she's your sister, and I love you, I just shut down a part of my brain and don't listen, or I start fudgelling."

"You do what?"

"Fudgel. It's an eighteenth-century term meaning to pretend to work when you're not actually doing anything at all. Can't you do the same?"

"I wish," Carla sighed.

The day was blustery, and the wind ran wildly through the trees, loosening the leaves much too early in the season. "Global warming," the cashier at the grocery store explained, as she leaned over and lifted a dead fly from Carla's heavily sprayed hair.

"Ewww," Carla shivered while watching the girl toss the insect into a trash can. "You don't see any more bugs in my hair, do you?"

The cashier studied Carla's teased blonde hair closely. She pulled the pencil from behind her ear and parted a few strands with it. "Nope, don't see any more."

"But you sure do need to do something about those gray roots," a loud familiar voice came from the next aisle over.

Seeing her sister, Jean standing in line, Carla cringed. "Thanks Jean, thanks a lot." Fluffing both sides of her hair, she grabbed her bags and dashed toward the door, waving a quick goodbye.

"What's the hurry?" Jean bellowed.

"Party tonight. Got to run!"

"Oh yeah, the one I'm *not* invited to," Jean huffed.

In the driveway of her brick home, nestled in the interior of an upscale subdivision called Lake Point, although there was nary a lake in sight, Carla unloaded the groceries from her car. Just when she closed the trunk, her friend, Betty, pulled up behind her. Betty yelled out the window, "Hey, tell me you're making those scrumptious peppermint mocha pudding cookies for tonight. They will go great with wine!"

"I was planning on something less decadent, like a cheese roll," Carla answered, moving closer to the car.

"Oh pleaseeeee," Betty whined, "Deena's already bringing a cheese roll. Can't you just bake a dozen of those fabulous cookies?"

"Betty, have you forgotten? It's not me that makes those cookies, it's my sister. It's her special recipe, and she refuses to give it out. And remember, you told me she couldn't come." Carla couldn't help herself, the guilt she felt the moment she saw her sister at the grocery store stayed with her all the way home. "That is…unless you've changed your mind."

"Oh, yeah, well…hmmm." Betty pressed her lips together in

deep thought. "I suppose she can come, IF...well, if she can bring a batch. And, of course, a bottle of wine, AND if you think you can control her mouth, that would be helpful."

"That's nice of you to invite her. I was feeling really bad about leaving her out, but honestly, you…."

And before Carla could say more, Betty revved the motor and loudly announced, "I'm leaving before I change my mind. See you later!"

That night while Carla was dressing, with Edgar propped up on a pillow in the middle of the bed reading a magazine, they abruptly stopped what they were doing when they heard Jean burst into the house talking loudly on her cell phone.

"Shut the door, hurry," Edgar whispered through clenched teeth, pointing wildly at the bedroom door.

Carla ran to close it and braced herself against the wall, listening intently at Jean's voice growing louder and louder as she came charging down the hall. Hearing her words softening within the confines of the guest bathroom, Carla let out a squelched breath and smiled awkwardly at her husband.

"Heeere's Johnny!" Edgar announced, flashing his teeth like Jack Nicholson in *The Shining*. "I can't believe you invited her after that speech you gave me this morning."

Carla bit her bottom lip, moaned and went back to the closet to finish dressing. "Oh dear, what have I done?" she muttered while digging through a rack of clothes, looking for the black shirt with the words "Group Therapy" embroidered in sequin below three full glasses of wine outlined in red rhinestones.

"Nice touch," Edgar said when she walked out of the closet fully dressed.

"Thank you. Although, I should know better than to wear

white pants. Every time I do, someone spills wine on me and there goes another pair. This time I'm going to distance myself from the spillers in the room."

"Oh, you mean like your sister?"

"Yes, she's definitely a known spiller." Carla sat at the edge of the bed. She ran her fingers through the clump of course hair on her husband's chest and smiled shyly at him. "Honey, what is that word you gave me this morning for my sister's ailment?"

"Logorrhea," he said, and then he said it again slowly. "Why? Are you planning on diagnosing her tonight at the party?"

"No, I guess I just like giving it a proper name. Somehow it makes me feel a little better. Hard to explain."

"No one can explain family, sweetie. Besides studies have shown that most talkaholics are aware of what they do and don't think they have a problem. It would help you, honey, to just remember one thing, she's not *you* and she doesn't represent *you*. Now, go enjoy the night and remember what I said. Let someone else handle your sister. You've been doing it for much too long."

Carla took a deep breath and exhaled. "You're right. Guess I'm a little tired of the job. And with our mother now living in Florida, she's not here to make me feel guilty." She kissed her husband on the forehead and bit the tip of his nose.

"Ouch! What was that for?"

"Just wanted you to remember me while I'm gone."

Edgar quickly sat up, grabbed his wife's elbow and pulling her toward him, he kissed her passionately. "Umm, how's that for a reminder?"

"Well," she cooed, "I might be home a little early tonight. Keep my side of the bed warm, will you?"

Just as Carla turned to leave the room, Edgar said, "And please honey, don't bring Jean home with you. Not tonight."

"WHAT did he say?" Jean barked, poking her head through the door, startling the couple.

"Nothing, he said nothing. Come on, we're late," Carla assured her sibling, glancing back at Edgar with wide helpless eyes.

"I made three dozen cookies," Jean boasted, as they walked toward Betty's home. "And I brought two bottles of Three Dollar Wally. It's surprisingly good I'm told, and I just love the name."

Carla tried to explain that the party was about wine of an exceptional quality but couldn't get a word in edgewise as her sister jumped subjects and ended up telling her a long, descriptive story about a man that nearly accosted her in the grocery store parking lot. She finished it just seconds before they approached Betty's front door and then she repeated the story verbatim as they entered the foyer. Carla darted toward the kitchen to unload the goodies in her bag. Jean's voice boomed from the two-story entry as she held Betty captive.

More ladies filed in and Jean told the story again, this time to the entire room. While Betty passed out glasses of wine, she looked over at Carla and gave her the look that said, 'Aren't you going to do something to stop her?'

Carla took a long sip and studied the captivated audience, their heads bobbing as they watched her animated sibling wave her arms around like a mad conductor. She knew she could interrupt Jean and move her to another subject, as she had done so many times before. Instead, remembering the advice her husband had given her earlier, she gave Betty a stiff smile and shrugged her shoulders in surrender.

Betty eventually took the matter into her own hands and stood directly in front of Jean. "Ladies, ladies, I'm so glad you're here tonight. Thank you, Jean, for that uh, that incredible story, but I do think we need to get on with our wine tasting."

Irritated, Jean plopped down on the fireplace hearth, the wine glass in her hand nearly spilling when she crossed her arms in defiance. Carla was relieved to see her sister far across the room at a safe distance from her white jeans.

"Now, everyone has a glass of wine, yes?" Betty surveyed the room, holding hers up in position for a toast. From their seats, the ladies held the glasses up high. "Cheers," she said cheerfully, and sips were heard all around the room. "This is a red wine, a fine blend of Merlot, Cabernet and a touch of Syrah. Now, would someone like to describe the taste?"

"Like a dirty dog," Jean spoke up. "Like a dog that has been rolling in dung and old wet leaves. I remember the first time I learned how to describe this kind of wine. I was in Las Vegas with a man, a beautiful man who took me to the Venetian Resort. It was *so* romantic. He was gorgeous. He looked like a mixture of Michael Caine and Pierce Brosnan. We were sipping a blend just like this one and gliding down the canal on a rickshaw under a soft moon."

"A rickshaw on the canal?" a small voice interrupted. "Don't you mean a gondola?"

"I didn't say rickshaw. My, my, is the wine getting to you already?" Jean sneered. "Anyway..." and the story went on and on and on, while Carla's thoughts strayed – trying hard to picture what a combination of Caine and Brosnan would look like. Feeling Betty's evil-eye on her, she turned toward her and silently mouthed, "Cookies remember, cookies?"

"So, what's the next wine, toots?" Jean asked, after finishing the story with a large gulp.

"Well, let's see, I've lost my train of thought," Betty said, shaking her head, as if to loosen her jumbled mind.

"Not to worry, let's try mine next," Jean grabbed two bottles of wine from her large vinyl bag. "Screw top!" she proudly announced lifting them up for all to see. "Three Dollar Wally!"

With tightened lips, all heads turned to see how Betty was reacting to the choice of wine.

"I, uh, well, Jean, uh, this is actually a fine wine tasting we're having here, emphasis on *fine*. I don't believe that Three Dollar Jolly falls into that category.

"Three Dollar Wally!" Jean corrected her. "It's only three dollars. Who can beat that? Shoot, that's less than fifty cents a glass. And you will appreciate its flavor." She filled the empty glasses sitting neatly in a row on the buffet.

"Come on ladies. I'm not going to serve you. Get over here and grab your glass of Wally." The ladies slowly rose from their seats and filed in line. Carla stayed put, savoring her drink, and avoiding Betty's glare.

"Now girls," Jean began as everyone sat back down, balancing the nearly full to the rim glasses in both hands, "I'm in for a surprise myself, as I haven't had this particular wine yet, but I was told about it by my masseuse. She's wonderful and has *huge* hands. Almost as large as my sister's. Show them your big hands, Carla."

All heads turned to look at Carla, who was now looking at her hand and questioning her sister's claim. "I have big hands?" she asked, a look of repulsion on her face.

"Well, maybe they're not as big as they used to be before you lost weight," Jean chuckled. "She had quite a set of meat hooks."

Carla opened her mouth to say something but stopped herself and snapped it shut. "Anyway, you get the idea," Jean continued. "The truth is, I think my masseuse might be a man. She has the hairiest arms, and she says she wears a size twelve shoe. I'm kind of afraid to ask. Nevertheless, she said this wine is fabulous. Bottoms up, girls!"

The ladies slowly tipped their glasses and hesitated, watching Jean take a large gulp and swish it around in her mouth. As she swished, her eyes grew wide, and a look of horror appeared on her face. All of a sudden, she leapt forward and spewed the wine all over the coffee table. Losing her balance, she turned to catch herself from falling and flung the glass of wine into the face of a guest. Horrified, the woman clumsily stood up, spilling the contents of her own glass on the guest next to her. A big splash landed on Carla's white pants. Betty came running across the room and tripped over the ottoman, falling face first onto Jean's hip, knocking them both to the floor. Two of the unscathed guests grabbed their bottles of wine and the appetizers they had brought and left the scene. The other two wine-soaked gals took off for the nearest bathroom. Carla sat in silence, hiding behind her empty glass, watching with exasperation as the red wine soaked deeper into her pants.

"Get off me, you cow!" Jean yelled, pushing Betty away.

Betty rose to her knees, her hands splayed out in disgust. "Look what you've done! You ruined my rug! You ruined my party!" Then she turned to Carla and said, "And you made me feel guilty about not inviting her!"

"Oh, buzz off," Jean blurted.

Carla rose to her feet. She had heard and seen enough. "*You* buzz off, sister. Betty's right. It's true, you aren't welcome to these events because you talk too much. You take over, you control, you don't listen. You have a problem. It's called, it's called… loga, logo, logorrhea. It's real and you have it."

"WHAT?" Jean looked at Carla dumbfounded. "I have WHAT?"

"Diarrhea of the mouth, Jean. Diarrhea of the mouth."

"That's for certain," Betty said, rearing back, considering Jean might take a swing at her.

"WELL! You can keep the wine. I'll take the cookies!" Jean flounced out of the house in a huff.

Carla dropped her head and slumped back into the sofa. "I'm so sorry, Betty. I know she's unbearable, but she *is* my sister. I'll gladly replace your rug."

"Family. I know, you can pick your nose but not your family," Betty sighed, sympathizing with her long-faced friend. "To hell with the rug. I've always wanted an excuse to replace this ugly Flokati. But you know, this might have been all worth it if she had left the cookies."

Carla let out a chuckle and lifted her glass. "You're a good sport, Betty. We really shouldn't let the *good* wine go to waste though. Right?"

After a futile attempt to sop up the huge red stain from the rug, the ladies hauled it out to the garage. Betty poured more wine and yelled out to the two guests hiding in the bathroom, "The coast is clear girls, you can come out now!" An hour later, most of the appetizers were gone and all but the Three Dollar Wally had been drunk.

A little intoxicated, Carla announced that it was time to leave. "I have a half-naked husband in bed waiting for me," she confessed. "I imagine I'll eat crow in the morning when my sister calls."

"Want me to walk you home?" Betty gently patted Carla on the back.

"No thanks, I'm good. And Betty, I'm really sorry about tonight. I've learned my lesson. I won't be inviting my sister to our gatherings in the future, and you don't have to feel guilty about it."

"I doubt I'll ever feel guilty again, my dear. But, what about you?"

"I'll deal with it. Maybe she'll check herself, now that I've given her a legitimate name for her problem."

"Well, maybe," Betty pondered.

Then they both shook their heads doubtfully and said at the same time, "Nah!"

The walk home gave Carla time to think about the evening. She was not as surprised by her sister's actions as much as she was surprised by her own silence, up until it all got out of control. She reasoned that letting Jean be herself, making a mess of things, should really be out of her hands. She just couldn't figure out why it made her sad, until she realized that this time she knew she could never invite her again. It was without a doubt, the final straw.

As she approached her driveway, she looked up at the moon and thought about her handsome husband anticipating the arrival of his slightly inebriated and lustful wife. She smiled in the dark and entered the house rather giddy.

An unexpected light was on in the kitchen and she heard talking. Tiptoeing down the hall, she stopped to listen when she recognized the voice. She heard Jean say, "I'll just be here a month, maybe two, until I find another job and an apartment — one where they won't evict me for playing the bongos at night. It's therapeutic. Helps me sleep. And don't worry, I'll sleep on the pull-out sofa, unless of course one of your boys wants to give up their cushy bed to good ole Aunt Jean. I can't believe they fired me. And all because I talk too much, they said. I disturb the other employees and make my boss nervous. Can you believe they said that? Pass the ice cream, will you? Aren't these cookies great with ice cream?"

Carla heard the scraping of a bowl with a spoon, but no other voice. She moved in a little closer toward the kitchen.

"And how was I to know that the wine was bad. I guess you just can't trust a masseuse with hands that big and feet to match. I think the worst part of the evening was when Betty tripped over me and caused me to spill my wine on her precious white rug. It was an ugly rug anyway. Looked like an albino Chewbacca. You can't blame me for telling her to buzz off. Right?"

Someone cleared their throat in a form of response.

"And you know what Carla said I had? Some kind of diarrhea that comes from the mouth. What in the world is she talking about? I have a lot to say, that's all. I'm not just one of those boring women who just sits there and looks pretty. I've traveled, I'm experienced, I've had several careers and a lot of fine men in my life. I'm an interesting gal with lots of stories. And I make a great cookie, don't you think?"

"That's one thing you do for sure," Edgar said.

Carla's mouth dropped open. *He's supposed to be waiting in bed for me, not eating ice cream and cookies with my crazy sister!* She started to go in and ream-out both of them, when Edgar spoke up.

"Jean, Carla told you that you have logorrhea. It's a form of diarrhea of the mouth. It doesn't mean that you have diarrhea, it means that you have no tools to control your constant talking. You..."

"I don't have logo whatchamacallit! What are you...?"

"Jean, shut up!" Edgar interrupted, pounding his fist on the table.

"Well, I never...!"

"Yes, Jean, you NEVER stop talking. Do you know what I've been doing while you were rambling on and on, chomping on cookies and slurping ice cream in between your words? Do you have any idea?"

"Well, sure. You were listening," Jean said smugly.

"No, I wasn't listening. I was singing the Weird Al's version of *Just Beat It* in my head."

"Why would you do something like *that*?"

"To keep from saying something rotten to you. Maybe even to keep from slapping you silly."

"What?" Jean pushed her chair back, making skidding sounds on the floor. "You're going to hit me? I'll tell my sister about this. She won't stand for that kind of talk."

"Jean, I'm not going to hit you. I'm trying to make a point. You have a problem. It's gotten worse, and your sister is beside herself worrying about you."

"She's never said anything to me about any *problem*," Jean scoffed.

"She tried tonight. You won't listen, just like you're not listening now."

"For goodness sake, Edgar. If you don't want to put me up for a few weeks, just say so. This is a pathetic way of telling me you don't want me here. Don't worry, I'll find somewhere else to stay."

"Oh yeah?" Edgar said, leaning back and crossing his arms. "Name one person right now that would be glad to have you stay in their home for more than a day. Go on, name one?"

"Lots of people. Lots of people like me. There's uh, uh, our grandmother. She loves me."

"Your grandmother is deaf, Jean and she's in a nursing home now. And by the way, she thinks you're Nancy, her old house-keeper. Name another."

"My sister. My sister would welcome me. When she gets home, just ask her."

At that moment Carla started to walk into the kitchen and tell her sister the truth. This time Jean will listen. Edgar had opened the door to a very unpleasant subject and now was her chance to finally tell her sister how much she annoyed her, how irritating she was to others, and how bad she felt when her friends made ugly remarks about her own sister...her only sibling. And worst of all, her sons ran and hid when she visited and made excuses to spend the night out. Only Edgar was able to tolerate her, and now, even he had reached his limit. Yet, something made her stand back in the shadows.

"Here's the deal, Jean. You can stay with us, but only on one condition."

"I won't clean your house. Those boys of yours are..."

"Jean, *please* be quiet!" Edgar pounded the table twice, this time for special effect.

"Humph!" she snorted.

Carla tried to keep from laughing, imagining Jean about to bite the tip of her tongue off. She wanted so badly to see their faces, but knew she'd be seen if she took another step.

"On one condition," Edgar leaned over, staring her down. "Are you listening, Jean?" he demanded.

"Well, of course. How could I not listen? You're practically in my face."

"You must listen carefully. You will not ask to go to any of Carla's social events. Do you understand?"

"Well, that's ridiculous!"

"DO YOU UNDERSTAND?" Edgar, now standing, leaned in and pressed his palms out flat on the table.

Jean said meekly, "Yes, I do." But the strange smile that came across her face told Edgar that she understood but had already figured a way out of the deal.

Edgar stood stiffly, in deep thought. "AND, you will not just happen to show up unexpectedly or make your sister feel guilty."

Jean held up her hands in submission. "OK, OK…whatever!"

"And Jean, if you decide you want help with your problem, I can direct you to a good psychologist. Until then, don't make me throw you out." Edgar got up, put his bowl in the sink and walked out of the kitchen. "Oh, and thanks for the cookies."

When he saw Carla standing in the dark, flattened against the wall, Edgar took her by the hand and quietly pulled her to the bedroom.

Behind the locked door, Carla jumped up and down on the bed and burst out in nervous laughter. "You are my hero!"

"You owe me, dear. Big time," he said and smothered her laugh with a long kiss.

"Wait a minute," Carla blurted, jolting back from Edgar's lips, "did she say a month or two?"

Back in the kitchen, Jean stood in front of the open freezer door spooning through a carton of ice cream. When she finished, she began reading the magnets and papers taped to the outside of the refrigerator. She spotted an invitation to John's birthday party and noted the date and time. "Ohh, great, I can wear my new slinky cocktail dress," she said to her reflection in the toaster. Glancing over her shoulder to make sure that she was still alone in the kitchen, she snatched a pen from the drawer and wrote on the invitation: Be sure and bring your SEXY sister, Jean.

ENJOY THE RIDE

Clare is spellbound watching the children playing make-believe together in the little playhouse on the playground. They are three to five years old, and they don't know one another, and they don't care. "Restaurant" is the name of the game, and they're all taking turns sitting on little stools shaped like mushrooms outside the playhouse window where they place their orders and wait to be served imaginary food in the form of bark scooped up from the playground's floor. Bark, pebbles, artificial grass, even chopped up tires are used nowadays in place of a soft grassy terrain with worn down paths naturally carved from droves of dirty bare feet running wildly around in circles, like it was when Clare was a child. She doesn't see a bare foot among them, except for one very unhappy little fella who removed his sandals to clean out the bark between his toes.

A little girl in ringlets and a prominent overbite that looks cute now, but will be a costly correction later in life − if she wishes to attract that doctor, lawyer or dentist − leans in and yells in a boy's face, "What would YOU like to eat?"

The boy stares at her, mesmerized by her Chicklet teeth and

corkscrew curls, and sticks his finger in his ear, not sure how to answer such a question because he's never had the option. His mother simply puts food in front of him that he has to eat, whether he likes it or not. 'Like a dog,' he might tell her someday when he realizes the disparity. But for now, he'll just run away and avoid this stupid game.

"What do *you* want for dinner?" the girl says it slower to the next little boy who appears out of nowhere. He doesn't seem to understand either, so she leans in closer, as her older sister does to her when she's warning her to keep away from her toys and repeats the question.

"Ske'ghetti," he says, wide-eyed and eager to please, not the least bit intimidated by her big teeth just inches from his nose.

"OK, here you go," she says, bending down, scooping up two handfuls of bark and tossing them on the windowsill now being used as a counter. "That'll be fifty dollars!"

The little boy stares at the piles and doesn't know what is expected of him, since he doesn't have a fork or money. But he doesn't run away. He looks to his right at the red-headed girl who has ordered imaginary pizza and watches her pretend to put the bark in her mouth. She chews, making a satisfied smacking sound and says, "Yummy, more please." The boy catches on and crams a handful of bark right in his mouth, as the girls squeal, "Ewww!" and the other boys watch open-mouthed with constrained admiration.

And the game continues, just like it always has.

Clare giggles and turns her attention to her boyfriend, Beau, who is pushing her grandchild on the swing. The four-year-old is demanding, "Higher, higher," and the frustration on Beau's face can't be denied. He doesn't have children, or grandchildren and his answer is said with a matter-of-fact directness that annoys the boy. "If I push you any higher, you'll flip over the top of the swing, hit the bar and knock your front teeth out and the dentist bill will be outrageously high, not to mention the painful surgery.

This is as high as you're going to get. Well, that is until you reach high school. So, for now, please stop yelling and enjoy the ride."

"Higher, higher, higher!" the little tyrant yells repeatedly. Beau sees Clare and flashes her a weary grin.

Beau has light hazel eyes that shift from brown to green, and usually green is dominant when he is being sincere. Not that he's not always sincere. Clare would like to think he's incapable of lying, but she knows that's naïve, because she thought the same about her ex-husband until his lies finally caught up with him and destroyed their marriage. She tries not to compare the two. Beau is such a fine man, and it's still strange to her that he's never been married. His reason, he said on their first date, was a simple and indisputable one. "I just never found the right gal." Two years and two months together later, Clare thinks she is the right gal and lately wonders why he hasn't proposed.

The thought annoys her so she turns her back on Beau just in time to watch an unusually tall preschooler in her perfectly starched cotton dress, rolled-down socks and practical shoes join the game. With a straight face that she no doubt borrowed from her mother, she says, "I'll have gluten-free toast." The boy serving her crumples up his face and freezes right there in his spot. Incensed, the girl charges toward him, her ponytail moving jerkily with her head, and he submissively lets her drag him from the playhouse to the toadstool. No verbal explanations are required, just a realization that they needed to change places and roles, and besides, she's bigger than him and wears glasses. So, the Sasquatch girl, as Clare used to be called, being the tallest girl in her class, is now on the server's side and proceeds to take his order instead.

"Pancakes," he proudly blurts, sure to wipe that frown off her face. "And syrup, too," he adds, pretending to have a fork in his hand.

The ambitious wannabe waitress, now with her hand on her

jutted hip, twirling her ponytail with her exceptionally long fingers says, "Oh, too bad, we're ALL out of those."

Clare looks around the playground to see who that little girl's mother might be. She easily spots her standing close by, erect in her tall, thin frame, arms folded, aligned with the elastic waistline of her stiff culottes, identical hair pulled at the scalp, looking pleased over the rim of her glasses at her willful daughter's behavior. The other moms catch each other's eyes and tuck the funny scene away to remember to share it next time they all gather for coffee. "Did you see that Sasquatch girl on the playground…?"

Clare winces recalling how being the "big for her age" kid wasn't all that fun and once again slips right back into useless thought.

Beau and Clare are in their mid-fifties, healthy, reasonably attractive, each with a savings account that will accommodate their old age. They are alike with small differences. Beau reads constantly, and she smiles to herself looking over at him now, armed with a magazine stuffed in the pocket of his jeans. He never goes anywhere without something to read, and once during the unprecedented presidential election, he pulled out a tiny book of The Constitution and read it right in line at the grocery store. Clare doesn't have political interests or the focus ability and prefers to study people, conjuring up her own lively fantasies about them.

Beau drives a newer model Toyota Avalon. Clare drives an uncommonly green 1979 garage-kept Lincoln Town Car in mint condition that her dad willed her. Even in its impeccable shape, it still smells like her dad. Cigar smoke is impossible to get out of leather. But she doesn't mind. She adored her father, a wonderful storyteller, and she is especially fond of the romantic one he told her about proposing to her mother under an enchanting harvest moon. She misses him terribly.

Beau's parents are in their eighties, alive and well living in

Florida next door to Beau's sister. He is grateful for her and that he doesn't have to be the one to look out for them. His cash contributions remove all guilt. Clare's mother is in assisted living. Clare's twice weekly visits aren't enough to remove all the guilt she has for not taking her widowed mother into her own home. Even if they got along better, she still would not have succumbed to the idea of two very strong-willed women under the same roof. Besides, Beau is at her home often and well, they do sleep in the same bed. Often.

Neither Beau nor Clare require lavish vacations, expensive restaurants, champagne, or the latest trends in clothing or furniture. Clare's ex-husband requires all those things, and his twenty-year younger girlfriend loves that about him. Beau enjoys a stiff scotch, while Clare relishes her gin and tonic. Gluten-free, paraben-free, preservative-free, none of those things or furry pets interfere with their comfortable lifestyle, and burgers and ice cream are a must. Beau sneaks a hot dog and bacon any chance he gets because Clare says they are artery hardeners and not allowed in her kitchen. Clare hides dark chocolate in her vanity drawer, only because Beau will eat it all if it's in plain view.

They each have a bicycle, good walking shoes and an appreciation for music. They are a fine balance of everything good and attainable and to top it off, they're both Democrats.

So, Clare says to herself again, while watching this compatible red-faced man sitting on the swing catching his breath after pushing her snot-nosed grandson for entirely too long, why won't he ask me to marry him?

Just that morning they received an invitation to a friend's wedding. The bride to be was in her sixties and marrying one of her clients. They'd met over an investment planning meeting held in a restaurant booth, and by the end of the meeting, they had closed their laptops and invested in a bottle of wine. That was only two months ago and when both Clare and Beau remarked at the same time, "Kind of soon, isn't it?" they laughed at their perfect synchrony.

At a friend's engagement party, they were asked throughout the evening if they were next in line. They cleverly avoided the question by answering with a question, "And ruin what we have together?" The high-five slap afterward was totally unnecessary, Clare remembered thinking.

And when Clare caught the bouquet at her sister's wedding, the men standing around Beau punched him playfully in the arm, teasing him relentlessly, while the ladies shamelessly taunted her with catcalls. Spotting the bridesmaid who was glumly standing to the side wishing she had caught the bouquet, Clare stuffed the clump of flowers in her sweaty hands and managed to slip out of the room unscathed.

They had conveniently ignored any opportunity to discuss marriage, as if they were living a drawn-out sitcom. Clare continued the conversation with herself. Maybe I'm being silly. Maybe I'm just getting old. Maybe Beau will always like being single. How ridiculous to imagine he'd trade in a lifetime of independence for her, a woman who has been married before with a rotten grandchild. What makes *her* so special? And yes, why ruin a perfect thing? And who needs to be married twice or for that matter, married at all?

"Humph!" Clare shook her head.

"What is it?" Beau asked, placing his hand on her forearm.

"Oh, nothing. I was just thinking," Clare answered as nonchalantly as she could.

"About what? You seemed to be a little perplexed." He turned her toward him and looked into her eyes. He had an uncanny way of knowing when she was bothered by something. Like right now.

"We can talk about it later," she chose to answer, knowing full well they would not have this awkward conversation. She patted his cheek and looked away. "Where's Jeremy?"

"Over there. Having a hard time reaching the drinking foun-
tain, isn't he? I'll help him...you go back to your thinking. I like
the way you look when you leave this planet." He slid his finger
softly down the crease in her forehead, kissed her nose and
moved quickly to rescue Jeremy from dehydration.

There he goes again, she thought, charming as ever. She
wondered if Beau knew that while she had been in such deep
thought and had left the planet, as he put it, that she had taken
him with her. Sometimes she thought he could read her mind.
He'd been known to leave little notes around the house saying
something cute or clever, and usually at just the right time.
Those notes were kept in a shoebox, and she imagined that
someday she'd be sitting alone browsing through them and
feeling once loved. Another box held all the cards her ex-
husband had given her for every traditional celebration manda-
torily requiring a visit to the Hallmark aisle. She hoped that
she'd remember the love they once had when the time came to
open his box.

Analyzing this man in her life, Clare's thoughts took her back
to the beginning when Beau was insecure and frustrated, cutting
his teeth on her grandchild. Now, he was building a relationship
with him, her family, her life. But what if we break up? He would
not continue to be a part of the family as such, because the truth
is, he is just a boyfriend, an extension, a person that could be
gone at any time, on any day. Boyfriend! I hate that word. I
wonder if he can read my mind now!

Beau looked back at Clare and caught her frowning at him.
He gave her a look that said, "Piece of cake. I can handle this."
But deep down inside, Clare questioned whether he could really
handle it, or was he merely mollifying her. He seemed to continu-
ally want her praise when he did what she considered an ordinary act of grandparenting. Or at the end of a day interacting
with Jeremy, he'd say, "I hope that gives me a few extra points."
The silly remarks were normally kind of cute, but lately they

annoyed Clare. She felt as though Beau had cheated life by never marrying. No baggage. And now he wants a family, and for free?

Suddenly Clare felt mentally exhausted. "Let's go home," she told Beau first. And then looking down at Jeremy whose face was all bent out of shape at the idea, she said, "and have ice cream."

"I don't like chocolate, and strawberry is yucky," he said, the frown still in place.

"Well, I have vanilla. That's what's in my freezer," Clare assured him. "Ben and Jerry's," she added, as if that would make a difference.

"Yum!" Beau blurted. And Clare could tell that he really meant that remark and didn't just say it to help her entice the disgruntled boy. She had always kept a pint in the freezer just for him.

Jeremy stomped his foot. "No, I don't want nilla. I want the three-color ice cream."

"But Jeremy," Beau bent down to explain, "the three-color ice cream has vanilla, strawberry and chocolate in it. All of which you don't like. You're not making any sense."

"Neither are you," Clare spouted out, looking at Beau as if he had just deprived her grandson of air. "Come on Jeremy, let's go get some three-color ice cream."

"What did I say?" he asked, standing there, his arms held out in confusion as they walked away.

Clare blew out a frustrated breath and rolled her eyes.

Two scoops later, Jeremy was dropped off at his home with dried glops of three kinds of ice cream smeared on his t-shirt. Clare had insisted that she take him in her car, alone, and especially since his clothes were so soiled, and she did not wish to dirty Beau's perfect leather interior. He agreed, too easily she thought, and he cheerfully went home to take a nap.

When she got back to her place, she looked at the grocery list on the kitchen counter and was reminded that she was cooking dinner for Beau, and the evening was designed to binge-watch a new espionage series he had read about. The list was deliberately dropped in the trash can on her way to her bedroom.

"Humph!"

The bed from the night before had not been made, and Beau's imprint in the pillow was still there. Most of the sheet was crumpled up on her side, which made her realize at that very moment, that he was right, she is a sheet thief. She kicked off her shoes, pulled off her shorts and unclasped her bra. Face down on Beau's pillow, she felt a sudden need to cry. Not a tear or two, but a necessary outburst, as if a gush of tears would cleanse her mind. She didn't want to think any more about Beau, about marriage, what was wrong, what was right, Jeremy. Sleep would do the trick, and the sound of rain would bring it on faster. On the nightstand, she pushed the play button on the compact CD player, and the soothing pitter-patter of a gentle forest rain soon had her sawing logs.

It was approaching dusk when the phone rang, Beau on the other end. "Should I grab anything at the store on my way over?" he asked, omitting the salutations.

We've gotten that comfortable, Clare thought, yawning into the phone. "I'm sorry. I fell asleep and if you hadn't called, I think I would have slept through the night."

"Want to go back to dreamland? We can do this another night, you know?"

"Hmmm." Clare yawned again and stretched out on the bed. "Maybe that's a good idea. For some reason, I'm really tired."

"Is everything alright?" Beau asked, the concern evident in his voice. "You said at the park you were thinking about something and would tell me later."

"Nothing serious. I'm alright. I just lost my oomph today."

"Ha, I bet. Imagine if I hadn't been around to help you with little Jer. Sometimes I come in handy, don't I?"

A long pause followed. There he goes again, wanting validation, praise, for what? For something I do regularly for no outward gratitude. She sat up abruptly. "I'm not just tired, Beau, I'm irritated, and…well, I'm not sure why. Think I need to work through this, so yes, raincheck, please."

"I understand. If there's anything I can do, you know where to find me. Sleep well, Clare."

"Will try, Beau." My good old practical boyfriend.

Clare let her legs dangle at the end of the bed and held her chin with her hands, her elbows digging into her knees, feeling as confused and ridiculous as a teenager. She couldn't get a grip on her emotions. She had been so defiant about never marrying again after her husband left her for that trollop. Beau, of all people, understood that, and it was never talked about again. Why now?

Is she cursed with the old adage, "Why buy the cow when you can get the milk for free?" Her mother was sure to keep that proverb alive and told her more than once. And to add to the conflict, her friend, Dolly had blatantly remarked, "Well, it's not worth buying the whole pig just to get a little sausage." What a mess she was in. Clare bemoaned the cruelty of it all.

"Alexa," she shouted on the way to the kitchen, "play songs by the Eagles." She hated the name of the sound device; the same name as the vixen that stole her husband. "Crap!" she yelled and went straight for the liquor cabinet.

"I'm sorry, I can't find a song called Crap," Alexa responded. Clare laughed out loud for the first time that day.

Several days went by without talking at length to Beau. She told him she needed some time alone, just something a woman has to do now and then. Blah, blah, blah! Throwing her off guard, Beau said he would miss her and would spend more time thinking about the queen and her quest to trap the king. Clare chuckled nervously at his comment, and if it hadn't referred to

Chess, she would have thought Beau was on to her. Chess was his favorite game, and he was known to spend entire afternoons in coffee shops in intense and extended face-offs with strangers and friends alike. Probably why he was so level-headed, she often surmised. An admirable trait, and one she could use. Especially now.

A week went by, and Clare still couldn't work through her dilemma. Her job kept her busy, as usual, and in the evenings she finished up small projects she had left undone for too long. She refused to watch television or read, or even talk to her friends. She played music constantly. When her daughter asked her to watch Jeremy on the weekend, she politely declined. Whatever she was doing, whatever she was going though, she couldn't stop it. By the ninth day of this routine, she had lost five pounds, and her patience with Beau was wearing thin. His calls lessened with each day.

Three weeks passed and Clare was now fifteen pounds lighter. During that time Beau had flown out to see his brother, since Clare was still not ready to resume the usual. Her sister had insisted on lunch together and after Clare told her the quandary she was in, her sister just smiled and said, "Why don't you stop thinking so much and enjoy the ride? That's what I did, and look at me, I'm happily married."

She left the restaurant feeling foolish, and as much as she wanted to take the simple advice offered, it wasn't possible. Faced with another Friday night without Beau, no prospects or plans, she dragged herself to the mall. She disliked shopping, but it was easier than she thought, as the pounds she had shed put her in the size eight category and everything she tried on fit well. No more oversized blouses, elastic banded skirts and shorts and thank goodness, no more Spanks! In less than an hour, she walked out of the department store with a bag full of goodies, in a new outfit, shoes to match. She should have felt great, but she couldn't even muster up a thank you when the saleslady said she looked better than when she had walked in. Her initial reaction was, "Geez, did I look *that* bad?"

She window shopped on her way out of the mall and stopped cold when she saw Beau standing in front of the jewelry store, next to him a lovely well-dressed lady, she guessed in her forties. Clare dropped behind a sunglasses kiosk and watched them. The woman pointed at some jewelry; the polished diamonds sparkling under the bright lights. They both leaned in, shoulders touching as they squinted through the glass. He smiled and they turned to walk into the store; Beau placing his hand gently on the woman's back, just above the sacral area. 'The most beautiful part of the back,' he had told her as he outlined hers with his finger the first time they made love.

At the brink of tears, Clare felt woozy. The scene was unbearable to watch. She nearly ran out of the mall.

"Oh, my God, oh, my God," she repeated, pounding on the steering wheel, as she watched tiny drops of rain fill up the windshield. She was shocked to see her man with another woman. And a younger woman at that! And wasn't he supposed to be out of town? How quickly he went from her to someone else. "No, no, no, no!" she cried.

Not a wink of sleep, not even a nap, Clare paced the house all night long. Her heart was broken, and she had caused it. She was tempted to call Beau, but what would she say? Scenarios crossed her mind one after another until finally at the break of dawn she fell asleep.

Thank heaven it was Saturday. No work. She slept till noon, awakened by a text on her cell phone: We need to talk. May I please come see you tonight? It's important. In case you don't remember who this is, it's me, Beau.

"I'm not sure I do know who you are," Clare whispered. She typed in a lower-case yes with a time of her choosing and drowned her fears and her tears in the shower. Afterward, she sat on the bed going through a box of Beau's little notes. One read: As ugly as that tattered t-shirt is you wore last night, I enjoyed tearing a new rip in it on your side of the bed. Have a great day thinking of that. Clare felt her face heat up remembering that moment.

Another, written in different colored crayons said: You, color my world, but Jeremy colored the guest bathroom wall!

A handmade birthday card drove her to tears: This makes two birthdays with the woman I'm crazy about. More, more, please give me more.

She crammed the rest back into the box and shoved them under the bed.

"First John leaves me, now Beau!" Clare yells at her face in the mirror, frowning at the ugly hot rollers clinging to her head. "I'm leavable!" she scoffed. "Is there such a word?" Beau would have given her the right word. 'Unworthy,' he'd probably say. He was always much smarter, and because he was so practical, of course, they would remain friends. Somehow, she knew that. After all, there was certainly no fear of him ever tying the knot. Even with me! The tears came too fast, and she had to reapply her eye make-up all over again.

After trying on every new piece of clothing she had purchased, Clare settled on a simple blue flowered sundress, and let her curls unfold on their own without brushing. She answered the door barefoot, as if nothing had changed in their lives. Beau's eyes opened wide when he saw her, then he looked puzzled.

"I dropped a little weight," she immediately explained, keeping him from saying what everyone else said so emphatically without thinking: "Wow, you've lost a *lot* of weight!"

"Oh, well, I really didn't notice that…you just look so lovely. It's been a while. May I come in?"

"Yes, of course." Clare moved aside, allowing his compliment to slip away after realizing he was waiting for an invitation. She stood watching him enter the house slowly, almost timidly, and then stop, awaiting instructions. Closing the door behind him, she asked, "Kitchen or living room?"

"Kitchen, I think. I've always enjoyed our talks in the kitchen."

She motioned ahead, noticing he had on what looked to be a new shirt. And were those new shoes, too? When she took note of the baggy cargo shorts that were his favorite, beginning to sag in the butt, she fought back a smile.

"Can I get you a drink?" she asked when he sat down on the stool at the breakfast bar.

"Still have some of that twelve-year-old scotch I left over here awhile back?"

"Matter of fact, I do. I had a couple of jiggers myself. Hope you don't mind."

"Of course not. But since when have you acquired a taste for anything else but gin?" He looked curiously at her.

"Just recently. Trying to broaden my horizons these days. I hear change does a body good." She winced at her silly remark said with a touch of irony.

Crystal glasses were filled, and the estranged couple toasted. "To changes," Clare said first. Beau cocked his head and agreed.

"I've missed this," he said, licking the wet remains from his lip.

"Surely you have scotch at *your* place."

"No, Clare. I miss *this*…sitting here in the kitchen with *you*." He took another sip. "Don't you?"

"I miss a lot of things." She bowed her head, avoiding his gaze. "Now, what is it you came to see me about?"

"Hmm." Beau usually started out like that when he was

about to give her a well, thought-out answer to a complicated question. "I've had a lot of time to think. Your absence has allowed me to think more than I have in a long time. Thanks to you," he toasted again.

Clare lifted her glass slowly, bracing herself for the harsh news that she swore she would not react to childishly. This is a good man in front of her, and she knew he deserved happiness as much as she did. If she had not seen him with the other woman, and in the jewelry store, of all places, she would have been telling him right now how she felt about her fears and marriage. Maybe they would amicably agree to something, but whatever it was, Clare was not certain she could carry on as *just* a girlfriend. It all sounded so ridiculous in her head, she wanted to scream. Here it is, the chance to be completely honest, tell him how she feels, but she'll look like a fool when after she says it, he tells her he's seeing someone else.

"Clare, I've never been married, and do you remember why?"

"Yes, you told me you never found the right woman, or rather the right gal, as you put it back then." *I know you found her. Go ahead and say it, damn it! She's young, she's lovely, I saw her, you bastard. Go on say it!*

"The right gal. Humph! I sound like something out of an old 1920's movie. What the hell is the right gal? I mean, the right set of tires, I understand. Even the right house, or the right doctor. You know what I mean?"

She could hear a trace of frustration in his tone after saying the word *right* five times. Not his style. Tempted to answer him with, "Right," she stopped herself, knowing it would have been said with derision. "Keep going, Beau. Elaboration is your strongest attribute. Eventually, I'll get it." She chuckled uneasily at admitting her shortfall.

"I guess what I'm trying to say is, I searched for the meaning of the right woman, and it dawned on me that there is no such thing. Just like many times there's no such thing as the right thing to do. Who determines what's right?"

Clare blew out some air and immediately caught a whiff of the malted barley riding the wave of her breath. Until now, she wasn't sure if she liked the taste. "You're bogging down, Beau. There's no hurry, because I would like to understand, but if you have something important to say to me, please just say it."

"There's a woman…"

Steadying the glass held beneath her nose helped Clare keep from gasping.

Beau took his time. He always took his time. "She's not perfect. She's not the most gorgeous woman on earth, and she's not the smartest. She's a lot of wonderful things, but it has occurred to me that she's probably not even the right woman. But what she is…is, she's just right for me."

Clare bit her lip.

"Look, I don't want to lose you, Clare." Beau paused to reach into his pocket, pulling out a small box. He opened it, got down on his knee and said, "Clare, my darling Clare. Will you marry me?"

Clare clapped her hand over her mouth. She could not believe what she was hearing. Marry me? What? Who is this man who ran from matrimony all his life down on his knees in front of me?

"Clare?" Beau closed his mouth tightly and gave a soft nod, urging her to speak.

"I, I have a few things to say before I answer you." She couldn't believe the practicality of her own words, much less the lack of tears.

"May I please get off my knees while you say them? This old gray stallion just ain't what he used to be," he chuckled.

"Yes, yes, sit down." Clare drained the rest of her drink in one big gulp. "Beau, dear, Beau," she began, removing the question about the other woman from the top of the list. "I've had plenty of time to think, too." She looked over at the ring. "My, that's quite beautiful." She stopped herself from touching it. "But listen, I don't want this if you just think it's the right thing to do."

"Do you love me, Clare?"

"Yes, I love you. And you're not perfect, or gorgeous either, and you're smarter than me, and wow, you can grill a steak better than any man I've ever known."

"Yes, even Jeremy likes my steaks…and my grilled cheese sandwiches." He grinned, searching for approval.

Clare nodded in agreement, and this time the cynicism wasn't there to make her eyes roll. "Do you love me, Beau? Because you didn't say it when you proposed."

"Of course, I love you. I would never have stayed that long on my knees for another woman."

"Speaking of another woman…" Clare looked away and then leaned in to look for the green in Beau's eyes. "I saw you at the jewelry store with another woman."

"Oh…you did? You were at the mall last night? Why didn't you come up and talk to me?"

"Beau, you were with *another* woman," she said, the suspicious tone unavoidable.

"My second cousin, Clare. June owns the store. I actually got a discount on your ring because of that, which gave me extra money to apply toward our trip to Hawaii we talked about." Beau's eyes lit up.

Clare's glare loosened and her eyebrows relaxed, but she was still determined to get the answers to her nagging questions. "Why did you come back so much earlier from your brother's?"

"Well, my very wise older brother and I had a really good talk, which made me want to get back as fast as I could…to you," he reassured her with a smile.

A look of embarrassed relief crossed her face. Thank God I can toss that other woman feeling out the window. "But back to my thoughts…Beau, I don't want this if you think it's just the right thing to do, or if you're just afraid of losing me."

"Clare, I *am* losing you. Nearly a month apart brought me to my senses. You rather forced it. But that's a good thing. You stood your ground. I had to come to you not only because it's the right thing to do, but because I realized how much I love you. So, I'll ask again, will you marry me?"

Even comforted by his words and the alluring green in his eyes, she wasn't surprised by her answer. "No, Beau."

Beau's face dropped. Clare couldn't tell if it read disappointment or relief. Not wanting to know either, she said, "But thank you, very much. I just needed you to ask." As she leaned in to kiss his worried face, she closed the tiny box and put the ring back in his hand. "But yes, to Hawaii," she whispered in his ear.

They slept together that night, the entire night in each other's arms. From there they slipped back into their comfortable routine, only Beau found himself calling Clare more often and asking to stay the night a lot more often. The trip to Hawaii was booked and turned out to be just what they needed.

Several weeks later on a Saturday morning, Clare stepped into a jewelry store and asked to speak to June. That evening, she brought home two grass-fed Ribeye steaks and a bottle of Silver Oak Cabernet.

"Steaks and wine? Wow, what's the occasion?" Beau asked.

"A most incredible full moon is on the horizon," she said, rather poetically.

After dinner they retired to the back deck to watch the harvest moon; so large, so close, it felt like they could draw their names on it. Clare led Beau to the railing and wrapped her arms around him from behind. She slipped something in his hand.

"What's this?" he asked, holding the round metal object up to the moon's powerful light. "Is this what I think it is?"

Beau turned to look at Clare, who had now dropped to her knees. "Will you marry me, Beau?"

He answered without hesitation, no long-winded speeches or questions that might or might not matter, but a pure and simple resounding, "Yes!" This, from a man who waited a lifetime for not just the right woman, but for an honest, rather complicated, sometimes ridiculous woman who knew without a doubt that he was just right for her.

When Beau lifted Clare from her knees and took her in his arms, their perfect kiss sealed the deal. Arm in arm, they stood before the magnificent moon. She spoke first, "You know, my dad proposed to my mother under a harvest moon, just like tonight."

"I remember the story." Beau pulled her closer. "I'm honored. But you know I have to ask…what made you change your mind?"

"I went to see June at the jewelry store. And when she said you didn't return the ring, I knew for certain that you were completely sincere about wanting to marry me, and that you were waiting for me to be sure. Funny how, at that very moment, I knew what I wanted."

The look on Beau's face was clear that he would never fully understand this woman he had chosen to be with forever, but he would settle with that, because he was for the first time in his life enjoying the mystery.

"June seemed to be tickled that I took down the only single man in the family and was quite generous. I'm curious if you got as good a discount on my ring as I did on yours." Clare laughed.

"Guess," he teased her.

"Five per cent?"

"Higher."

"Ten per cent?"

"Higher."

"Twenty-five per cent?" Clare gasped.

"Higher."

"Higher? You're kidding?" Clare was delighted.

Beau took the engagement ring in question from his pocket and slipped it on her finger. "I've been nervously carrying this with me every day since I bought it. I am so pleased to know that you'll be wearing it from now on. Besides," he grinned, "the thirty-day return policy has expired."

Even in the glow of an electric orange harvest moon, Clare could see the green dancing in Beau's eyes. "You're a funny one," she chuckled, gently pinching his lips together and pulling them to meet hers. "Let's stop talking and enjoy the ride."

RANDOM REFLECTIONS

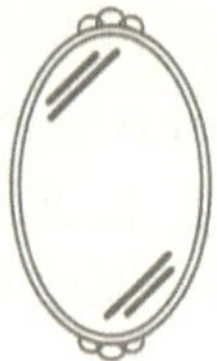

My mother never went anywhere without her lipstick. Today, I feel naked without it. A woman has her own claim to what brings her to life — whether it's lipstick, a push-up bra, or high heels — it's hers to own. Just try taking it away from her ... you'll never feel closer to death than that very moment.

BIG HAIR HIGH HEELS

The man stepped out of the shadows. He had not expected the rain and was unprepared for the sudden downpour. When he paused to look up at the second story window, he saw that the lampshade was tilted. Cursing under his breath, he wished he had been more careful while searching the woman's apartment. He couldn't possibly go back in, now that he was dripping wet. The stupid blunder would bother him the rest of the night and leave him in agony, tossing and turning in his sleep. If, he slept at all.

Medrith had been the community watchdog for nearly fourteen years. As she lay on the porch, sporadically dozing off and on, she heard the man curse. She saw his shadow first, casting a long, black figure against the white stone wall, before she spotted him hurrying past her. Lifting her nose high in the air, she detected a scent she had learned to hate. It reminded Medrith of her owner's ex-husband who kicked her regularly when no one was looking. Every instinct she had left in her old worn-out body said to alert the neighbors, but the last time she barked after midnight she got whapped on the nose with a newspaper.

Instead, she let out a slow, grinding growl, which caused the man to quicken his pace. With the tenacity of a Pit Bull, she followed him to the parking lot.

Just when her target opened his truck door, Medrith clamped down on his leg and biting hard with all her might, three teeth flew from her mouth to the ground like snowflakes. She tugged at the man's wet pant leg until it slipped from her tired gums. Dumbfounded, the old girl turned and walked away, looking back only once with a weak yelp as if to say, "So, there!"

The man wiped the slobber from his pants and checked for damage to his prosthetic leg. He was relieved that the decrepit canine's broken teeth were not embedded in the flesh of his good leg, and if he had not been so terribly sleep deprived, he might have laughed.

It was nearly five o'clock in the morning when Sylvia Rodriguez collapsed onto her bed without unpacking or brushing her teeth after four days of endless fun in Las Vegas with her best friend, Francine. Completely exhausted, she slept soundly to the pitter-patter of the rain outside her window.

The bells from St. Mary's Cathedral woke Sylvia up much too early. They were loud and abrasive to the ear, she had complained to the priest the last time she attended mass. He cautiously agreed but explained that God would be sorely disappointed in the Catholics if they stopped ringing the bells that had been rung at the same time every day for over a hundred years. "That's why they call this town, Merry Bell, my dear," he said, smiling and patting her on the top of the head. People were always doing that, and every time they did, she felt like a little kid.

Sylvia vowed that if she ever found a genie in a bottle the first thing she'd ask for is to add an extra eight inches to her petite five-foot frame. Most of her life she had felt ridiculously small, and in her younger years she teased her hair as high as she could get it, often dressing in two-inch heels – anything to create height. If the forever changing fashion industry had not frowned on big hair, and if she hadn't developed an awful set of bunions, she'd look taller today. Grudgingly, she stored the heels in her hope chest and threw her teasing comb away.

Glad to be back in her hometown, Sylvia lazily sipped coffee in front of the television. Reaching for the remote control, she found it wasn't there. It had always remained in the same spot, like everything else in her small apartment. She looked around the room and noticed that her college graduation picture was crooked on the wall. Sylvia was a stickler for tidiness, and things like this bothered her. Directly beneath it, she saw a trail of smoke coming from the lampshade that was tilted too close to the bulb. Francine had insisted that she leave it on to discourage break-ins, and now it was about to catch fire. She jumped up so quickly the coffee cup went flying across the room, but she had the lampshade in the kitchen sink in seconds flat.

As a skilled social worker, Sylvia was practiced at remaining calm, so she carefully and methodically combed the apartment for any other surprises that might be waiting for her. Everything else seemed to be in order, except for the strange odor in her closet. The scent was unusual, sweet and pungent, with a touch of charcoal. Had someone been in her apartment while she was gone? She was absolutely certain when she discovered that the magnetic letters on the refrigerator door were all askew. And the letter "V", along with some vowels were definitely missing.

Mack Finnegan was still grieving over a loss that hurt so deeply it often woke him up in the middle of the night; never fully recovering from the break-up with his high school sweetheart. It had happened shortly after prom. He had spent an entire year's worth of savings – money he had earned from working weekends at some of the worst odd jobs ever – on a tux, corsage, and a rental car. And not just any ordinary car, but the finest car in Merry Bell. It was owned by his uncle, the richest man in town. He charged Mack a hefty fee for the Corvette and even charged him for the new leather scent thingy that hung over the rear-view mirror. The crazy uncle with eight children managed to throw in a package of contraceptives for free, along with a twenty-minute lecture about gonorrhea. The prom had been beyond wonderful for Mack, and his date was the most excited girl there. How she could leave him after such a magical evening baffled him for years after. Even still, no one could replace her, and the bouton-niere he wore that night sat decayed and lifeless in a plastic cubicle on a shelf next to the picture of his one and only love, Sylvia May Rodriguez.

Mack pulled the blanket up to the bottom of his chin and opened the Yearbook to the pages that were marked with straws from every root beer float he had ever bought Sylvia. He slid his finger down her picture, tracing the gown she had worn at prom, recalling how soft it felt to his touch. He remembered sitting on the floor watching her tease her hair – her bedroom door left respectfully wide open so that Sylvia's mother could stick her head in and say something clever; when she was actually keeping a close eye on her seventeen-year-old daughter, determined that she remain a virgin longer than *she* had. Slowly and hypnotically Sylvia had lifted and sprayed each strand, forming a beehive tall enough to reach Mack's nostrils. He couldn't take his eyes off her, and he was completely unaware of the goofy look of love plastered on his face. Sylvia's mother, however, knew that look well – it was the same look her husband had worn when they hid in the barn after the Sadie Hawkins dance in their senior year. That roll in the hay cost her mother the lead role in Camelot, four years of college, and her baby fat. Sylvia May was born two hundred and seventy-three days later, two months after graduation.

~

"Who do you think broke into your place?" Francine asked, the minute she heard Sylvia's story.

"I can't even imagine," Sylvia replied, sipping on her third cup of coffee. "It gives me the creeps though, even if nothing was really disturbed."

"But Syl, your apartment could've burned down, and with you in it! Maybe you should call in a detective."

"Oh sure, what would I say? Officer, my lampshade was tilted, and I nearly burned to death. I'm sure someone is out to kill me!" Sylvia rolled her eyes.

"I don't know," Francine whined, "If it were me, I'd have my cousin Ernie investigate. He's always wanted to be a detective, and he has that second sense like that guy on TV does. You know, what's his name…the Columbian guy with the rolling eye?"

"Columbo," Sylvia corrected her. "His name is Columbo, and he's not Columbian…I don't think. Well, anyway, funny you should bring him up. I was thinking of that show when I noticed the remote control was gone. I found it later on the kitchen bar. I don't remember putting it there at all. Hmmm," she sighed and looked off in the distance.

"Unlike you, I have to get back to work. At least change your locks," Francine insisted, ruffling Sylvia's hair on the way out.

"What am I, a dog?" Sylvia grumbled, wondering again why everyone seemed to have the need to touch her head.

In the quiet of the room, she pondered the current situation. Recalling that her overly cautious mother had five apartment keys made the day Sylvia moved in, she decided to take a drive out to her parent's home.

"You look tired," Lily said to her daughter the minute she

entered the door. "Must've been *some* weekend," she winked, grabbing her hand and leading her to the kitchen. "I was just cooking dinner for myself. Your dad is on one of those dull business trips, and I'm dining alone. You *will* stay for dinner?"

"Of course, mother," Sylvia hid her aversion to her mother's cooking behind a fake smile. "Do you need my help?"

Lily placed a knife in Sylvia's hand and a cutting board in front of her. "Yes, start chopping these onions. I have always hated that job."

"Mother," she began, sniffing loudly as she hacked at an onion, "do you remember who all has a key to my apartment?"

"Well, let's see. I have one, of course. Your dad has one, you have two and well, what did we do with number five?" Sylvia watched her mother's tongue move across her lips as it always did when she was concentrating. "Oh yes, I remember. We left one out for the plumber when your toilet overflowed last week. But you got that back from him, right?"

"No, mom, I thought *you* did," she answered, holding the knife in the air while fighting back a sneeze. "You mean, you mean to tell me that the plumber still has access to my apartment?"

Lily looked up at her daughter, confused by the sudden change in her tone. "Well, if he has it, we'll simply get it back."

Sylvia contemplated not telling her mother about the possible intruder, expecting her response to be even worse than Francine's. "Mother, don't worry about getting the key. I'm going to change the lock."

"Whatever for? That plumber has been in practically every house in Merry Bell. I doubt you have to worry about him. Save your money, and I'll get the key from him."

"Mom, I didn't want to upset you, but I guess you should know…it seems that maybe someone entered my apartment while I was in Las Vegas. By chance, was it you or dad?"

"Well, I know *I* sure didn't," Lily said defensively, "and definitely not your dad. Are you thinking that the plumber came back?"

"I almost hope it was him, or someone else has a key to my place. But it doesn't matter. I'm changing the lock tomorrow."

After Sylvia explained to her mother over dinner, the reasons for her concern – the odd smell, the missing letters and finally the burning lampshade – Lily vehemently agreed. "Tomorrow's really not soon enough, but they're closed by now. I'll take care of it in the morning, so you won't have to leave work." Lily patted Sylvia on the head and hurried out of the kitchen. From the hallway she yelled, "And I insist that you stay the night! Please clean up for me sweetie, while I wait for your dad's call."

Sylvia stood alone in the quiet, sniffing the onion remains on her fingers, feeling oddly like a child.

By noon the next day, Sylvia had accomplished so much at work she decided to walk to her favorite café. She was delighted that Merry Bell had not changed a bit the ten years she'd been away. Strolling past the old shops she had often visited, she remembered that Arthur's Plumbing Company was down one of the side streets and decided to stop in.

The door jingled loudly when she entered the shop and just before she tapped the little bell on the counter, Arthur stepped out from the back with a toilet lid in one hand and a screwdriver in the other. "Well, hello Ms. Rodriguez, long time no see," he greeted her with a nod. "I bet I know why you're here. Your mother called earlier and asked if I had the key to your apartment."

Relieved, Sylvia smiled and said, "Oh great, she thought you had it."

"Oh no, I told her I didn't. I didn't know until just a few minutes ago that my assistant said that he gave it to your boyfriend who was at the apartment when he arrived. Be sure and let your mom know that. She seemed pretty concerned."

"My boyfriend? I don't have any men friends in this town, Arthur. I just recently moved back, and I've only reconnected with one or two girlfriends from school," Sylvia's voice cracked. "Something's not right. Is your assistant available to talk to?"

"Well sure, hold on." The plumber put the toilet lid down, leaned backward and yelled, "Dennis, Dennis, up front, please!"

Dennis lumbered into the room, holding both hands up to keep them from touching anything. They were coated in a greasy substance slowly dripping down his boney arms.

"Miss Rodriguez here would like to know who the guy was that you gave her key to last week," Arthur said.

"Well, I didn't ask him his name. He was standing at your apartment door when I arrived. I assumed he was your boyfriend because he said that it'd be safe underneath the mat." Dennis shrugged, pulling his mouth down as if to say that was all he had to offer.

"There you go Miss Rodriguez. Now, back to work, Dennis." Turning around to follow his employee, he looked over his shoulder to ask, "Does your toilet work well now?"

Sylvia leaned against the counter, too deep in thought to hear Arthur's question. She was trying to imagine who the person at her door could be. Feeling slightly dizzy and increasingly uncomfortable, she said, "Wait a second! Call Dennis back please, I have another question for him."

Dennis peeked around the door, his hands still held high.

"You didn't by any chance go into my closet, or take, I mean borrow some plastic letters from my refrigerator, did you?"

"Uh, nope."

"Can you describe this man you gave my key to?"

"You don't remember what your *own* boyfriend looks like?"

"I DON'T HAVE A BOYFRIEND!" Sylvia growled.

"Oh, well then, he was just a regular guy, clean shaven, nice smile and, oh yeah, he had a cigar in his front pocket. I noticed that right away because it's the kind I like to smoke."

Sylvia rushed around the counter, leaned toward the assistant and sniffed him. Then she turned around and ran out of the shop, leaving Dennis and Arthur looking mildly confused.

When Sylvia got home, she slowly lifted the doormat that read *Your Place or Mine?* – a welcome home gift from Francine. Underneath it was the missing key. She studied it to make sure it was indeed hers, and then she put it under her nose and smelled it.

Mack Finnegan had given nine years of his life to the Marine Corps – a snap decision made shortly after Sylvia May had broken up with him. Returning to Merry Bell, after the accident that discharged him from Special Forces, only intensified his desire for his high school crush, and before he knew it, he was lying on a chaise lounge crying like a baby in front of one of the only two psychologists in town, Dr. Nicholas Barfield.

"Mack," the doctor gently spoke, "it's time to address this issue with Sylvia. It's very possible that she has something important to say that will get you past this feeling. You may also find that you don't care for her as much as you think. Or, not," he quickly added, as psychologists never want to assume anything. "But I don't see the harm in you meeting up with her. After all, it's very common for high school friends to get together in their later years. That's why they have reunions."

"OK, Doc, I'll think about it," was the last thing that was said for the duration of his visit, as Mack instantly fell asleep.

The Merry Bell High School ten-year reunion was just around the corner and Francine was frantic about what to wear. "Do you realize that Gus Henderson is single again after two marriages, and he'll be there? I have to look especially sexy!"

Sylvia folded the last towel and placed it in the basket. "Wow, you still have a crush on him?"

"Well, of course." Francine cocked her head and looked at Sylvia as if she had lost her mind. "Don't tell me you've forgotten that time I cried all night when he asked Debbie to the prom. I thought I was going to die. By the way, if you can remember that awful chapter in my life, I want to thank you for talking me out of joining the Peace Corps because I was so upset."

"Well, dear, that's what friends are for."

"Yeah, well, if you recall, you were ecstatic about going to the prom with Mack. I still don't understand why you broke up with him. I guess you knew what was best."

Sylvia had thought a lot about Mack since she arrived in Merry Bell. "I didn't break up with him. He broke up with me. Don't you remember? It happened while I was at camp."

"Oh, yeah. I kind of forgot that little detail. But, to this day I can't understand why. You should've seen the two of you on the dance floor. Gosh, I thought he'd be down on his knees proposing before the weekend was up."

Avoiding Francine's eyes, Sylvia turned away to reach for a glass of water. "Well, that was what I call *graduationitis*. I think we were all pretty much in love with everything at that moment."

"I suppose," Francine moaned. "Well, who cares what clinical term *you* wish to call it. Gus is single and so am I. I'm going with rings on my fingers and bells on my toes. I have a chance at love, sweetie, and I'm going to take it! You should find out if Mack's going, too. I heard he's back in town."

"HE IS?" Sylvia jerked, so surprised to hear the news the glass of water slipped right out of her hand.

Francine threw a clean towel her direction. "Anyway, he's

back and Debbie said he's gorgeous, muscles and all, but she also said he was wounded in the war."

"Oh no," Sylvia stopped sopping up the water and looked despondently at her friend. "I hope it wasn't too serious."

"What do you care?" Francine said facetiously. "Got another case of *graduationitus*?"

"Oh, shut up!" Sylvia threw the wet towel at Francine and ran to the bathroom in time to hide the tears.

Waiting impatiently for Mack to wake up, as this was the first time anyone had ever fallen asleep during one of Dr. Barfield's sessions, the doctor sat somewhat befuddled studying the teeth marks in Mack's shredded pant leg. When the time was up, he gently nudged the snoring soldier awake. After an awkward apology for sleeping on the job, the doc assured him that he'd only charge for the minutes he was awake. He asked, with a chuckle, "Have a bout with a dog, Mack?"

"Oh, uh, yeah…you could say that," he answered through a yawn and stood up to leave, hoping to avoid an embarrassing explanation. How in the world could he explain running into the plumber with Sylvia's key and taking that opportunity to look for signs of a boyfriend in her apartment? No harm done, but still.

When the doctor suggested again that he go to his reunion and meet up with Sylvia, Mack promised him that if he could keep from crying, he would do just that.

"Try to get some sleep, and just remember, young man, you're not in high school anymore." When Mack was out of earshot, Dr. Barfield whispered to his assistant, "That boy has got it bad, really bad."

Back at his own place, encouraged by his doctor's advice and finding no evidence of a man in Sylvia's life, Mack stood naked and flexing in front of the full-length mirror, pleased with his lean body and especially the outline of the muscles in his biceps. He decided that the unmentionable part was a respectable size – quite adequate he had evaluated, after showering with his Marine buddies. But when his eyes reached his leg, he dropped his smile, seeing the metal casing clamped below his knee. The longer he stood gazing at his reflection it occurred to him that Sylvia might find him repulsive and half the man he used to be. A hot shower helped shake off the impulse to cry, and afterwards he applied an extra coat of polish to the prosthesis. "I am a Marine, oorah! I am a Marine!"

When Lily heard that her daughter's key had not been safe in the hands of the local plumber, she was naturally concerned and scheduled to have the lock changed. After she ran into Dr. Barfield, and he told her that Mack was back in town, her worries intensified. The old doctor had to be very careful what he shared with Lily – patient's confidentiality and all – but he alluded to the idea that Mack still had designs on her Sylvia. His smile when he said it did not make Lily feel any better.

Lily's husband arrived home just in time for dinner. She rushed to the door and welcomed him with a warm hug and a kiss that lasted longer than the usual perfunctory peck on the cheek. "I missed you," she whispered in his ear and carefully removed his jacket before leading him to the kitchen.

"Oh, this is nice," Hubert said, looking down at the beautiful place setting and lit candle. "What's the occasion? Did I forget our anniversary?"

"No, darling. I just thought you'd like something special. Now, take off your shoes and settle in for a lovely meal. I've prepared a new dish that I can't wait to have you try."

Hubert pretended to like the casserole that Lily had painstakingly created, and after a second glass of scotch, his tongue slightly numbed, he decided that it wasn't all that bad.

"Honey," Lily cooed, "Mack Finnegan's back in town."

"Oh? Is he on furlough?"

"No, he's back for good. He quit the Marines because of a leg wound."

"That's a shame. Well, I wonder if Sylvia knows he's here. I bet she'd like to see him," her husband said, poking at the under-cooked broccoli stem that kept slipping out from under his fork.

"Oh, I hope not," Lily winced.

"Why would you say that, Lily? I thought he was a fine kid. So did Sylvia. If I remember correctly, she was *ga-ga* over him and pretty darn broken up when he left her."

Frustrated, Lily rolled her eyes and stabbed at a carrot, so hard it flew across the table. "Yes, well, in case you've forgotten, *ga ga* is what *got got* our little Sylvia into this world."

"Yes, I remember dear. You sound as if that's a bad thing." Hubert put his fork down and stared concernedly into his wife's eyes. Lily saw the hurt on her husband's face and looked away.

"What's the matter honey? Is something wrong?" he asked.

"Well, yes! Don't you understand that I missed out on college because of YOU?" she yelled. Throwing the bright red napkin on top of her plate, she stood up and stormed into the bedroom.

Hubert sat quietly at the table and thought carefully about his next move, which was not to take the last three bites of the casserole in front of him. He stood up and blew out the candle, then pulled off his belt and carried it to the bedroom where he found Lily sprawled out on the bed crying. He removed his slacks and shirt and crawled into bed next to her. "Sweetheart," he whispered, "talk to me."

"I, I just wanted my little girl to have what *I* didn't."

"Well, she did. She finished college and got a good job. What has this got to do with *you?*" Hubert gently turned Lily over and looked down at her blotchy face.

"She's going to find out, and she'll hate me. I know she'll just hate me!" Lily wailed.

"Find out, what?"

"That I lied, that I wrote the letter she thought was from Mack. I made her think he didn't want her anymore." Lily turned her head and sobbed into the pillow. "And," her voice muffled, "and, I did the same thing to Mack!"

"Oh, honey, you didn't," Hubert sighed heavily, remembering how crushed Sylvia had been when it ended and wondering if she really would forgive her mother. Hubert sat up and looked down at the tortured woman he thought he knew so well. "Well, come on…that was ages ago. Surely she's gotten over him, and it won't matter now."

Lily looked up hopefully. "I'd like to think that, but Hubert, Mack still loves our daughter. Dr. Barfield practically told me so. Mack's seeing a therapist because of Sylvia, and I'm the one that crippled him!" she shouted, thrusting her face back into the pillow.

"*You* crippled him? Lily, he was injured in the war."

"Yes, only because I sent him there by taking Sylvia away from him. And do you realize that our daughter hasn't been in love with anyone since? I've ruined two lives. Not one, but two! No, make it three! I ruined my life, too!"

"Because you didn't go to *college*?" Hubert quickly stood up and stared down at his pathetic wife. "Well, guess what sweetheart, why don't you go ahead and make it four lives you've ruined and include me! I didn't get to go to college either, and I had a scholarship!"

Lily rolled over, brushed the hair back from her face and looked at her husband as if seeing him for the first time that day.

"Oh, Hubie," she said, not having called him that in a long while, "I'm such a fool. You're so right." Reaching out for his hand, she pulled him toward her.

"Look," he began, snuggling up next to his wife, "I'd change some things if I could, but I wouldn't change having you and our little girl in my life. So, we did it backwards, so what? We have a wonderful nest egg. Why don't we *both* go to college? Shoot, I'd love to quit my job and get a teaching degree, and you can, well maybe you can get a job working in politics. Seems you have a knack for writing convincing letters," he laughed and then groaned when Lily jabbed him in the stomach with her elbow.

"You'd really do that?" she said, wiping her tears on the sheet.

"Heck, I think I still have my Varsity jacket, and don't you still have those penny loafers?"

"I think I do." Lily looked dreamily at her husband and climbed on top of him. "I'm feeling frisky just thinking about that jacket." Lowering herself onto his chest, she whispered, "By the way, I'd do it all over again, exactly the way we did it. You're the best thing that's ever happened to me." She kissed Hubert lightly on the neck. "And, I'll tell Sylvia the truth. They say confession is good for the soul."

"That's what I hear," Hubert sighed, staring up at the ceiling. *College at my age? What the heck am I thinking?*

"Gosh!" Francine squealed, "it's finally here, our ten-year reunion! I've been dieting all month to look good in this dress. Got any of those bra pads that I can tuck in here to make my cleavage pucker, like we did in high school?"

"No, I threw those out with my teasing comb." Sylvia grabbed a box of tissues. "Here…try these."

"Do you think Mack will be there?" Francine asked, while stuffing the soft tissue inside her bra.

"I imagine. He *was* the quarterback. I suppose he'd feel obligated."

"What if he has a date?" Francine dropped her arms by her side and stared at her pumped-up bosom, looking very pleased.

"What if?" Sylvia shrugged. "I'll be civil. I'm sure he will be, too."

"I'm glad we're going solo," Francine sighed. "I just hope Gus isn't with anyone, either."

"Hey wait a minute. I thought *I* was your date?"

"No thanks. You're pretty and all, but much too short." Francine saw the disappointment in Sylvia's face. "But we can fix that. Let's tease your hair up, and why don't you wear those shiny black high heels you used to wear? I bet Mack will fall in love with you all over again!"

"You think?" Sylvia ran to the mirror, imagining her hair six inches higher. "Gosh, I miss wearing my hair like that. But you know it's out of style now."

"Who cares? You look great in big hair and high heels. Let's do it! I've got a teasing comb in my purse. I use it to clean out my hairbrush."

"Ewww," Sylvia scrunched up her nose.

"Don't worry, I'll wash it first. Now sit down…this is definitely going to take a while."

The high school gym looked exactly as it had nearly ten years earlier. The reunion planners had done a fine job of stringing out-of-season Christmas lights and colorful streamers from hoop to hoop. Sylvia and Francine were some of the first to arrive. As she had done at her senior prom, Francine poured a flask of vodka into the punch bowl. The old high school counselor saw her do it. Francine looked at him in horror, suddenly feeling like an eighteen-year-old facing suspension. She was instantly relieved when the counselor winked and gave her the thumbs up. Francine poured herself one and another one for the old gent. What she didn't know when she handed it to him, is that he had also added his favorite spirit to the punch. He didn't bother to share that bit of information and thanked her with a "Bottoms up!"

Within the hour the gym was practically full. Sylvia's hair received rave reviews. She beamed when someone compared her to Brenda Lee, the cute little singer from the fifties. Francine spotted Gus, who came solo, and she pushed her way through the crowd of women to get as close to him as possible, abandoning her best friend to the shadows at the far end of the bleachers where she could covertly keep an eye on the entrance. Sylvia wondered if Mack had any intentions of showing up, considering he might think it silly since he had been a hard-core Marine. It is rather silly, she thought, as she looked at her school chums dancing as if they were teenagers. She was glad that she wasn't out there making a fool of herself.

"Hey, Sylvia!" a man shouted while crossing the room coming toward her. "Remember me?"

Sylvia squinted into the crowd, partially blinded by the overhead light. Hoping it was Mack, she gave him a big smile until she realized that it was Barney Weiner, the nerd that chased her all over the school when Mack wasn't looking. "Oh, hi, Barney."

"I'm surprised you recognized me," he said. "I've gained a few pounds. I own a string of donut shops, and it's my job to make sure that each batch tastes just like a Weiner donut should."

Sylvia looked sideways at Barney, wondering how in the world he could name a donut after himself.

"Yes, I know that's a weird name for a donut, so I stick hot dogs in the holes and wah-lah! A Weiner donut it is!" he laughed, snorting through his nose, his stubby fingers slapping his thigh.

"Well, that's, um," Sylvia cleared her throat, "very clever. Say, I'd love to chat, but nature calls."

"Save me a dance?" Barney yelled after her, his voice squeaking like the sound of basketball shoes grabbing onto a wooden court.

The line for the restroom was long, so Sylvia left the gym to find another one. The halls were barely lit, and she felt strange walking through her old school in the dark. The place felt much smaller than she had remembered it, just as her parent's home did when she had first arrived. Sylvia remembered that the teacher's lounge was just around the corner, and she fumbled through the dark corridor to find it. When she opened the door, a small light was on in the room. She snickered, as if Francine were sneaking in with her, and she knew that they would both be thinking the same thing – how cool it was to finally get to see where the teachers lounged and took off their scholastic masks. She smelled what she thought was tobacco and imagined them enjoying a smoke while sipping an alcoholic beverage the coach had smuggled in, disguised in a tall thermos. She stood hesitantly at the door, taking in the setting that looked like a comfy living room. When she stepped forward and scanned the contents, she jumped back seeing a man lying on the sofa with his arm draped over his eyes. "Oh my, I'm sorry to disturb you," she said softly.

The man sat up, clearly disoriented from being awakened. "Wow, I must've fallen asleep. Hmm, where am I?"

Sylvia's eyes opened wide when she recognized the bewildered man. "Mack, it's me, Sylvia."

Mack looked up with half-closed eyes and grinned from ear to ear. "Well, hello, Sylvia May."

With both hands on her cheeks, Sylvia giggled. "My goodness, I haven't been called that in years. Hello, Mack."

Suddenly realizing that it wasn't a dream, Mack stood up. "Boy, it's really good to see you." He was standing so erect, Sylvia thought he was about to salute, instead he offered her his hand. When their palms met, they locked eyes. Sylvia felt her heartbeat pounding against her bare chest. Mack pulled away, hoping she hadn't noticed that he had stopped breathing.

"You haven't changed a bit," he said. "I'm glad to see you still tease your hair."

"Well, I did it for tonight, anyway. But look at you. I'm glad to see that you can still wear your prom tuxedo. I guess Marine life has been good to you." Remembering that he had been wounded, she dropped her head to her chest.

Mack realized then that Sylvia knew about the injury. "Have a seat, and I'll tell you all about it."

Sylvia moved to the small chair next to the sofa.

"No, sit over here by me, if you want the full effect," Mack urged, moving over to give her room.

She timidly sat next to him and crossed her legs, pointing her patent leather high heel toward him.

"Nice shoes," he said.

"Thank you. I wore them to prom, if you remember."

"No, I really don't. I just remember how beautiful you looked and how I couldn't take my eyes off you." Mack turned away and tightened his lips, hoping to stop an oncoming tear.

"It was a wonderful night. I'll never forget it. I felt like Cinderella at the ball, and that car you rented was fabulous! Honestly, I think we were the coolest couple there."

Mack smiled and dared himself to look deeply into the eyes of his old flame. "We were. Yes, we really were, for a while."

"Well," Sylvia swallowed hard, "you were going to tell me about..."

"Yes, yes, well, it was kind of stupid, actually. Nothing to be proud of. We were making a delivery to another regiment. A routine mission we did often. The driver had just gotten a *Dear John* letter from his fiancé. When I asked him about it he started crying, and the next thing I knew he was bawling. He yelled out his fiancé's name just when he lost control of the jeep. I was pretty upset myself when I heard her name." Mack cleared his throat. "Well, with both of us losing it, neither of us saw the big rock until it was too late. The jeep hit it sideways and rolled over, first throwing us out and then landing on my leg. My buddy walked away with a few scratches. I wasn't so lucky."

"I'm so sorry." Sylvia put her hand on Mack's firm shoulder. "What was the name of the girl he was supposed to marry?"

Mack crossed his wounded leg over the other one, pulled up the pant leg and revealed to Sylvia his metal prosthesis.

Sylvia gasped at seeing the contraption, and then her mouth dropped open when she saw the name, *Sylvia*, written vertically with the missing magnetized plastic letters that used to be attached to her refrigerator door.

Keeping his pant leg pulled up, Mack stood and showed the stunned classmate the other side.

Sylvia tilted her head sideways to read the words – this time written in permanent ink – *I love you.*

Much, much later, after lots of explanations, hugs and tears and apologies, with a few juicy kisses in between, Mack and Sylvia strolled hand in hand onto the gym floor where they danced to Al Green's, *Let's Stay Together.* Mack swooned when he felt the densely teased hair grazing his nostrils and fought back a sneeze when he inhaled the thick layer of hairspray. Neither of them cared how hot the gym had become, and not a shred of light passed between them – holding each other tightly, just as they had ten years earlier on the very same wood floor. Even with aching bunions, Sylvia never lifted her head from his chest throughout the entire song, and she decided right then and there that she loved the smell of a cigar mixed with sweat and Old Spice aftershave.

The couple didn't want the reunion to end, but when the class president stood in front of the microphone to introduce the *Most Likely To* students, they agreed that it was time to leave.

Sylvia looked high and low for Francine. She guessed that she had gone outside to sneak a smoke, trying to relive the guiltless bygone days of their precious youth. She and Mack walked through the parking lot arm in arm looking for her. When they reached Francine's car they noticed that the windows were fogged up and wads of tissue were scattered on the ground below the back-door window.

"Oh, gee whiz," Sylvia whined. "I hate to break up this love scene, but she's my ride home. Well, here goes." Faking a cough to give her friend a fair warning, she tapped lightly on the front car door window knowing full well that they were in the back seat. The couple stood a respectable distance from the car and waited.

The window slowly went down, and Francine peeked out. "Is it time to go already?" she asked, clearly disappointed.

Then, up popped Gus Henderson's head – his long hair mussed and hanging over one eye. "I sure hope not," he grinned, revealing smudged lipstick on his mouth and teeth.

"Not a problem," Mack spoke up. "I'll take Sylvia home."

"Why thank you, Mack. Glad to see the cutest couple from the Class of '62 back together againnnn!" Francine squealed, just when Gus started tickling her and both heads went down as the window slowly went up.

Sylvia looked up at Mack and made a funny face, feeling a little awkward just standing there watching the car. "Thanks for offering me a ride. Can I make a quick phone call before we leave?"

"Of course, I'll wait outside by my truck."

"Sure you don't mind?"

"I think this is something I can handle, Sylvia. I've waited for years. I think I can wait a few minutes more…but only a few."

Sylvia was certain that she had turned fifty shades of red as Mack placed his hands around her waist and effortlessly lifted her high into the air and lowered her down to his lips.

Barefoot, with her heels slung over her shoulder, she felt like she was being carried by balloons on the way to the teacher's lounge to call her mother.

"Mom, I'm sorry to wake you," she spoke into the telephone, unknowingly twirling the coiled cord tightly around her fingers.

"Oh, you didn't dear. Dad and I are going through our high school memorabilia. Aren't we, sweetie?" Lily puckered her lips and sent kissing noises to her husband sitting at the foot of the bed wearing only his football letter jacket and a pair of boxers. "Matter of fact, he's wearing his Varsity jacket right now."

"Oh, that's uh, cute. But mom, listen. Since you're already up, I'd like to bring an old friend by for a little visit."

"An old friend?" Lily leaned over and twisted the hair on Hubert's chest to get his attention.

"Ow!" he blurted.

"Shhh!" Lily pointed vigorously at the phone, her face contorting with the pending news. "Dad and I are dying to know who it is. Tell us, darling."

"It's a surprise. See you in ten minutes." Sylvia quickly hung up, knowing full well that her relentless mother would not be the first to end the conversation until she got her question answered. On the way out, she caught a glimpse of her impish grin in the mirror and feeling like a dizzy teenager in love again, she couldn't wait to get back to Mack.

Lily slowly put the phone down and stared worriedly at her husband. "You don't think it's. . .well, do you?"

Hubert eased his body to the edge of the bed, leaned in and kissed his troubled wife. Then he carefully bit her bottom lip and gave it a sensual tug. Slowly letting it go, he looked into her half-closed eyes and said teasingly, "My, my, you get to apologize twice. Do you still think confession is good for the soul?"

"How about I make it three confessions," she said, nibbling on his upper lip.

"Ohh, please do. I can't wait."

"I've decided I don't want to go to college after all."

"Oh, really?" Hubert sighed with relief. "I was hoping you'd get past that silly notion."

No longer in a playful mood, Lily shoved him away and began to pout. "It wasn't all that silly."

"Aww, come on sweetie," Hubert pleaded, clinging to the mattress, determined to appease his troubled wife. "I'm still looking forward to seeing you in those cute penny loafers."

"Well," Lily huffed and crossed her arms, "don't you even want to know why I changed my mind?"

"OK, why did you change your mind?"

"I think I'm pregnant."

Dumbstruck, Hubert fell off the bed.

THE GUNTHERS

I'd never been to Betty Soo's house. She goes to the university where I attend and some of my friends say she's kind of spacey, so when she warned me that her household was different, I didn't think much about it. Whose isn't? She said that hers was more different than different, and kind of left it at that. I didn't let that faze me, because what could be more different than being the youngest of nine? I was sure hers was nothing unusual. Besides, she is a very pretty girl with a nice body, although the dark circles under her eyes say something about her I don't understand.

We pulled up to her house, me following behind in my uncle's extra car and her in a rusty green 1967 Plymouth Belvedere that she said she used to share with her brother. I stood at her car door and waited for her to get out, but she just sat there, kind of mumbling something incoherent, like she was talking to someone, and it wasn't me.

"Well, are we going in, or what?" I thought maybe I should ask.

"Yes, we are, but I always say a little prayer before I go in… just in case."

"Just in case, what?"

"Just in case," she said, followed by a breath of exasperation, and then she got out of the car.

I followed close behind, watching her head jerk nervously from side to side and behind her as if something was going to jump out from nowhere. By the time we got to the front door, she acted relieved, and said in a whisper, "Be very quiet."

"OK," I said, nodding my head with lips tightened, willing to play along. Slowly she opened the door, inch by inch and when it was opened enough to stick her head in, she did.

"Coast is clear, so far," she said and grabbed my hand, leading me inside.

A small lamp was on in the corner of the room, and the rest of the house was dark. She pointed for me to sit down on the sofa. On one end a large pile of wrinkled clothes took up half the seating. She sat opposite me in an overstuffed armchair, so big her feet dangled as she fell into its deepness.

Something moved under the pile of clothes. A skinny hairy finger came out and pointed at me. I looked over at Betty Soo, who was now reading the movie guide, and said, "Betty Soo, there's someone underneath these clothes."

"Oh!" she exclaimed, freezing in place. "Whatever you do, don't make any sudden moves."

I had no problem following her instructions, since her eyes were open so wide, I was now afraid to even breathe.

Betty Soo reached underneath the cushion and pulled out a tennis ball. She threw it across the room and down the hall. "Fetch!" she yelled.

Out of the pile, came a small figure, the size of a baby chimp with feet as large as mine. It leapt into the air, scattering the clothes about, and ran down the hall after the ball. When it didn't come back, I asked, "What was that?"

"Gunther," she spoke softly.

"Gunther? What do you mean?" I tried not to act too freaked out, which I surely was.

"Hard to explain, really, but he's...he's, well, he loves to play fetch. Only thing is, he never brings the ball back."

"Why is that?" I asked, as if our conversation was as normal as talking about school.

"He eats them. Well, I mean, he peels them, then eats some of the insides, and I'm not sure what he does with the rest." Betty Soo made a yuck face and continued reading the guide. "Want to watch a movie?"

"Uh, OK."

"First, let's go make some popcorn," she said, moving awkwardly out of the chair. I followed her, of course, just in case Gunther should come back. I peered down the dark hall and could have sworn I saw two sinister eyes beaming in the blackness. Not really wanting to know if I did or not, I followed close behind my new friend.

"Stand perfectly still," she demanded when we entered the kitchen and she switched on the light. "Don't make a move." She tiptoed toward the pantry and slowly opened it. Inside sat a small creature with big, black-bottomed feet feasting on a bag of lima beans. Its eyes were closed shut while it chewed rapidly. Betty Soo reached for the popcorn and the thing spit a mouthful of beans at her. She slammed the door and turned to look at me, a weird smile on her face, beans stuck to her chest and chin.

"What was that?" I stepped back and grabbed the doorknob for a quick escape if need be.

"Gunther."

"Again?" I asked, now wondering whose eyes I thought I saw in the hallway.

"He likes to sleep in there. Sorry, no popcorn. How about some coconut milk?"

I wasn't sure what to say, since I've never tasted that beverage, so I just said, "OK."

I glanced around the kitchen, painted an odd color yellow I can't quite describe and stained with big splashes in various colors dripping down the wall. On the countertops food and opened boxes and bags were carelessly strewn. I stepped on a pile of potato chips and spotted the torn-open bag at the edge of the countertop. I leaned over to pick up the bag, and just when I had it in my fingertips, a hand came out from inside the breadbox next to it and snatched it from me. The rolltop door was snapped shut so quickly, I don't know what I actually saw. But whatever it was, it was small enough to fit in there.

"Don't tell me," I looked at Betty Soo, standing there frozen, biting her bottom lip with an alarmed look on her face. "Gunther?"

"I guess." Her face relaxed when she was sure nothing was coming out of the breadbox.

"Are there more Gunthers in the house?" I suddenly realized to ask after seeing three of these things so far.

"I don't know," she said despondently. "I haven't been able to count them. I can't tell them apart and they're so fast, I can't keep up with them." She opened the refrigerator door, and two hands came out, pinched her cheeks, and like a flash of lightning, it disappeared from the kitchen. Again, it happened so fast, I could barely tell what it was I saw.

Betty Soo braced her back against the refrigerator and looked at me discombobulated. I felt like leaving, but she still looked cute even with that helpless pathetic expression and, well, I'm not a coward. "Why'd you bring me here, anyway?" I asked, thinking all along that she was just wanting to get to know me.

"I think because you're such a nice guy, and well, I do like you, but I also thought maybe you could help me. Truth is, I wasn't so sure I was really seeing these Gunthers, but now that you see them, well…you did see it, right?"

"Yes, I saw something. This is *really* weird. Want to talk about it?"

"I should. Well, yes, I need to. So, a few weeks ago, I can't remember for sure, I was coming in with groceries and this thing, Gunther, I call him, was lying on the kitchen countertop. I hit him with a broom, because I didn't know what else to do, and he got so mad, he threw a whole drawer of utensils at me, one by one until I ran outside and sat in my car for a while. It's been crazy like this ever since. I don't know what to do."

"Call an exterminator?" I let out a small laugh. "Does anyone else know you have this visitor, or visitors?"

"No, just you. I don't know who to turn to, and I guess I just couldn't take it anymore, and that's why I asked you over. Can you help me?"

"Well, other than throwing stuff at you, pinching your cheeks, and eating your food and your tennis balls…and wrecking your house," the crunching sound under my foot provided a timely sound effect, "what else does Gunther do? Has he harmed you?"

"No, I mean, well, psychologically, yes. I can barely sleep at night. Sometimes he just sits at the foot of my bed and stares at me. He doesn't talk, but he has this high pitch sound that hurts my ears so badly, I have to run out of the house to get away from it."

"When does that happen?"

"Whenever I look him directly in the eyes. So, I try to avoid that, as you can imagine."

"How long does the sound last?"

"Not too long, but one time I ran outside, and my neighbor was walking her dog. The dog went bonkers and rubbed his ears in the grass and cried like he was in pain. So I guess the dog heard it but when I asked the lady, she said she didn't hear a thing. She hasn't talked to me since. Kind of gives me a lame wave when she sees me, and now she walks on the opposite side of the street."

"So, where do you think Gunther is now? Maybe I could try talking to him."

"He could be anywhere. He pops up when and where he chooses. I'm a little more used to it now, but I'm sick of it, too. I can't even take a shower without him in the bathroom."

"Wait, how can he get in if you lock the door?"

This question made poor Betty Soo so uncomfortable, she shivered and said, "Come with me and I'll show you." She took my hand, which felt nice, although it shouldn't have at that very moment, but again, she is so cute. She led me to the bathroom, closed the door and locked it. "Now look around the room, in the cabinets, behind the shower curtain."

We did, and there was nothing. "OK, sit on the toilet while I wash my hands," she said.

I did that, too, although it was a weird request. The second she turned on the water, a pair of purplish colored eyes popped out from behind the shower curtain. I made the mistake of staring into them and sure enough, that high pitched sound she talked about earlier pierced my eardrums so badly, I grabbed two towels off the rack and smashed them against my ears. Betty Soo ran out of the bathroom to who knows where. I stayed behind and stared him down, the way I used to stare at my brother to get him to give me back something he stole from my room.

I stared until the creature fell backwards into the tub with a loud *thunk!* The sound immediately stopped, so I slowly pulled back the shower curtain, and there he was, on his back, eyes closed, a tiny, hairy man-thing, big feet and small hands, his head the size of a soccer ball, his torso the size of a store-bought talking Elmo. Ugly. Poor thing was downright ugly.

"But how did he get into the bathroom with the door shut?" I whispered to myself.

"Invisible," Betty Soo said, standing at the door, scaring the bejeezies out of me, I nearly fell backwards, too. "There's no other explanation, he just vaporizes or duplicates himself or something like that. Jeez, what'd you do to him?"

"Nothing. I just stared him down instead of running away

like you did, and he ended up like this…fainted, I guess. Ever seen this before?"

"No, but wow, you're on to something. Let's see how long he stays out."

We both sat on the edge of the tub, gazing at the creature, looking back and forth at each other quite flabbergasted. As we watched, I noticed the creature had grown smaller. "Look, he's shrinking."

"Oh my, he is." Betty Soo stood up, backing away as if she knew what was about to happen next. "You should probably stand back, too. This can't turn out good."

Not sure what that meant, or anything else that was occurring at Betty Soo's house, I stepped back. What happened next, well, it's hard to explain.

Like the air seeping out of a balloon, Gunther's body began to shrivel and then it shot up, hit the shower walls several times and ricocheted off the toilet, landing at my feet. What was left of him looked like an old banana that had decayed at the bottom of a garbage can. Afraid to touch it, I kicked it across the tiled floor where it slid and stuck in the corner.

Betty Soo stood there staring; a tear drop clung to her thick eyelashes. I didn't know what to do, except hold her hand in mine. As I did, she bowed her head in prayer. I respectfully dropped my own.

"OK," she blurted, a nervous smile crossing her lips. She reached over and unrolled a wad of toilet paper and handed it to me. "Will you please flush that thing down the toilet?"

"I, uh, are you sure? Shouldn't we bury it? Or donate it to science, or something like that? I mean…it looked at me."

"I never thought about that. This thing has been nothing but a nuisance. I think it should be somewhere safe, away from people," she pleaded with her eyes and stuffed more toilet paper in my hand.

I reluctantly wrapped the gross glob of matter in the tissue paper and walked over to the toilet. It was heavier than I thought it would be, and I couldn't tell if it had a heartbeat or if it was my own rapidly pulsating in my hands. I don't know why I could not drop it into the water, but I just couldn't. Instead, I asked Betty Soo if she had a shoebox.

Secure in the shoebox, duct tape wrapped around it five times, we stood staring at it, neither of us wanting to keep the thing. My answer to everything is to flip a coin, so I pulled out a quarter from my pant pocket and flicked it. I picked tails.

I sat the box containing Gunther in the back seat of my car and went back inside. Betty Soo was frantically checking closets, drawers, under the chairs and beds to make sure there were no more Gunthers in the house. Convinced that the one and only Gunther was in the box in the back seat of my car, she hugged me like a woman who had just been given a ticket to Maui. Of course, I hugged her back. Then, on cue, like we were in a romantic movie scene, we kissed.

The kiss lasted longer than I had thought it would, and we ended it while sitting on the sofa. Looking at Betty Soo now, there was a whole new light in her soft brown eyes, and her smile melted my heart. I asked her out, and we planned to have dinner soon. But when I tried to leave, she began to cry.

"What's the matter, Betty Soo?" I took her in my arms and consoled her.

"I'm a little scared to stay here tonight. I mean, I'm relieved that Gunther is gone, but I guess I have been so wound up…"

"I understand. I can't even imagine living with that thing for more than one day. You've been very brave, but why did you take so long to share your secret?"

"It's really hard to understand, even for me. I felt a very strange pull to it, as if it were controlling me. Or maybe I am so lonely here, I needed something breathing to be around. I can't explain it, but when I met you, I was so attracted to you, and you have such a trusting face, well, I knew I had to do something."

"Are you really lonely?" I asked, suddenly aware of this lovely girl's sadness.

"Yes, terribly."

"And, really attracted to me?"

"Oh yes, very."

"Hmm." My mind began racing. I asked her if she'd like to talk some more, and she did. She told me her whole life story, and at the end of it, she said that her brother who had shared the house with her had suddenly dropped out of college to travel America with an older female guru and her followers, all packed in an old VW bus. She admitted that she was depressed and again expressed how lonely she felt. With her parents living in China, and her only sibling gone, she had taken too many courses to have time for friends, and a boyfriend was just not in the cards. Yet with all those sad feelings, she was extremely grateful for the privilege to attend a university in the United States.

She asked about me, and my life was so simple, I almost felt embarrassed to share. Middle class parents, my big unruly family, college on a scholarship with a pile of student loans, still plagued with leftover adolescent acne, some friends, but no girlfriends to speak of, at the moment.

Naturally, we kissed some more, and before I knew it, I was sound asleep in her bed, my arms wrapped tightly around a very cute, but very sad young woman named Betty Soo. It was then that I realized I, too, was lonely.

We awoke to a beautiful morning, and I helped her put the kitchen back in order while she told me all the crazy things that Gunther did to her while living in her home. We planned to meet the day after. When it was time for me to get to class, we kissed again at the door, and I drove away having completely forgotten about Gunther in the back seat until I ran into my science teacher. I attempted to explain what had happened, the creepy creature in the shoe box, leaving out the details about Betty Soo.

He reacted as if I were pulling his leg, said something about today's hallucinogens, and shooed me off. I decided to go home after class and think about my next move.

I brought the box into my apartment and left it on the coffee table. Behind in my studies, I made myself a sandwich and hunkered down at my desk, books open, pen in hand. Hours passed and I fell asleep, my face on page nine of my biology report, the pen still between my fingers. When I finally opened my eyes, I saw a small figure sitting at the edge of my desk. I closed them tightly shut again, thinking my imagination was still sparked by the events of the day before. When I opened them, the figure was gone. *Phew!*

The clock read six in the morning. When I looked at my face in the bathroom mirror, ink smudges from drooling on my hand-written notes were spread across my cheek. While I chuckled, I saw movement in the corner of my eye. I looked over, and the shower curtain moved ever so slightly. "Get a hold of yourself, man," I said to my reflection. Still, I pulled the curtain back to see what may or may not be behind it. Nothing.

A hot shower later, my stomach growled. Walking past the living room on my way to the kitchen, I glanced back at the coffee table. The shoebox wasn't there. Frantically, my eyes darted all around the room. I retraced my moves the night before when I entered the apartment and back to the car. Convinced that it must be somewhere inside, I made a thorough search through the apartment. The box was nowhere to be found.

I was late to class and could barely concentrate thinking about that shoebox and how I would explain its disappearance to Betty Soo. I was completely baffled.

After my last class, I rushed back to the apartment and searched one last time before heading to Betty Soo's house. I hated to bring her this strange news, and I toyed with the idea of not telling her since she had been so relieved and comforted by the thing's death and removal from her home.

When I arrived, it was nearing dusk. There was no porch light on and no lights coming from the windows. I knocked and knocked and called out her name until the neighbor next door came out and yelled, "She's not home. She moved."

"What do you mean, she moved?" I asked, approaching him on his front porch.

"She moved. I helped her put a few boxes in her car and load up some heavy suitcases. She seemed pretty happy to be leaving."

I stood there staring at this stranger as if he had just told a stupid joke and forgot the punchline. "Are you kidding?"

"Why would I kid about something like that? She said you might come by. You're Josh, right?"

"Yeah, I am." I felt my body slump. "Did she say anything else, like where she was going?"

"Something about China. She was late for her flight, so that was about it." The man tugged at his t-shirt that had slipped above his large abdomen. "But hold on, she did leave you something," he turned and picked up a box on a table next to his rocking chair. "Here," he walked toward me and handed me the shoebox – Gunther's tape-sealed coffin.

"My dinners on the stove, got to get back inside. Hope she left you something nice," he said and let the screen door slam behind him.

I'm not sure how long I stood there holding that box, but long enough to realize that I had been duped into believing that I was Betty Soo's hero and her new boyfriend. I put the box back in the car and drove home, and as I drove, I realized what I should be concerned about is how the thing got out of my apartment.

As I sat there eating, yet another sandwich, I eyed the box curiously on the kitchen table. "I'm losing my effing mind," I said to no one and left it sitting there in the dark as I studied at my desk, thoughts of Betty Soo and Gunther slipping in and out of my mind. Exhausted, I crawled into bed and decided to drop the box off at the school's science lab in the morning and let the teacher figure it out for himself.

In the middle of the night, I felt something move on the bed. I sat up and looked around the room. Two illuminated eyes were peering at me in the dark. I kicked the blanket off, jumped from the bed and switched on the lamp. Sitting there as still as a statue was a smaller version of Gunther. I looked into its eyes and the shrill started out soft and then became so loud, I had no choice but to run out of the apartment.

Several days of nonsense with Gunther, pinching my nose when I peered into my closet, unraveling rolls of toilet paper and wetting them down with who knows what, spreading a jar of jelly along the toilet rim, silly, annoying things, and the worst, staring at me while I slept, I had had enough. I packed my ears with cotton balls, put earmuffs on, and covered them up with a thick beanie. I went to the bathroom and pretended to be going about a daily routine of brushing my teeth. Just as before, Gunther peeked around the shower curtain and stared at me. I stared back and the siren noise began, louder than ever, increasing by the second. Holding my hands over my padded ears, I stared him down until he fell backwards and landed face-up in the tub. Eyes closed and gradually shrinking, I braced myself against the wall and waited for him to blow about the room like a balloon losing air. He didn't disappoint me.

With Gunther back in the cardboard box and back in my car, I drove like a bat out of hell to my school. I knew a girl that works in the admissions department and after a few flirtatious minutes, I convinced her to give me Betty Soo's forwarding address in China. I triple taped the box, wrote *Fragile* on the outside and shipped it first class to an address in Shanghai. No return address.

Everything went back to normal and after a few weeks of hard studying, the Gunther episode had begun to fade. Still, sometimes when I'm thinking about that crazy night at Betty

Soo's, I get a little sad. I think about kissing her and spooning her in bed. I think about how I couldn't flush Gunther down the toilet. I even laugh a little about some of the pranks he pulled and really how harmless he was, until he made that god-awful sound. I often wonder why she named him Gunther, and if he was really even a "he." I guess I'll never know much more than I do now.

The semester ended, I passed my classes and worked the entire summer to start paying off my student loans. When I went to my advisor, she pulled my file and informed me that my loans had been paid off and that all my future classes were prepaid. She would not tell me who did this wonderful thing, as the donor was to be anonymous. Not only had my college been paid for, but my apartment lease was covered for two more years. One morning I even woke up to a nice, gently used car. Along with my parents, I was deliriously happy and utterly confused.

One day, I don't know why, but I drove to Betty Soo's home. I knocked on the door and stood there waiting. Waiting for what, I'm not sure. When no one answered, I went next door to the neighbor.

"Can I help you?" he asked.

"Yes, do you remember me? I'm Josh, a friend of Betty Soo's who used to live next door to you."

The man stepped one foot out the door and looked over at the house. "There?" he asked.

"Yes, there. Remember, she left a box for me when she moved awhile back. You gave it to me."

"I'm sorry kid, but I've never met you, or Betty Soo. For that matter, there hasn't been anyone living in that house for years. Sure you got the right house?"

I turned around and looked at the street, the house, the

leaning mailbox I nearly ran into when I first visited. "Yes, I'm sure."

"Hmm," the neighbor grunted, scratched his belly and closed the door behind him.

I went back over to Betty Soo's house and peeked in the window. It appeared to be vacant inside. But when I scanned the room, my eye caught something on the living room floor. The shoebox.

I can't tell you how fast I jumped into my car and sped away. Some things are just *un*explainable, *un*fathomable, *un*reasonable, and honestly, I can live with those *uns*. Besides, I need to concentrate on school and there's no time for pondering foolish stuff like what lies beyond the Twilight Zone.

Thank goodness I stuck to my guns and now, two years later, I am finally graduating. As I stood there looking at the sea of caps and tassels, I felt a sudden sadness that Betty Soo was not here enjoying this special moment with me. She had told me how much she loved being here. It must have been hard for her to leave right in the middle of school. I couldn't believe that of all the things I should be thinking about, she popped into my head.

When my name was called, and I walked across the stage, I heard my parents and siblings yell out, "GO JOSH!" with a hoot and a holler. When I looked their direction, sitting right next to them was Betty Soo. I felt sure that I was hallucinating and quickly exited the stage. I ran to the restroom and threw cold water on my face. Was I that stuck on the girl to imagine her in the audience? I waited until the ceremony was over to go back inside the auditorium. Wading through the happy parents and beaming students, I found my own parents standing by the wall, their backs to me as they stood talking to someone.

I tapped my dad on the shoulder, and he turned to hug me.

My mother grabbed me around the waist from behind. My siblings nearly piled on top of me, and when they finally let me go, Betty Soo wrapped her arms around my neck and kissed me on both cheeks. Still as pretty as a sunflower, she held her hands on my shoulders and smiled at me. I nearly swooned.

"Surprised to see me?" she asked, her eyes brighter than ever, the dark rings gone.

I looked over at my parents whose grins were frozen in place, my brothers giving me the thumbs up. My mother said, "Son, you never told us about this beautiful friend of yours."

"Well, I…, well, we didn't know each other all that long, but wow, it's good to see you, Betty Soo."

"Long enough," she winked, and stepped aside.

After photos were taken and another round of hugs from my big family, they finally made excuses to leave and said they'd see me at the dinner party planned the next evening.

"I'm sure you and your friend here have a lot of catching up to do. All the way from China…," my mother squeezed Betty Soo's hand and walked away with my dad, both looking back wearing silly smiles of approval at seeing me standing next to such a nice girl.

Betty Soo waved goodbye and then turned to face me. "Congratulations, Josh. You did it. I'm totally proud of you."

"Thank you. But why are you here?" I had to know.

"Why not?" She looked at me impishly. "Come on, let's go to dinner. I have a car."

I pulled off the cap and gown and followed her outside. When the crowd began to dissipate, a long, white limousine pulled up. I looked around to see what super wealthy student would enter that beast. When the driver opened the back door, Betty Soo reached for my hand and pulled me inside.

"What the heck?" I exclaimed, slightly resisting, until she yanked me in.

"I've missed you," she said, and planted her lips right on mine. I let her kiss me until I gave in and took over.

When we broke apart, I had to say, "You left. You left without a word. You stood me up."

"I know, I know, and I'm sorry it had to be that way. You paid me back, though."

"How did I pay you back?"

"You sent me Gunther. I hated you for that, but the strangest thing happened. I couldn't hide him from my parents now that I was living at home. It seems they weren't as intimidated by him as we were. My mother, being Chinese and very strict, trained him…to a point, anyway. Then she sold him to the wealthiest family in Shanghai for more money than you can imagine. I think he's now being used as a secret weapon or something, but something worthwhile instead of just driving people crazy."

"So," I said, looking around the limo and at the back of the driver, hatted and dressed in black, "and now you're *rich*?"

"Very," she said, blushingly sweeping her hair back to reveal her solid gold earrings.

"Wow, this is crazy, isn't it?" I sunk back into the luxurious leather and sighed deeply. Then it hit me. "You, you are my nameless donor?"

"Yes."

"Oh man, this is really getting crazier. I should thank you. No, I *do* thank you. Why, though, did you do that for me?"

"Josh, if it weren't for you, *we* would not be so very wealthy. Gunther would be in the sewer system, and I wouldn't be here sitting next to you feeling so happy to see you."

"We? *We* would not be so very wealthy?"

"Yes, *we*. Your fortune awaits you now that you graduated. And if you wish, you can have me, too."

❦

Four years have passed, and I am a happily married financially comfortable man. Betty Soo's parents have arrived to enjoy our first Halloween together at our lovely new home near the university where I teach now and where my wife is enrolled.

They have brought bags of Chinese candy, and we are sifting through the many colorful varieties spread out on the kitchen table while drinking hot ginger tea and spiked apple cider cocktails. It's a happy scene, and I have never felt such joy. The doorbell rings, and I run to answer it. Expecting trick-or-treaters, I encourage everyone to come with me.

I open the door, and we stand there looking at an empty porch. My mother-in-law opens the door wider, and we all peep out. I look back at them and shrug, and at the same time, I catch an odd look on my wife's face as she is fixated on something near my feet. I'm thinking, oh no, not the flaming bag of poop prank!

It's worse. Much worse! Everyone follows her stare and looks down at the familiar battered shoebox wrapped in duct tape. I hurriedly gather them up, shut the door and double bolt the locks. Wide-eyed, we stand there staring at one another, my back braced against the door, afraid to say his name, even to whisper it, much less think it. Gunther.

"Heee's back," Betty Soo sings, throws her hands up in the air and starts laughing. Then her stepfather slaps his knee and bellows out a string of laughter that echoes in the tile entry. When her mother's frown turns into a crooked smile and she begins with the titters, her fingers pressed against her lips trying to prevent the infectious laughter from bursting out, and my wife is now wheezing with hilarity, I put my head in my hands and nearly drop to my knees howling in a kind of inexplicable amusement only the four of us could possibly understand.

When we finally settle down, I toss a coin to see who will take the shoebox. I pick tails.

IN THE SCHEME

She had smelled the bloated carcass long before she tripped over it, while watching the vultures soaring high above the prairie that stretched for miles along each side of the two-lane farm road connecting one dusty town to the next. Running from the stench, Edith turned around to take another look at the carnage left rotting on the side of the road. She swore this would be the last time she'd ever see roadkill again.

Earlier that morning the air had seemed fresh and full of hope while packing her meager belongings, along with a picture of her mother that she kept on the nightstand in the rickety old house where she had lived the past year. The decision to leave lifted a weight the size of a ten-pound sack of potatoes that she felt she carried every day she awoke from a bed other than her own.

She would erase the ugly past as easily as she did the blackboard in the third grade – one of the few pleasures she remembered as a child – writing numbers with a fresh piece of chalk and then wiping them clean with a swipe of her tiny hand, leaving chalky imprints of equations soon forgotten by girls like her that never intended to use math except for measuring ingredients for cookies and birthday cakes on those perfect sunshiny days.

As she walked under the blistering sun, she tried to stay focused on the new life ahead but could not help thinking about what she was leaving behind. Hanson was a good man. In fact, there was not one evil bone in his body. Devilishly handsome, too, and it didn't bother Edith that he was older than her. They took an instant liking to one another, yet he had never taken her to his bed. Extremely shy, he had been raised by two spinster aunts who worked a lifetime producing cheap table wine from a withering vineyard on the outskirts of Roswell, New Mexico. Suddenly inheriting a substantial sum of money, the old gals gave the house, the land, the whole shebang to Hanson and high-tailed it to the Galveston coastline where they planned to spend the rest of their retirement on cruise ships drinking everything but wine. Hanson would remain content spending the rest of his life working to produce a better-quality grape with higher goals than simply providing a cheap way to keep the locals inebriated. Edith could not understand why a young man of twenty-six could be that unadventurous, spending all his energy on something that boring, and with little income to support his dream.

"Crushing grapes might be enough for you Hanson Whitaker, but not for me!" she yelled into the dry wind.

Shaking her head free from the bandana that was giving her a slight headache, she stopped to look for the car she imagined would carry her to a new, more exciting life. There were no clouds to hide the west sun, but in the brightness, she thought she saw dust rising from the road several miles away.

Quickly, she dug into her big denim purse, applied new lipstick, and threw her head forward to loosen the hair that had stuck to her scalp. Widening her eyes for that innocent look, as she did many times to get Hanson to notice her from across the table while he gulped down the evening meal, she puckered her wet lips and lifted her thumb to hitch a ride.

Through squinting eyes, she saw the outline of a car that she imagined was a limousine, until it became apparent that it was merely an old Ford, on the hood an ornament of a mermaid with pink lily pads on her perfectly chiseled breasts. With thumb still high in the air, she coughed from the dust that rose when the automobile finally came to a stop, the passenger door just inches from her knees.

"On my way to College Station, Texas," the boy yelled over the loud humming of the engine. "Heading my way?"

"Well, as long as it's nowhere in New Mexico, I think so," she responded with a brand new confidence that turned her frown upside down.

"Alright then!" Leaning over to open the passenger door, he warned, "Watch out for that spring poking out of the seat. Last hitchhiker I picked up turned out to be heavier than a cow, and this old car's leather is worn thin."

Anyone that opens the door for a girl can't be all that bad, Edith surmised. Besides, he is kind of cute, and now I won't have to spend any money on a bus ticket. Things were already looking up. She slid carefully into the seat, keeping a close eye on the metal spring.

The boy introduced himself as Larry, known as Lawrence by his teachers and Lar by his friends, and he was on his way to Texas A&M to study agriculture and everything that grows with it. They exchanged a few pleasantries, leaving out their last names and settled in for a long nine-hour drive.

Larry turned on the radio and picked up an occasional signal filling the car with oldies but goodies and the latest and greatest. When the Righteous Brothers crooned "Unchained Melody," Edith could barely hold back the tears that had been building up since she tripped over the dead coyote. It was all becoming very real now: her life in the hands of a stranger, heading back to

Texas with no particular plan, and hearing her stomach grumble, reminding her that in her haste she had forgotten to eat.

Having heard the growling, Larry reached over the back seat to grab from a paper bag the most beautifully ripe apple Edith had ever seen. She smiled gratefully, wiped her eyes, and stared at the luscious fruit, so shiny she could see her reflection in its skin. Three crisp bites later, the tears were gone and her spirit renewed.

"I'm about to turn twenty-one," she boasted, ready to tell her story to this nice boy.

His eyes trailed her body from her knees to her flushed face. "Yeah, I would have guessed around that."

"I bet you're kind of wondering why a young woman like me is hitchhiking in the middle of nowhere."

Larry shrugged off the question, seeming to not care. All that really mattered to him was that she was pretty and had no wedding ring on her finger. Edith took his shrug as an invitation to explain.

"A year or so ago," she began, pondering the time that had lapsed, "I was living with my stepfather after my mother passed away. It was her heart. Just gave out, I guess. But anyway, things got a little uncomfortable, and since I was nineteen and about to graduate, I started working on a way to move out. Ed, that's my mother's third husband, he, well, he had other plans for me. Plans I didn't like." She paused to look over at the driver to see his reaction after delivering such a big dose of her life all at once.

Larry stared straight ahead, uncertain how to respond. He decided the best thing to do was to keep an eye on the road.

Edith was relieved that Larry didn't ask personal questions and continued with the rest of the story. "Ed took me to the county fair, and I met a guy that I got to know really well during the three days we stayed in that town." She didn't feel the need to give names or places or reasons. "He lived a quiet life on a vineyard. The way he described it sounded like a dream come true from the kind of life I was living. So, the day he packed up to leave, I hid in the back of his pickup under a tarp and rode what must have been about two hundred miles. I didn't care where we were going, just anywhere away from Ed." Hesitant to share too much, she paused and nervously flattened the cuff on her blue jean shorts.

"Well, you can imagine his face when he saw me pop out from under that stinking tarp, my hair matted to my head and a big, ugly wrinkle in my cheek from sleeping on my arm."

Larry decided now might be the time to respond. "Yeah, I guess he was pretty upset."

"On the contrary," Edith objected, "he was glad to see me. Matter of fact, we went straight into his house where he fixed me a sandwich and a glass of some fairly decent wine, I guess…well, I don't drink that stuff, but anyway. I waited while he unloaded his truck and did a few things around the vineyard. I sat on his porch swing and watched him for at least an hour, when he finally came and sat beside me ready to listen."

Minutes passed before Edith started where she left off, as if during the silence, she was rewriting her history. "So, after I told him why I ran away, he didn't say a thing. He just asked me if I wanted to stay there as long as it took for me to figure out what I was to do next. And so, I did, and all that time I helped with the vineyard, cleaned house, watched a lot of television, and tried to figure out who I was. I even wrote a book…well, more like a short story."

"Really? What's it about?"

"It's about me. But I don't have it. I left it on the kitchen table for my friend to read so that he would know all about me, since he never really asked for details. Talk made him feel odd, he used to tell me, but he loved to read."

"So, you wrote your life's story?" Larry cocked his head, calculating. "Well, a quarter of your life, anyway."

"Yes, I guess you could say that. I spared nothing and wrote as if I were talking to God. Writing it helped me move on. After I was finished, there were no more excuses. Said and done and no more excuses."

"So, now it's your turn," Edith prodded, holding the spring steady as she reached over to shake Larry's free arm.

"Hmm, I'm not sure if my story is near as exciting as yours, but in all fairness, I'll summarize best I can. Does the name Lawrence Whitaker mean anything to you?" he asked without turning her direction.

Surprised to hear the name, she eyed him closely. "Um, well, yeah, are you talking about the Senator for New Mexico? The *very* rich senator?"

"Yes, that one. He's my father. I'm his namesake."

Uncrossing her legs, Edith suddenly had a flash of intuition that was usually followed by a deep breath and the feeling that someone had walked right through her. She thought a second before speaking. "I've seen pictures of him." She remembered teasing Hanson when showing him the Senator's picture in the newspaper. "You two must be related, looking so much alike and having the same last name and all." Hanson just rolled his eyes and responded laconically, "I doubt that."

"So, I'm riding in the car with a celebrity," she joked.

"Yeah, well," he sighed, staring at the empty road ahead. "Dad died this year and kind of left me in a dilemma.

"Oh, I'm sorry. I don't watch the news, so I didn't know he… well, do you want to tell me about it?"

"Are you sure you want to hear. I mean…"

"Larry, I just told you everything there is about me." Edith reached across the seat and softly caressed his shoulder. "I trusted you, so you can trust me. Besides, now we have something in common. We both lost a parent."

Larry scratched his head under the baseball cap and settled back into his seat as if he were about to begin a long story while sipping a beer in a rocking chair under a soft November sky.

"Well, one day I was messing around in the attic, and I ran across a picture of a teenager that looked a lot like my father. When I asked him about it, he grabbed it from me and told me it was none of my business and walked out of the room. My mother died when I was a kid, and my stepmother had already moved out, so there wasn't anyone I could ask about it anyway. I kind of forgot about it until after my dad died."

Jerking the wheel to miss a dead skunk on the road, Larry pinched his nostrils closed. "Better cover your nose, the stink is so powerful it goes right through the car!"

A waft of the foul odor had Edith covering both her nose and her mouth. They stayed that way until Larry started singing in a funny nasally voice, "Dead skunk in the middle of the road, stinkin' to high heaven!"

They laughed for the longest until they couldn't laugh anymore. When all was quiet, Edith insisted that Larry finish his story.

"Oh yeah, well, it turns out I have a brother that I never knew about."

Edith cleared her throat. Inquiringly, she thought to ask, "The boy in the picture is your brother?"

Larry studied her face and seeing that she was seriously interested, he pulled over to the side of the road. He went to the back of the car, opened the trunk, and looked in his suitcase for a cigar box stuffed full of photos; some black and white, some faded and some in full color, a mixture of generations gone by. He took them to the front seat and filtered through them.

Edith watched anxiously as beads of perspiration formed across the line of her upturned nose. He handed her a stack of discarded photos. She shuffled through them until she reached a picture of two ladies, identically clothed in flowered dresses, each holding a glass of wine while the sun shone down on the vineyard behind them. She let out a gasp and at the same time, Larry placed a photo of the mysterious boy on her lap.

Swallowing the next gasp, she sat transfixed on what was clearly Hanson Whitaker, at least thirteen years earlier.

"Do you see how much he looks like my dad?" Larry asked, placing a picture of the Senator on her knee. And then looking in the rear-view mirror, he added, "Maybe a little like me, too. The thought of having a mysterious brother out there sure is weird, and he may be the only relative I have left in this family. And then there's the money…and at the bottom of this cigar box, a letter my dad left for me."

Edith's thoughts were whirling out of control. "Larry, please, since you've gone this far to share so much, you can't leave me in suspense. What did the letter say?"

"It read that the picture I had found was my half-brother, and his name is Hanson Whitaker. He told me that I could identify him by a birthmark behind his right ear and that if I decided to find him, then he was the rightful heir to half my inheritance. He wrote that he wanted to tell me more, but it really didn't matter after all these years, and that I should do the right thing." Larry sighed and focused on a bird flying low in front of them.

Beside herself, Edith suppressed the excitement in her voice. "So, what *will* you do? I mean, have you tried to find him?"

"No. There was so much to do after the funeral and getting into A&M has been my top priority. I've already lost a year, and, well, to be honest, I'm not ready, and I'm not even sure if I ever will be. It's a big task, and I don't have the time or even the money."

"What do you mean? Didn't your father leave you a big inheritance?"

"Oh yeah, I'm set for life," he said, stalling to think it through. "More money than I need, but I won't get it all until I'm twenty-one, except this car I'm driving – this was his pride and joy. It's a classic, you know. All original, even the paint."

Turning the wheels to head back onto the road, the two not-so-strange strangers anymore sat in silence thinking; one was fantasizing finding his brother, and the other calculating exactly how much money would it take to be set for life.

More talk ensued, lunch at a rusty diner, and a stop at Dairy Queen on the south side of Waco where Larry and Edith took big licks of each other's ice cream cones and laughed hysterically when it got on their noses and landed on the hot cement. The long drive together was stimulating a new friendship, and by the time they reached College Station, Larry had found a place to rest his hand, comfortably on Edith's thigh.

Larry's father had bought him a small house near the east campus of A&M long before he had died, in hopes that his son would carry the Aggie tradition and graduate with high honors just as he had before becoming a politician. When they entered the brightly, painted maroon door, Edith squealed with delight over the furnishings: leather chairs, rich tapestries, and hardwood floors. "It's absolutely gorgeous!" Running her fingers across the cool, granite kitchen counter, her eyes widened with curiosity. "May I look at the rest of the place?"

Larry led her to the bedroom. Never had Edith seen such a grand bed, draped in a luxurious brocade bedspread with the letters A & M embroidered in the middle. It was even lifted an extra foot off the ground. She couldn't resist throwing her body across it and burying her face in the soft pillows stacked against the cowhide headboard. With her eyes closed, she thought about her grandmother's smelly old house, and the cramped bedroom where she would have to sleep amongst her vast collection of old dolls, their glassy eyes constantly judging her. Home to Ed was definitely out of the question. The nearly two-hundred dollars she took from Hanson's coffee can would last for only so long. But standing at the foot of the bed was someone who had everything she needed. She gave Larry a woeful glance and let out a cry of despair.

Edith's sobbing into the pillow took Larry by surprise. They had spent the last few hours of the trip easily flirting and laughing. And more than once the urge to kiss her overwhelmed him. How naïve he felt watching her now, helpless and frail, her tan slender legs pulled up to her chest in a fetal position. He remembered seeing his mother like that when she had her 'fits of depression', his father would call them. He was only nine years old when they carried her from the house to the graveyard in the city, and by the time he was ten, he had a second mother that he rarely saw, as she and his dad would go for long trips to other countries and come back just in time to plan another. He couldn't recall why that stepmother disappeared and was replaced with numerous women who would come and go like the housekeeper. The sudden reminder that he was now an orphan lurched ahead of his thoughts.

Overcome with sadness, he found himself spooning Edith, his thighs pressed against hers, fighting back his own tears. Before he knew it, he felt a pulsing sensation between his legs. It happened quickly, along with a tiny burst of sweat at the base of his spine. When he slowly began inching away, Edith's crying came to an immediate stop. She reached behind her and caressed him gently but firmly, enticing him to stay. Soon, accelerated breathing was all that was heard, and within seconds they were engaged in heated foreplay, moving rapidly to ripping off their clothes and finally to a full-bodied mounting that ended abruptly, leaving them breathless beneath maroon and white sheets.

Not knowing what to do when Larry fell instantly asleep, Edith rolled over, placed her head on his chest and listened to his rapid heartbeat gradually subside to a perfectly steady, *tu tump, tu tump*. When she heard her own heartbeat in rhythm with his, she smiled and allowed herself to drift off, only to awaken an hour later to Larry whispering in her ear, "Again?"

～

The next morning, Larry jumped to attention and hastily made excuses to leave the house. Edith frantically paced the smooth hardwood floors while he showered. He had made it clear on the long drive that he had four grueling years ahead and could not take on extracurricular activity, including and above all things, a girlfriend. He reminded her again on his way out the door. Edith hid her disappointment and assured him that she had other plans. She had been so sure that the romp in the hay the night before would change Larry's mind, but any hope of being a part of his life was unquestionably not in the cards. She would have to switch gears.

Leaving a thank you note on the refrigerator full of beer, Edith made the bed and searched through the luggage Larry had left open on the bathroom floor. She found three hundred-dollar bills in the centerfold of a Playboy magazine. Shaking it loosely, another hundred-dollar bill dropped at her feet. She contemplated taking it all, but in the scheme of things to come, she decided only half of it would be all she needed for now. Before she closed the door behind her, she went back inside to get the pictures Larry had shown her in the car. She took his father's letter, too.

Edith stopped at a department store and bought a brightly colored sundress with a scoop neck, earrings to match, and a new pair of sandals. On her way out, she snatched a pair of bikini panties off the shelf and stuffed them in her purse. Finding the nearest bus station, she purchased a ticket to Waco. From there she would hop the next bus to Roswell, where she would catch a ride back to Hanson's home.

Arriving just after dark, she spotted Hanson sitting on the front porch, reading. As usual, he was so deeply engrossed in the subject matter, he hadn't noticed her approaching. When she was close enough, she saw that he was disheveled, with red swollen eyes and a box of tissue next to his bare feet. She stood still in the shadows and waited for him to look up. He continued reading, and when he finally got to the last page, he lifted his chin slowly and smiled at her. A tear trickled past his nose.

"Welcome back," he said, moving over to make room for her on the bench. Timidly, she dropped her bag and sat down, eyeing the literature in his lap. It was the book she had written, neatly bound in a loose-leaf folder, just as she had left it, only the pages were now slightly lifted at the corners where they had been turned more than once.

Edith put her hand on his cheek and studied his face. Then she smiled and reared back to say something. Hanson gently placed his hand over hers and spoke before she could. "I understand. Your book says it all."

She kissed him deeply, passionately, until he surrendered in her arms. Discreetly, she looked behind his ear for a birthmark.

Later that evening when all the stars came out to brighten the half-moon night, Edith lay wide awake in Hanson's bed while he slept soundly next to her. Listening to his barely audible breathing, she felt at peace knowing that soon she would become Mrs. Edith Whitaker, all the while pregnant with a Whitaker baby.

BATHROOM MATERIAL

I came from a one-bathroom family, and there were seven of us! That room was our library, our escape, the most coveted hideout in the house. These stories are crafted for those untimely leg tingling visits when the bathroom is truly all yours. And at the dentist office while waiting for a root canal. They're fun to read on a plane, on a hammock, on the beach, or in the middle of the night when you just can't sleep.

Untether your wonderful imagination, let go, and enjoy!

CONDITIONING THE CONDITION

Every time Gordo got aroused or very upset, he would begin to hiccup. It had been like this since he was fourteen years old when he first noticed changes in his gangly young body in places, well, places only he could see. The first time it happened he was in the corner drug store reading comic books when a teenage girl brushed by him to reach for a Glamour magazine. Her long blonde hair grazed his cheek like the tail of a spirited pony quickly turning around to follow a butterfly. The girl's bare armpit was just inches from his nose, and he could see her lace bra beyond her sleeveless shirt. Feeling flush all over, the first round of hiccups exploded. They came rapidly within seconds of each other and would not stop until several minutes after the girl had walked away covering her mouth with both hands to hide uncontrollable giggling. Needless to say, Gordo was crushed.

Now, at age twenty-four, with no sign of relief, his problem had only worsened. No doctor, therapist, or even his mother could find a remedy. So, he spent most of his time with his head deep in books, hanging around libraries where nothing exciting happened, short of an occasional loudmouth being escorted out of the building. To be on the safe side, he took a job in the basement of a university where he filed documents in a windowless room under cold, florescent lighting. He lived with his widowed mother and led a very simple life, void of social activity.

Gordo's mother decided to marry her second husband after a whirlwind romance. He had never seen his mother quite so giddy, and he found it unnerving. To top it off, his stepfather was twelve years younger than her and only eight years older than him. This made it extremely hard to live comfortably under the same roof together. And then there was the flirting in the kitchen as they eased past each other, patting bottoms and sighing under their breath, as if they couldn't wait for him to leave. Gordo could barely keep from gagging and tried hiding behind the newspaper loudly crunching his cereal pretending not to notice, but it seemed to spur the couple on to even more silliness. Finally, after three days of this nonsense and quite disgusted, he chunked his spoon into the half-empty bowl, causing a clanking noise that made the newlyweds jump to attention. Then he sent the newspaper flying across the table, slammed the chair against the wall, and hurried outside just before the hiccups arrived. Angrily, he marched pass his usual bus stop and walked the fifteen blocks to work, hiccupping the entire way.

That night when he returned home, he avoided the frisky couple and took his dinner to his bedroom. He completed the final chapters of a Ken Follett novel, turned off the lamp and slid into the bed he had slept in all his life. Lying there thinking, it occurred to him that he might be jealous of his mother's happiness. She was on her second time around, and he hadn't even experienced his first. As he had for a while now, he pondered what it would be like to live in his own place or drive his own car with a cute girl by his side. Slipping into a similar dream, he was suddenly jarred by a bumping sound from somewhere in the house. He stared blindly into the dark, listening closely to what sounded like something banging against a wall and then a faint squeal of laughter as if a child were hiding in a closet waiting to be found in a game of hide-and-seek.

Gordo quietly tiptoed to the door and opened it just enough to peek down the hall. The thumping got louder, followed by a couple of squeaks. Inching his way toward the sound, he froze in his footsteps just feet from his mother's bedroom door. He realized at that moment what he had heard and quickly flattened his body against the wall. Feeling his face redden and a hiccup forming right below his Adam's apple, he sneaked back to his room just before it burst from his throat, hitting the back of his teeth so fiercely it knocked him into bed. Smothering his face in a pillow, it took ten minutes for the hiccups to subside and another ten for the thumping to finally stop.

Gordo woke up earlier than usual. Distressed by the idea of having breakfast with his mother and her stud, he left a note telling them that he was eating in town and looking for an apartment. When he arrived home that evening with a lease in his hand, his mother was waiting alone in the living room to greet him. She gave him her blessings, kissed him on the forehead and dashed out the front door to meet her husband at the YMCA where he was employed as an instructor for a senior citizen weightlifting class.

In his new apartment, at the end of the building with access through a private stair in the back, Gordo settled in by first lining up his collection of over one hundred books on the floor along the wall. For the next few days, he slept on a sleeping bag stuffed with towels. He missed his twin bed with the star-studded sheets and aqua blue pillowcase that had softened over the years from numerous washings. But his mother insisted that it remain in her home as a guest bed for her new husband's friends. Before the month ended, he had collected things from consignment stores and garage sales to make the place his own – including a double bed with a Star Trek sheet set. Gordo thought he was happy, but the daily routine from work to apartment began to get old after the second month away from the familiarity of his childhood home. Realizing that there was no turning back, he settled into a solitary and predictable life. Days went by without a peep from the hiccups that lay dormant just waiting for him to drop his guard.

One evening just before dusk, Gordo was hauling groceries up the three flights of stairs to his apartment. He heard a loud scream from the unit next door. Stopping to listen, he heard another scream, this time higher and longer. Feeling the hiccups marching toward the escape hatch, he put the bags of food down and swallowed hard. He knew he had to do something, so he held his breath and knocked harder than he had intended on the neighbor's door. The door flew open and there stood a young woman standing on the kitchen countertop wrapped in a towel, her hair tied loosely in a bun nearly touching the ceiling. She pointed nervously to the floor. Her eyes were wide with terror. Holding the towel tightly around her breasts, she let out another scream, and when she jumped up her head hit the ceiling and shook the light fixture above, sending Gordo flying backwards against the wall where a rapid release of hiccups came flooding from his mouth.

"Look, look!" she yelled, so frightened she obviously didn't feel the bump rising on her head.

Gordo followed her index finger straight to a small table next to a sofa. "What...hiccup...is it?" he asked, "I...hiccup...don't see...iccup...anything!"

"Look, look, right there!" she scowled, her face reddening in anger.

Fearing he'd find a dead body or worse, a snake – he hated snakes – he slowly walked around the sofa and spotted a small brown mouse chewing on a potato chip. Its beady, little glazed-over eyes looked up as if to ask if he wanted a bite. Amused, Gordo started to laugh but the hiccups forced the laughter into a corner and held it there.

The girl lowered her voice and begged, "Get it, please, get that disgusting thing out of here!"

Gordo looked around for something to throw over the hairy creature. He spotted a bowl full of salad on the countertop next to the girl's stomping feet. He dumped the salad on the floor close to the mouse. Within seconds, the hungry varmint began fearlessly chewing on the feast of leaves, never looking up once to notice the plastic bowl hovering like a flying saucer over its quivering body.

"There!" Gordo turned to face the girl. "You're, *hiccup*, safe for the time being." She appeared to be quite an ordinary girl, but as his eyes scaled her body, he saw that she was in beautiful shape, with ample breasts and muscular calves that suggested she might be a dancer. Turning quickly away, he looked back at the scene of the crime.

"Thank you, but could you *please* take it far away from here? I refuse to get down as long as it's in my apartment," she whined.

Gordo found a magazine and slid it under the bowl, safely capturing the mouse and some of the lettuce. Trying not to drop it in between hiccups, he carefully walked out the door, down the stairs, and into a thicket of woods that surrounded the complex where he left the furry intruder happily dining on salad.

Picking up his groceries, before the ice cream melted and ruined his plans for dessert in front of an old black and white movie, he hurriedly put them in the refrigerator and ran back to return the magazine and the bowl to the girl next door. She was still standing on the bar. He supposed she was waiting for him to give her the thumbs up, that her home was now safe and rid of unwanted guests.

"Could you help me down, please? I'm shaking so much, I'm afraid I can't do it alone."

Hesitating, not certain where to put his hands, the girl fell forward into his arms. He caught her just in time to brace her fall and stepped back to prevent them both from crashing to the floor. Hoping to adjust the situation he lifted her higher to get a good grip, and when he did, the towel opened, exposing her right breast. He fumbled for the end of the towel and fell forward against the back of the sofa where he attempted to set the girl down with towel intact. His plan failed when she slipped from his arms and landed bare bottom up, her face embedded in a big, purple cushion. Gordo tossed the towel over her naked body, let loose a rapid stream of hiccups and stumbled out of the apartment back to the safety of his own unit.

He locked the door behind him and threw himself on the floor, flat out on his back, waiting for the spasm to end. Minutes later he heard another scream. Recognizing his neighbor's voice, he once again ran to her aid. This time she was stark naked standing on the toilet stool. Before Gordo could move away from her view another mouse ran past him into the living room. Though he knew he shouldn't look at her beautiful body, he stole another glance, and then the involuntary inhalation began. Attempting to swallow the hiccups, he turned to chase the little critter down. He found it under an ottoman and luring it with a leaf of lettuce he scooped the little rodent up for a ride to the woods.

Climbing the three flights of stairs again seemed to help the hiccups calm down. "It's all clear, you're safe now!" he yelled while placing the bowl and magazine in front of her door, knowing better than to go back inside.

While in his kitchen, Gordo thought about how funny the situation had become and wondered if there would be more screaming. Thinking about her lovely body, he caught himself hoping that her apartment housed a whole family of mice. But as the sun began to set, the night promised nothing more than Ben and Jerry's Chunky Monkey and Cary Grant with his devilish smile. Hours later, Gordo went to bed thinking about the ordinary girl – picturing her hiding under the covers, afraid to get up in the dark. He fell asleep remembering everything about her but her face.

Tuesday was uneventful, and by the time Gordo arrived home from work he realized he was exhausted from the exciting night before. Sinking into a hot bath, he lingered a little longer while he read *The Weekly*, a magazine that saved him from buying the daily paper. As he rose from the tub to reach for a towel, he heard another scream, a wretched cry, much worse than before. Tightening the towel around his waist, he banged on the door until the tenant finally quieted down and responded with a weak, "Come in."

"I can't, it's locked!" he bellowed into the crack between the door and the casing.

"Look under the plant, there's a key, and hurry!" she demanded.

Feeling around in the dark, Gordo found the key and entered the apartment to find the horrified girl sitting on her knees in the center of the bed. This time she wore a short t-shirt that read, *I slept with the Conductor*, and a pair of shiny red panties. From the corner of his eye he saw several mice scampering around the room. Suddenly they ran over his bare feet, sending him leaping onto the bed next to the trembling girl, his towel now being drug across the floor by panicking mice captured underneath it.

The hysterical girl grabbed onto Gordo's neck and climbed onto his back – her breasts pressed firmly against him, while her legs dangled wildly on each side. Seeing her bare feet made him even more excited, and the hiccups began tumbling out, creating a sharper sound than usual as he held her in that particularly awkward, yet erotic position. Crying in his ear to take her out of the apartment, he jumped from the bed clutching her slippery bottom and ran through the scurrying mice toward the door.

When he got to his apartment, he let go of the girl, and without looking back he rushed to the bathroom for his robe. She stood there shaking and whimpering as she watched his very white rear-end move gracelessly across the room – the hiccups exploding with a vengeance, causing him to trip over his own feet. Between gasps of air and nervous laughter, she sat down on the couch, and tucked her feet underneath her – just in case one of the creepy little bastards had followed them in.

Gordo stood in front of the bathroom mirror holding his breath in a vain attempt to open the glottis in his throat. He watched his distorted face in agony until the last hiccup escaped. Angry at his weakness, he turned away in disgust and went to check on the girl. She had calmed down considerably, and as he approached her, she held out her hand. "Hi, my name is Caroline. Gosh, you're my hero."

When he felt her delicate hand in his and looked down at her smooth thighs, the hiccups exploded all over again.

"Shhh, don't say a word," she whispered, placing a warm finger on his lips. "I know exactly how to stop those lousy hiccups."

Pulling him toward her, she giggled and proceeded to show him how.

STICKY INSULTS

"Hi, I'm Sandra," she said, glancing nervously around at the room full of strangers.

"Welcome Sandra," everyone in the circle of Leslie's living room responded in unison.

"As a newbie, Sandra, we all abide by the rules written on the wall over there," Leslie, the leader said, pointing to a neatly printed sheet of paper taped over a framed picture that had stayed hidden since the meetings began nearly two months earlier. "I begin our meetings with a reminder that what we say here stays here."

"Humph," Stanley groaned, rolling his fifty-nine-year-old bloodshot eyes. "Just how do you propose you stop folks from telling others what we say?"

"Now Stanley, we've been over this before. Trust, it's all about trust. So, moving on, I think since we all have come in from a long day of work…or play," Leslie looked over at Bernard, who had retired recently, "maybe we should do a few shoulder shrugs first. OK, everyone, start rolling."

Bernard's shoulders popped loudly every time he made the

full rotation and when they did, Stanley would groan. Everyone else in the circle tried their best to muffle the titters, while Leslie shamed them with stern eyes. "Alright, I think that's enough. Now, we all know why we're here. Insults from the past have hurt us, and we have carried them into our lives as if they were made for us. We are here to exterminate those insults that stick to your gut, to your brain and to your heart. And how we begin this journey," Leslie paused to look at each person in the circle, skipping over Sandra who was concentrating on twirling the tiny diamond ring on her finger, "we start by exposing these ugly insults and telling how they have altered us. So, to help our newcomer along, I would like for us to share. Who will go first and bring Sandra up to date?"

A sudden hush came over the room while everyone looked down at the floor and waited.

"I will," a petite lady in her early thirties volunteered. "Uh, let's see. When I was in high school, I dumped my boyfriend, Gary, for a guy from another school. He was really hurt, but I figured he'd get over it. I mean, after all, we were just teenagers. Oh wait, I'm sorry, I forgot to say, hi, my name's Marcie."

"Hi Marcie," everyone said in unity, except for Bernard who said it last as he was engrossed in chewing off a hangnail.

"Well," Marcie continued, "this year was my high school's ten-year reunion and Gary showed up. He was gorgeous. Even his bad skin had cleared up. My husband and I had just separated, since, well, you all know…he cheated on me, and I guess I was lonely and seeing Gary brought up some old feelings. Well, to tell you the truth…he turned me on. So there! We *were* a little frisky back then, to say the least. But, anyway, we danced some and then went outside to talk. I leaned against his car, just like in the old days, and put my arms around his neck. He kissed me long and hard." Marcie closed her eyes, reliving the moment. "It was wonderful, and he was a much better kisser than before, so naturally I melted. But then, he put his hands on my breasts and handled them as if he were examining them. I pulled away and asked him, 'What the heck are you doing?' He said, 'I don't remember your breasts being this small.' Then he laughed and walked back into the building."

"Awww," the group sighed.

"And so, Marcie, tell us what that insult has done to you," Leslie encouraged.

"Well," she said, looking down at her B-cup breasts, "I feel inadequate. Something I never felt before, but now I do, and it feels bad. I don't feel sexy or that a guy would appreciate me. Let alone my own ex-husband."

"Thank you, dear," Leslie said, moving on before Marcie started her usual crying. "Now, who would like to share next?"

"Well, hell, I can beat that," Stanley smirked, all heads whipping his direction. "I've been the best bowler in my league for five years. The night of our final tournament I had a very bad case of gas. I blame it all on my wife's sister who brought over a pot of chili. She knew I loved chili, but she didn't tell me that she put sage in it. Sage gives me the worst case of bloating ever. It didn't hit me though until I went up to bowl. Normally I'd have had a strike the first time out, but no, I had gas so bad, it blew me over the foul line and the lane is so slippery, I fell and broke my arm." Stanley searched the listeners for sympathy. Having heard the story before, everyone but Sandra was expressionless. Her look of disgust encouraged Stanley to finish the story.

"That wasn't the worst part. Oh no! One of my team members…I won't say his name, but the initials are K. T. Well, when I was being walked out to go to the emergency room, I heard him say loud enough for me and everyone else within earshot, 'Bout time he got a taste of humiliation.' That one lousy remark made me stop bowling. I haven't played a game since. Really hurt. Yes, it did."

"Awww," the circle repeated, as if this was part of the meeting ritual. Sandra caught on and offered a weak sigh.

The room grew quiet. Sandra glanced at the others pensively and when Leslie caught her eye, she quickly looked down.

"Well, Bernard. Your insult was a doozie, too. Please share with the group," Leslie urged the old retiree.

"You know, I'm not sure if I can remember it anymore. I think now I just come to these meetings to forget mine."

"That ain't fair," Stanley jumped in. "We're here to share, not to use each other to forget. I'll share your insult for you and if I'm wrong, you can just correct me along the way."

"But I…." Bernard's protests fell on Stanley's oily and selectively deaf ears.

"Bernard tends to leave certain pieces of clothing off sometimes when he goes out in public. Or he might do something as simple as wear different colored socks. Usually, his wife catches it before they get out of the house. But one time she wasn't there to help. Seems Bernard was invited to church by the minister himself, and he wanted to dress snazzy for the big occasion. Well, he certainly did, alright. He wore his favorite suit, starched white shirt, fancy jacket and pleated pants. Only thing he did wrong was he wore his boxers over his pants instead of under them. That wouldn't have been so bad, except the pair he wore was a joke gift he had gotten for his birthday. His brother-in-law bought them at a sex toy shop, and they were a big hit at the party, but not at church. Unfortunately, the boxers had fifteen different sexual positions, all in color, with the numbers 69 splattered everywhere, like daisies." Stanley laughed into the palms of his hands. "I love this story," he choked, "makes me crack up every time I tell it." Looking up at everyone's sneers, he corrected his remark, "Oops, I meant…every time I *remember* it."

"Yeah, well, you wouldn't be laughing if you had been there when it happened," Bernard argued defensively, eyeing the newcomer in hopes that she would ask him to finish the story. When nothing was said, he continued anyway. "They let me sit through the entire sermon and at the end, as we were all leaving the church, my wife whispered in my ear, 'If you could even do one of those positions, I'd have gotten rid of my vibrator years ago.' Then she walked out of the church as if she didn't even know me."

"Awwww," everyone sang. "Awwww," they sang again. Some stories deserved a double or even a triple "Awwww".

"The thing is, I wasn't all that insulted until I found out later what a vibrator was. I thought she was talking about her vibrating recliner."

The women bowed their head, holding back giggles, but Stanley fell off his chair laughing.

Leslie frowned at Stanley and waited until he was through making a scene before she continued. "Thank you all for sharing, but now it's time to get down to why we're all here. Our goal is to look the insult right in the eye and decide that it must die. Barb, over here, has chosen to be the first in the group to bravely tackle that task." Leslie patted her on the back, like a mother soothing her child just before the doctor thrusts a needle in her upper arm. "Tell us your story and how you are going to accomplish this."

Barb sat up straight, lifted her chin up high and began. "I think it's important that you all know that this is not easy for me, just as Leslie said it wouldn't be. Everyone here knows that I had an affair with a married man."

Marcie's head popped up higher, and she glowered at Barb in disapproval.

"Well, it's over, and that's what's important. As you all know, he left me with some very harsh words. What hurt the most was when he compared me to his wife, saying that unlike me, she had the perfect breasts." Barb glanced over at Marcie who was looking down at her B-cups again.

"He made me feel so bad, I ate to my feelings and as you can see, I'm heavier now. But one day it came to me that he's not the reason I hate myself. What I did, you know, with a married man is wrong. So I decided that to make things right, I need to ask his wife for forgiveness."

"Better make sure she doesn't have a gun on hand," Stanley whispered to Bernard.

"So," Barb paused and suddenly did the strangest thing. She slowly got down on her knees in front of Marcie and reached for her hands. Startled, Marcie let her take them into Barb's sweaty palms. "I'm sorry Marcie, for having an affair with your husband. I'm very sorry. I hope you can forgive me."

Marcie's eyes and mouth popped open so wide, Stanley could see the silver fillings in her molars. The circle let out a trembling "Awww," that abruptly ended in silence, and everyone watched in perfect stillness for Marcie's response.

Looking even more uncomfortable, Barb squeezed harder on Marcie's hands as she realized that her bad knees were aching, and she was beginning to doubt if her sphincter muscles would hold out. Despite the increasing agony on Barb's face, Marcie's uncertainty held tight, and not a word left her compressed lips.

Stanley broke the silence with a loud intentional grunt. Marcie jerked free from Barb's grip and scooted her chair back. Everyone held their breath, certain that something bad was about to happen. Then Marcie stood up and began unbuttoning her blouse one button at a time until she got to the last one which at that point, she ripped the blouse open, and the button flew across the room and hit Bernard on the nose. The old coot was so excited watching Marcie disrobe that he didn't feel a thing.

Marcie, now standing in front of everyone in her white padded Maidenform bra, reached behind and unclasped it. Letting the bra drop from her shoulders and land at Barb's knees, she stood up taller and cupped her hands beneath her bosom. "Perfect breasts, he said? These are perfect breasts?"

"Yes, indeed," Stanley said, raising his thick and hairy eyebrows up and down.

"I concur," Bernard saluted, and then the rest of the group

agreed with a long, bleating, "awwwwww." Leslie remained tight-lipped.

Barb timidly picked up the bra and handed it back to Marcie. Then she painfully lifted her body from the floor, and with head bent, she turned to leave the room.

"Wait just a minute," Marcie demanded, "I have something to say to you, Barb."

Barb stopped in her steps and kept her focus on the floor.

"Turn around," Marcie ordered, slipping back into her bra, to Stanley's disappointment.

Everyone but Leslie pressed their backs into their chairs and waited for the slaughter to begin. "You know, I should slap you silly…but all I want to do is hug you." Marcie rushed over to the sinking woman and gathered her fleshy body into her arms. Applause filled the air.

"Boy, I didn't see *that* coming, did you?" Bernard leaned over and nudged Sandra.

"And neither did Leslie," she replied, looking over at the odd expression on Leslie's face." Leslie looked quite tense, just the opposite of the composed, confident leader she often portrayed at these meetings.

"Well, this has been a remarkable session," Leslie began, pushing chairs against the wall and making room for the group hand-holding circle that ended each meeting.

"Wait a second," Sandra turned to face the nervous leader. "Don't I get to tell *my* story?"

"Perhaps next time, Sandra," Leslie said.

"No!" Bernard blurted. "I want to hear. Don't you all want to hear?" He surveyed the room with his droopy eyes that had remained wide open since Marcie's bosomy display.

A confirmed yes filled the air and everyone sat down and looked toward Sandra. After all, this was so far, the best group meeting they had ever had. Leslie stood uncomfortably against the wall.

"About two years ago," Sandra began, "I was engaged to a very fine man who I loved dearly. It was a whirlwind romance, and we were set to be married only six weeks after we met. The wedding was small, unpretentious and exactly how I wanted it to be, with only our best friends and family attending. I wore a simple white chiffon dress that my fiancé had picked out for me. I was surprised by his excellent taste in women's clothing and even more surprised when he elected to apply my make-up. Needless to say, he made me look fabulous. How lucky was I to be marrying not only a handsome man, but a man with refined skills, to boot. He explained that having four sisters helped a lot."

Appearing quite bored with these details, Stanley crossed his legs at the ankles, slid down in his chair while folding his arms tightly against his hard gut and noisily cleared his throat.

Marcie whispered, "Don't mind him, please continue."

Avoiding Stanley's anxious leg thumps, Sandra sucked in her stomach and a deep breath before giving her audience what they were waiting for. "Well, everything was going smoothly until we stood in front of the minister. We both had prepared our vows and had them written down. I was asked to read mine first. They were really lovely words. I have a copy in my purse if you want to hear them." Sandra's eyes lit up as she scanned the room looking for approval.

Bernard held his watch up inches from his eyes, hoping to remind Sandra that they were already past their allotted time, while Barb squirmed in discomfort on the small hard chair that accommodated only half of her sizable rear end.

"Well, never mind. They were beautiful though." Sandra looked around the room one more time for at least one taker. The participants remained allied with their leader.

"So, what happened next surprised everyone in the church. My fiancé turned white as a ghost and stood staring at me as if he had forgotten who I was or where he was, or who he was, is more like it. Then he screamed, "I can't!" and ran out of the church. Just like that, and I never saw him again. No apology, no excuse, no letter, no phone call, no nothing. Gone. Just plain gone."

"Awwww," the voices were higher this time, and everyone shook their heads sympathetically except Leslie, whose shoulders had seriously drooped.

"So, I guess you could say this is the ultimate insult. Not that he dumped me in front of Mother Mary and my whole family, but because he wouldn't tell me why he couldn't marry me. And for two years, even though I felt dejected, I tried to find him. He was nowhere to be found…until today."

"Ohhh?" the women in the group queried, unadulterated curiosity plastered across their faces, as the men sat with furled brows waiting to be chastised for being a part of the male species.

"Yes." Sandra stood and walked purposely toward the wall, her eyes transfixed on the rules taped to the picture behind it. "Yes, I found him," she said, ripping the paper from the frame, exposing an oversized photo of a handsome man standing next to a woman who looked exactly like Sandra, only without the deep crease now embedded in her forehead.

The group stood and slowly walked toward the picture, squinting in confusion. "Why, that's *you*," Barb said, pointing from the picture to Sandra.

"Who's the guy?" Bernard asked, suddenly interested again.

"Who cares who he is," Stanley grumbled. "Why is this picture on Leslie's wall?"

All eyes turned toward Leslie, who had stepped away from the scene and was bracing herself against the door jam.

"Are you guys related?" Barb asked, trying to piece the puzzle together and looking closer at the picture and then back at Leslie. "You do kind of favor him."

"That's because," Leslie stalled and let out a long sigh, resting two brightly painted fingernails against her lips, "that's because, I *am* that guy."

"WHAT?" Stanley's nose crimped in disgust. Catching himself looking up and down at Leslie's long body dressed in a full skirt, white fluffy blouse, and black pumps, he quickly turned his head, hoping that the others hadn't seen him gawking.

The room was now full of apprehension, as everyone looked back and forth from Leslie, the so-called woman, to Sandra, the woman scorned, all of them anticipating a reaction of some kind.

After many seconds of hearing only each other breathing, Barb's rough voice pierced the cramped air. "I think maybe we should adjourn at this point. Perhaps these two have things to say to each other that may consist of more than just an apology."

Everyone in the room agreed, and while they filed in line to exit, Barb said to Marcie, "Want to grab a Margarita? We can talk about what a bad lover your ex was." Marcie giggled, and arm in arm they followed Bernard out the door. Only Stanley remained seated.

"You, too, Stanley." Bernard stood in the doorway, motioning him with a jerk of his head.

"Awwww." Stanley reluctantly stood. "This was just getting good. Thanks for a helluva meeting, uh, Leslie," he said, walking around the chairs and peering down Leslie's blouse. When he got to the door, he put his hand on Bernard's shoulder and said, "Hey, I feel like bowling a game or two. Want to join me?"

"Sure," Bernard answered with enthusiasm.

"Can we first stop by my house and get my bowling shoes?"

"Yeah, that'll give me a chance to turn these stretch pants around." Bernard pulled at the tight fabric twisted around his crotch. "They're on backwards and have been rubbing me raw the whole night."

Stanley looked over at Bernard's pants and asked with that same crinkled nose, the distain forever etched in the creases, "Are those your wife's?"

"Yeah, so what? I'd rather have this little quirk than that weird one Leslie has. You couldn't pay me to wear those heels."

When the door slammed behind them, Leslie and Sandra rushed toward each other and kissed like they'd never kissed before.

NO MORE CARNATIONS

She was tired of the nonsense. You know, when a marriage becomes meaningless – struggling to be kind, or civil and nothing is spontaneous anymore but merely routine, like plucking that same stubborn hair on your chin or walking outside half asleep to get the newspaper. When a couple is indifferent to their misery, mindlessly muddling through the days – trapped in their vows.

It was Margaret who came to realize that there was nothing more to say that had any value, and while she shared the same bed with Clyde, sleep was the only thing on their minds. Just lately she had become aware that she was staring at his back that was always turned toward her, lying restlessly in the dark pondering how they had deeply disappointed each other, until she finally gave in to sleep, only to wake the next morning to an empty bed and an empty heart.

Sixteen years together and Margaret couldn't remember the last time she felt flushed around her husband, or the last time he kissed her on the mouth, instead of the fleeting peck on the cheek, or worse, on the forehead. Matter of fact, she couldn't remember the last time she even wanted him to kiss her. Mechanically passing each other in the evenings and finding separate projects to do on the weekends, they drifted lethargically through too many uneventful years.

She hadn't realized how far down into the well she had fallen until one day she heard herself comment to a friend who was crying about her bad marriage. After listening intently without interruption, Margaret calmly replied, with arms tightly crossed, "Why don't you just leave him?"

At that very moment, hearing those careless words sling out of her mouth and ricochet right off the wall and back to her hypocritical tongue, Margaret knew it was herself to whom she had addressed the question. And when her friend looked up with weepy eyes and said, "I'm afraid to leave him," Margaret felt an indescribable ache and wanted desperately to cry along with her.

But nothing else was said as they politely finished the last sip of coffee, and both women quietly returned to their ordinary lives, except, Margaret was not the same. Tired of drivel, tired of the hollowness in her heart, weary from days without love or fighting, or something as simple as missing each other, she knew without further questioning that it was time for change.

When she arrived home, a vase of yellow carnations – which she recognized from each anniversary before and every Valentine's Day thereafter – was sitting on the kitchen table. A mirthless chuckle emerged from her throat, realizing that she had forgotten their anniversary. She sneered when she read the note, "Happy Anniversary - Clyde," written on a plain note card yellowing at the edges torn from a pad that sat in the kitchen drawer, used mostly for grocery lists and phone numbers, and by her husband every year on occasions like this. "Well, at least this time the carnations aren't dyed bright pink!" She forced another laugh, stuffing the card inside her purse instead of in the garbage pail, where she really wanted to dispose of it.

Margaret was feeling wild inside and unusually anxious. Anxious to end the pretense and anxious to disturb the flow of two lives that were no longer dancing together or even walking together but were merely hanging onto unraveling ropes tied at separate ends. She grabbed the flowers that he knew she never liked, preferring roses instead, and starting at the front door, she tore off pieces of layered petals, dropping them one by one on the floor and with each one she said, "He loves me, he loves me not."

She spread the petals from the living room to the kitchen and finally ended at the foot of their bed where she stood with the last petal in her hand. Taking a deep breath, she tossed it onto the faded, blue bedspread and whispered, "He loves me not."

That evening, Margaret made her husband's favorite dinner – meatloaf, mashed potatoes, and broccoli smothered in Velveeta cheese. She left it in the oven on warm, took an ugly note card from the kitchen drawer and wrote a message to her mate. On the linen tablecloth, she placed her best China setting that had not been used since her mother gave it to her. She dusted a crystal champagne flute glass with her name engraved on it, a wedding gift from her grandmother, and sat it next to the plate. At that moment, she revived a scene she had long forgotten: Clyde's name on the matching glass had been misspelled, and when she playfully laughed about it, he turned to her in anger and thoughtlessly threw it away. She remembered hearing the glass shatter in the garbage can and a feeling of hurt that stayed with her for the longest.

A candle was lit, and a bottle of Brut Champagne opened. Outside, she cut a large bunch of gardenias and placed them in a vase in the center of the table. Setting the note next to the fork, she grabbed her things and slipped out the back door.

Like clockwork, her husband would soon be arriving. She parked her car around the corner, walked back to the house and hid behind the large gardenia bush next to the dining room window where she could easily see the entire contents of the kitchen and all the way to the entry.

While she waited, she inhaled the marvelous scent of the gardenias, remembering when she had first smelled them as a child. She recalled how much her mother adored the intoxicating fragrance of the beautiful white and hearty flower and, when in season, she placed them throughout their home and always in Margaret's own bedroom. Clyde disliked the scent, so she limited herself to growing one bush, which she would cut large bunches from annually and bring to her aging and fragile mother.

Margaret heard the squeaky brakes from Clyde's pick-up truck and then the familiar sound of boots clomping across the front deck, his large lumbering shadow arriving at the door first. As usual, he entered slowly as if he were carrying something heavy, letting the screen door slam behind him and tossing his keys on the table nearby. Instead of sitting in his recliner and bellowing for a beer, he stopped and stared at the floor laced with petals. He scratched his head and stood there a few seconds longer looking mildly puzzled. Then he proceeded to continue his daily ritual of removing first his boots, then his socks.

Outside, Margaret observed the scene. Crouched behind the bush watching her husband through the window, she felt an odd sensation, almost as if she were seeing him for the first time. It was a creepy feeling, like a perverted peeping Tom.

Still scratching his head, Clyde followed the trail of petals to the kitchen. He looked ahead, surveying the stove for signs of dinner. He sniffed the air like a bloodhound and went to open the oven door. The smell of freshly baked meatloaf wafted throughout the room. "Good!" he said, like a strict piano teacher would blurt out to a student who struggled through *Heart and Soul* for the first time. Then he looked around the house for Margaret.

"Margaret, I'm home!" he yelled from room to room, stopping to lean against the wall, plucking petals from the bottom of his sticky bare feet. Hearing no response, he looked in the garage for her car. "Humph!" he grunted on the way back to the kitchen.

Clyde opened the refrigerator and stood in front of it for longer than usual, glancing back over his shoulder at the table, noticing a setting for only one. He grabbed a can of beer from the twelve-pack box and took a long stream of gulps. Then, he did something that didn't surprise Margaret, but disappointed her, although she expected nothing different, nor had she fantasized anything more. Her husband pulled out the dinner that was neatly arranged in a casserole dish, took it to the table, shoved the gold-rimmed plate to the side and sat it down in its place. He then took the bottle of champagne and emptied it in the sink. Margaret swallowed a gasp when he grabbed the gardenias and threw them out the back door, just a few feet from the window where she was hiding. She was certain the vase cracked after he plunked it down hard on the tile countertop.

Clyde sat at the table, blew out the candle and reached for the fork where he spotted the note. Picking it up, he read aloud, "No More Carnations. Margaret." With another loud grunt, he nonchalantly tossed it onto the lovely piece of China he refused to enjoy and proceeded to eat the dinner right from the casserole dish.

Margaret slid out from under the bush and quietly picked up the gardenias from the yard. She took one last look at her husband chomping away at his favorite meal and turned to walk to her car. The sun was setting, and the streetlight popped on just as she reached for the door handle. She took another long sniff of the beautiful flowers before placing them on the car seat next to her suitcase. Then she drove west, down the highway toward her mother's home.

FLUMMOXED

THE "IN THE PINK" ADVENTURES OF FUMELDA FLATTERLY

How is it that a woman can manage to lose her shoe twice in one day? If her name is Fumelda Flatterly, it's easy.

Here's exactly how it happened: The plane to Sheboygan, Wisconsin via Milwaukee was due to leave in less than five minutes. Frustrated with her tardiness, Fumelda hurriedly mowed through thick crowds of passengers, bumping shoulders, and nearly knocking over a blind man and his chubby yellow Labrador. Just seconds before she reached the gate, a rather broad, foreboding, orange-tanned woman hit her from behind with a purse the size of a sofa cushion. Clutching her precious totes full of goodies, Fumelda's willowy body fell forward, toppling over a row of seats where her bright pink high heel shoe flew from her foot right into the hands of the snickering perpetrator who quickly stuffed it in the nearest trashcan and casually walked away.

Spread-eagle on the floor, pink-laced panties askew, Fumelda yelled to the hostess to hold the plane. Readjusting her clothing as best she could, she frantically searched for the missing shoe. With no help from the others rushing past her, Fumelda gave up the search and hobbled as fast as possible toward the closing door.

Taking pity on the disheveled young woman, mainly because the hostess loved the color pink and Fumelda was drenched in it, she was mercifully allowed to board the airplane. Pink outfits, pink roses, pink icing, you name it, Fumelda adored the color. Then it would come as no surprise to learn that her hair was dyed a punky pink that matched her pink parfait lipstick, and rosy pink cheeks.

As Fumelda made her way down the aisle, banging her bags against several heads, she came upon her seat, now occupied by a very frail, old man who was fast asleep. She double-checked her boarding pass and looked up and down the aisle for an empty seat only to find that the plane was full. Gently nudging the snoring fossil, she whispered in his hair-filled ear, "Sir, please wake up. You have my seat." Lazily prying open one eye, the elderly man awoke with a jolt upon seeing Fumelda's oversized pink glasses within inches of his face. He instantly shrieked a pathetic cry for help.

The flight attendant rushed to his aid, while the passengers moaned and growled at Fumelda. In her defense, she claimed loudly for all to hear, "But stewardess, that man has taken my seat, and I can prove it!"

"Excuse me! I am a flight attendant!" the woman in the dark blue uniform bellowed.

"You're excused," Fumelda said, waving her hand dismissively. While digging through her bubblegum pink handbag for the ticket, the old man grasped at his heart, let out a dramatic guttural farewell, and dropped his head to his chest.

"Oh, *pleeease*. You've got to be kidding!" Fumelda scoffed, poking at the old man's arm. The passengers hissed and booed at her while the flight attendant grabbed her by the elbow and insisted that she exit the plane. The old codger looked up and watched the scene with barefaced audacity.

"This is outrageous!" she yelled at the pilot who quickly slammed the cockpit door upon seeing the indignant passenger being shoved toward the exit.

Within seconds, an exasperated Fumelda found herself escorted by a security guard on one side and a custodian with a mop in hand on the other. Her loud protests were hushed when they dragged her outside and left her standing on the hot concrete in a state of shock, with one bare foot, her purse, and an empty shopping bag.

Upon seeing her bedraggled reflection in the plate-glass window, the flip in her hair now flat, she dropped to her knees, and let the tears pour. She was not crying because of the lost shoe, the missing articles, the mean woman who whacked her, or the old man who faked a heart attack. She cried because now she would miss her ten-year high school reunion, Sheboygan High class of '94, and the boy that had promised to save her a dance. She had clung to his pledge for all those years, and nothing could have prevented her from returning to her hometown to claim that dance with the only man she had ever loved, Freddy Alan Titler.

Her crying vacillated from sobs to sniffles, and having to blow her nose on her favorite pink, polka-dot skirt only made matters worse. She wasn't sure how long she would sit there – her back against the hard, glass wall, knees pulled to her small chest, her eyes nearly swollen shut – until a hand touched her shoulder and startled her out of the crying jag. With fists raised, squinting through a gummy layer of tears mixed with mascara, she saw the silhouette of a man, the sun shining brightly beyond his small frame. He offered her his hand. Unfurling her knuckles, she allowed him to lift her from the ground. While balancing on one heel, she adjusted her clothing, brushed the loose hair behind her ears, and cleared her throat. The kind man smiled and waited patiently and silently for her to collect her wits. When she did, he handed her the missing shoe. Slipping it on, she felt a resurgence of strength and thanked the man with a warm hug.

Still without speaking, he took her hand again and walked her to his white limousine, parked just feet away. That she got in without faltering, surprised Fumelda. She even accepted a chilled drink of Vodka and pink lemonade as if it were a daily ritual. While he watched her sip, motioning with his slender fingers to drink it all up, she became wary of the cool and mysterious gentleman. Before she could gather up her questions, he took her hand again, looked deeply into her eyes and asked her, "Where would you like to go, dear lady?"

Fumelda didn't have to think twice about her answer, and like a participant on a game show panel, she blurted out, "Sheboygan!"

Three hours later, Fumelda found herself exiting the Good Samaritan's private jet on a private runway and entering another one of his limousines. Giddy, she arrived only an hour late to the reunion.

With freshly applied pink lipstick, she adjusted her wrinkled skirt one more time, glanced at her figure in the revolving glass door, glad to see both high heels intact, and boldly walked toward the ballroom entrance.

The room was full of chatter, shrills from women as they ran toward each other, men straining their eyes to find their old high school girlfriends, a Backstreet Boys song streaming from the live band on the brightly lit stage. She noticed that the wallflowers, just as they had been at the school dances, clung to the walls at the far end of the ballroom where the light was dim and close to the restrooms. A line of men and one woman dressed like a man waited eagerly at the bar. Fumelda combed the place carefully, again and again, with no sign of her handsome, childhood crush. She felt the annoying tears revving up behind her eyes. To avoid further embarrassment, she moved toward the shadows to blend in with the shrinking violets.

Realizing she was again without a tissue, she slowly slid down the wall and bent over to wipe her dripping nose on her skirt. At that moment, a hand holding a handkerchief appeared before her. Sucking in a sniff, she looked up to see a very large completely bald man smiling down at her. Through the blur, she looked closer, straining to see who he might be. The face seemed vaguely familiar; smooth skin stretched over layers of hard fat, green eyes lost in swollen eyelids, with a smile that revealed two large dimples where once there were none.

"Fumelda Flatterly, good lord, is that you?" he asked, his eyes full of hope.

While blowing her nose on his soft, cotton offering, she noticed the initials, *F A T* embroidered in pink. It can't be, it just can't be, she nearly said aloud. Her eyes slowly traced his humongous body from the unpolished brown loafers, hurriedly past his bulging stomach, up to his bulbous nose and lingering smile. Frantically searching for the right words, she answered shakily, "No speaka Engliz." Then she lowered her head to conceal her lie and quickly maneuvered around his enormous torso, shielding her face as she slipped past a girl she recognized from gym class, and rushed outside where she discovered, through the pouring rain, that the limo she had arrived in was still there.

"Oh, joy!" she yelled. Running toward it, she slipped in a puddle, and her shoe went flying over her head. Looking back, she saw Freddy's body pushing through the revolving door. He seemed to be stuck. When he missed the exit and circled around again and again, she dismissed the lost shoe, climbed inside the limo, and slid down to the floorboard to hide.

"Where would you like to go, Miss?" the driver asked robotically from behind the wheel.

Fumelda whispered hoarsely, "To the nearest shoe store, please...and hurry!"

to be continued…

SILENT UNDERSTANDING

Except for the light seeping through the closed bathroom door, the room is dark and murky like my mood. I find myself sitting on the edge of the bed listening to you while you shower. The water beats down hard on the top of your head, splashing against your back and trickling down that slim white bottom I've seen many, many times. No one has ever accused you of being shy.

I wonder if you are tempted to bathe with my pure Lavender soap – sudsless, natural minerals, a unisex scent – instead of scrubbing with that manly toxic blend of chemicals that reddens your flesh to a harsh crimson. Any minute now I expect you to belt out Irish tunes that causes anyone within earshot to stop and listen, including me.

But this time, you're not singing. You are standing still. I can tell because the water is pounding in the same rhythm, and I hear you sigh. Intrigued, I lie back on the bed, my feet planted on the floor, and listen to you release the frustration stemming from the absence of our lovemaking. I allow myself to remember when my entering the bathroom unannounced would have excited us both.

Behind my closed eyelids the fascination fades, and I see a hand reaching out to me; a hand that is not yours. I am cruelly reminded of my own sensuality, and the decision to restrain it saddens me. A low grunt erupts within the acoustic chamber, rescuing me from thoughts I should not be having while lying on a bed we still share.

Your unbridled sigh of relief sends me sneaking out of the bedroom like a child who had been hiding behind the door listening to her parents argue. This feeling is unsettling, yet I am eager to put it in words, so I rush to my writing desk instead of sharing it with you.

I write the first two words of a poem – silent understanding.

I like you. I like your name. Joseph. I have liked you since the day we met. You were telling a joke to a group of people at a party, and I was standing by, drink in hand, watching you. After the punchline, no one was laughing but me. I'm not sure if I got the joke either, but the faces on the confused listeners and yours was so funny and priceless, I burst out in a guffaw, and my loud snort caused everyone to turn around and look. Then when you looked, you saw the same funny scene I did and started a whole new kind of laughter. As your audience gravitated toward a saner group of partiers, you fell into my space, and we laughed together. We've been laughing with one another ever since.

Our lease will expire soon, and after three years in this cute little bungalow we must decide if we want to renew it. More importantly, as we do every year, we must decide if we want to continue living together. We agreed from the beginning that we would not take each other for granted. We would discuss it thoughtfully because we both know that life changes on a dime. You're hesitant this year. I sense it, because so am I.

Our friend, Ethan, lives nearby. He's a funny guy, laughs a lot like we do and enjoys our music the same. The first time he dropped by to deliver a package inadvertently sent to his address, we fell in love with him. He's been a fixture from that day forward, and we've watched him go through two loves, a broken ankle, a parakeet, and land by the seat of his pants on the New York Time's Best Seller list. But out of nowhere, he tells us he needs to take a hiatus from anything breathing, even us, and he buries himself in his writing. His dedication to his work is admirable, and I miss him so much, I, too, have decided to make sacrifices and spend more time on my poetry. Joseph understands.

Fall is nearing the end of its colorful season – a time to dig deep in the bowels of my soul. The gray days, wet mornings, and lifeless trees bring out the macabre and the Edgar Allen Poe in me. I wonder if Ethan feels the same way.

While in this mood, I decide to enter the depths of writing hell unencumbered, naked. Prickling with goosebumps, I wrap a blanket around me, cross-legged on the floor in front of my laptop. This makes me feel raw and creepy, and that is where I want to stay until I've written something worthy or until I'm hungry. A soft knock on the door disrupts me in mid-phrase, and I curse under my breath as an idea evaporates.

"Who is it?" I speak into the crack of the door.

"Me, Ethan. Have you got a minute?"

"Oh! Of course." So delighted to hear his voice, I answer without thinking, forgetting that I'm undressed underneath the blanket. Too late, I open the door.

"Oh, I'm sorry Elaine, did I catch you at the wrong time?" he asks, stepping back from the threshold.

I pull him into the room, or rather yank him in and shut the door with my foot. "Well, no and yes. No, because I'm really glad to see you. Yes, because I was writing and had a fantastic thought in my head, and now it's gone. But come sit down and make it up to me."

It's when I grab his hand and lead him to the sofa that I notice the dark circles under his eyes, enhanced by a five o'clock shadow and a wrinkled blue plaid shirt. "Gosh, Ethan, I've… we've really missed you. How's the writing going?"

"It was going just fine until I got stuck. And by the way, I've missed you, too…I've missed you both." He leans in for a hug. I can only hug back with one arm, so it's a bit clumsy. He inhales deeply, like he always does when near me, as if he's breathing in my essence. "I really have," he says, gently releasing me from the awkwardness. "I've been stuck like this for days, and it occurred to me that maybe you could help."

"I'll do my best. Let's have a cup of hot tea and talk about it. I have not had any fluids for hours, and I bet you haven't either. I'll go change first."

I notice he's looking curiously at the blanket. "Please don't change. You look almost wise wrapped in all that fabric. Kind of like a priest. Stay the way you are. I won't stay long."

But I want him to stay as long as possible, and I've got to get that priest idea out of his head, so I bow like a Japanese geisha, hands in prayer mode, puckering my lips, batting my eyelashes, eager to please. He laughs. I love hearing his laugh. "Make your-self most comfortable," I say in character, humbly backing out of the room in small steps. "I prepare hot, soothing drink, for good master."

I quickly pull my hair out of the matronly bun and toss the blanket over a chair as I prepare the tea. It feels wonderfully naughty being naked with only a thin wall between us. I let that thought linger for much too long.

One leg tucked underneath me and cocooned in the blanket on the old recliner that Joseph left behind, we sit and talk like the good friends we are. I am enjoying becoming familiar with Ethan's voice again. During his absence, I was afraid I might forget it.

"The book is almost finished," he says after we catch up on three months of trivia.

"Oh, how exciting. You must be feeling such relief."

"I'm not there yet. I'm without an ending."

"Endings can be hard," I say with empathy. He's clearly lost and reaching out to me for help. "No ending at all?"

"Actually, there are lots of possible endings, but they aren't meant for me alone to decide."

Confused, I sit back and wait for him to explain.

"If you recall, the book was about relationships, how they develop, and a lot of psychology behind the concept of friendship. I used lots of different examples from people I've met and, of course, my own experiences. Then I began writing about my friendship with you and Joseph, and the book took a whole different turn." He hesitated when he saw my brows arch over the teacup. "Don't worry, I've changed all the names to protect the innocent."

"Fair enough." But that was not at all what I was thinking. I wrapped myself tighter in the blanket, my bare feet exposed.

"It seems that, well, as I was writing about how we met, our trips together, the blurry morning political satires over coffee, taking turns cooking on weekends, and staying up all night writing those goofy songs, and the time you took care of my parakeet and accidentally turned on the fan…."

"Oh, please don't remind me, Ethan. I swear I think it was as hard on me as it was on you. I still feel rotten about killing that poor bird. I was really afraid you'd hate me for that."

"And that's just it, right there," he blurts, pointing a finger in the air. "You *still* feel bad about it. And I do, too. But not so much about losing Clemens, as much as your hurting from it."

I stared at Ethan's wrinkled brow, caught the seriousness in his face and decided I should suppress the giggle rising inside me, recalling how he named the parakeet after Samuel Clemens – the runner-up, Vonnegut, barely winning over Nabokov. "OK." I bit my lip and left it at that.

"Yes, well, that's one example. There's more. As I journeyed through our friendship, I also realized that I gave up the girl-friends I had because I compared them to you. They couldn't even come close."

"Now, wait just a minute. That last girlfriend was an up-and-coming dancer, beautiful, and may I add, the only woman I know who could stretch her leg around her neck! A perfect catch. No comparison, I assure you." I was certain my clever comeback would muster up a smile.

"She hardly laughed, Elaine," he said, his sober expression unchanged. "I think she was afraid she'd wrinkle her perfect face. When I broke my ankle, she was nowhere to be found until it healed. You were the one that ran endless errands for me and brought me meals, and..."

"That's what friends do, Ethan. I loved helping you."

"You see. There it is, again. You loved helping me."

I knew, watching Ethan perched on the edge of the cushion carefully considering his words, studying his hands, that he had much more to say. Those hands of his, always ready to gesticulate his unsullied enthusiasm, like a conductor leading Beethoven's Fifth Symphony.

"What I've learned while drafting this book is everything you've ever done for me showed that you genuinely cared. You seemed happy to go out of your way for me. Including our conversations. I don't recall you ever leaving one unfinished. You exhausted yourself with each topic."

"I appreciate your awareness of my qualities, I really do. But what does this have to do with your ending?"

"I'm getting to that. You see, not only am I aware of those things about you, but I am also aware of the same about me.

That's why I had to go away for a while and think this out. I realized that I love being in your life on any level, for any reason. I love laughing, talking, eating, even suffering with you. I love inflating your bike tires, picking you up from the mechanic's shop, our long walks, the funny way you're looking at me right now…all of that. And…I deeply miss it."

As hard as I'm trying not to let his words reach my heart, what he's telling me is what I already know, and even Joseph knew. I decide to help him get back on track just in case I'm wrong. "I imagine many friends grow close like we have."

"You're putting a practical spin on it, Elaine. Let me ask you this. Have you thought about me often?" He swallows a small gulp and takes a chance. "I mean more than you thought you would?"

"I have. Both Joseph and I talked about you all the time… for days after you were gone."

"And after that?" He could see clear through me, his eyes coaxing me for an honest answer. He's out on a limb and wants to take me with him. I hesitate. "I, well, I became sad, frankly. Things felt like they changed more than I had expected. I felt… disconnected." I heard what I said, loud and clear, and it sounded so sincere, felt so completely right, I had to repeat it. "Yes, disconnected."

He let my words sink in, and then he said ever so softly, "I felt the same."

Our eyes locked, tears welled up, the silent understanding between us taking its hold. I squeezed my tingling fingers, afraid to move, frozen in this precious moment. His stayed firmly pressed between his knees, as if, should he set them free, he would say too much. Instead, he smiled. That beautiful boyish smile that always made my face soften like a child looking up at a star-filled sky. I held my breath, and when I released it, my smile came with it.

"How will your book end?" I ask.

He stood and took a step toward me. "We shall see." And there it was, just as I have imagined it many times, his hand reaching out for mine. How natural this feels, our palms meeting, as he leads me into his loving arms.

I let the blanket drop to the floor.

OWN THE NIGHT

She moves toward the ladies' room, sashaying in slow motion, as if there were many eyes beholding her bouncy buttocks and bountiful breasts. While she is gone, murmurs are heard throughout the bar.

Facing the poorly lit mirror, she regards her reflection from the shoulders up; the mirror too short to reveal the whole plump package. A rehearsed smile, a wrinkled pucker, with half-closed eyes she blots her freshly applied lipstick that the girl behind the drug store counter guaranteed would bring out the gold in her tawny brown eyes.

Taking one quick glance at her exaggerated cleavage before she abandons the safety of the locked room, she practices several seductive poses and rehearses her re-entry, assured that her audience is eagerly anticipating her glorious return. "Alright, Mr. Demille, I'm ready for my close-up."

Bending over to shake her hair free for that ravishing wind-blown look, she hits her head on the ceramic basin. At the same time comes a knock on the door, alerting her that another is waiting to use the facility. Bellowing "Occupied!" she quickly shakes her hair again, this time avoiding another bang on her already throbbing skull. A cigarette is what she needs, and as she lights up, she cautiously scans the area for a smoke alarm. Whoever is behind the locked door, impatiently jiggles the handle.

"Occupied, I said! OCC-U-PIED!"

Feeling a little dizzy and losing a perfectly good buzz, she breathes deeply from her diaphragm and exhales through her teeth with a "ssssss" sound. She imagines exuberant applause and expects to find a fresh glass of wine delicately breathing just for her own sensitive palate, indubitably sent over by a handsome devotee sitting in a dark corner admiring her from the moment she planted her shapely rump on the swiveling vinyl bar stool. Yes, he would be the one who announces her fame to all.

A waft of cigarette smoke follows her past the irritated woman standing outside the restroom door, arms tightly folded, eyeing her in disgust. "Pfft, pfft!" She is accustomed to women being jealous of her alluring attributes and purposely dismisses her. As she approaches the bar, she is sorely disappointed to find an empty glass, identified as hers by the lipstick smudges on the rim. She flippantly waves at the bartender with a look of displeasure, pointing her finger at the Bordeaux now back on the shelf. Annoyed, he pours her another, as the patrons sit idly by.

No doubt, fear of rejection is what keeps them from approaching her. The married men are afraid to look her direction with their wives sitting so close. She is certain the bartender is now angry at himself for being gay and missing a perfect opportunity to woo her. Her stardom leaves them stupefied, humbled at her feet, for it is well known that porn stars never die, even long after they've retired, as they can always be revived on command – forever etched in the minds of her fans. Forever.

"Yes, no one ever leaves a star. That's what makes one a star," she tells the bartender, who apparently has no interest in her brilliant quote from *Sunset Boulevard*, stiffly turning his back to her while he polishes yet another wine glass.

One more drink, and in her mind these dismal souls will transform into sex-starved sycophants, and then she will once again own the night. But first, she must somehow, carefully and inconspicuously, pull up the silk stocking that has wriggled free from her pudgy thigh, now clinging pathetically to her ankle.

ACKNOWLEDGEMENTS

Always, a big thank you to those who have ever crossed my path. It's you, friends, family, and everyday people, who give me the ingredients for these stories.

My warmest hugs for Rob Radmer, Mary and Dave Dekker, Vivian Green, Martha Collins, Herb Koene, Simone and Chris Guidry, Glen White, Wendy Savage, Barb Butzen, Mary Fitzpatrick, Kay Radmer, Patricia and Bo Lebo, Christopher Walsh, Jackie Yancey, Dennis Wiesner, Jack and Emily Jensen, Jeanie Matthews, Liz Stotts, Tonya Bills, Kelli Rea, Scott Vreeke, Steven McBrearty, Barbara Slade, Patti Mirehouse, Lark Beaugureau, Dianne Feudner and so many others for your encouraging cheers.

A heartfelt thanks to my late friend, Billy Wilson who even while terminally ill, read my first book and shared his sincere response to each story. I wish he could have stayed around for these.

And a profoundly special thanks to Don Tassone and Evelyn M. Turner, fine fellow authors whose passion for writing continuously inspires me.

Thank you, my son Jake Bryer who sponsored my first book signing at his fabulous Austin Art Garage, and the Reel Sheboygan band who made it come alive.

Sharing my stories is a dream come true, made possible by all of you.

ABOUT THE AUTHOR

Libby Belle lives in Austin, Texas, a city that thrives on weirdness – a perfect place to nurture her vivid imagination. It's also where all six of her beautiful children, ten grandchildren, and a bunch of wonderful wacky friends and relatives reside.

She has written over a hundred stories, a book of poetry, and a half-dozen songs. If she's not writing, she's conjuring up her next story.

"I even write in my dreams," she says. "It's a most wonderful curse!"

Her stories have been published in London and New York

magazines and Texas newspapers. Her first collection of short stories was published in 2020. Look for *The Juicy Parts and other Quirky Stories* on Amazon, Barnes and Noble, and at Austin Art Garage.

Visit LibbyBelle.com